DUXBRIDGE MYSTERIES

RECIPE
FOR
MURDER

by
Annie DeMoranville
and Avery Whitney

Deco Skyline Publishing
Boston, MA

www.AnnieDeMoranville.com

Deco Skyline Publishing
Boston, MA

Publisher's Note: This is a work of fiction. Names, characters, places, and incidents are a product of the author's imagination. Locales and public names are sometimes used for atmospheric purposes. Any resemblance to actual people, living or dead, or to businesses, companies, events, institutions, or locales is completely coincidental.

Cover by Larissa Gibson
Photos by: TaMara Rullo, Carol Reposa, Mary Dozier and Mark Gibson

Recipe for Murder/Annie DeMoranville and Avery Whitney -- 1st ed.
ISBN: 978-1-7325070-5-0

Hi Dad!

To everyone who thinks this is about them.
It is.

CONTENTS

ONE

"Come on. The sun'll be up soon." Tina grabbed Jacob's hand and led him away from the dying bonfire.

"Ooooo!" cooed a group of teens sitting in the sand around the fire, accompanied by someone making smoochy sounds

"Oh, grow up, Denny," Jacob called back as he struggled to keep up with Tina.

Tina dragged him up and over the dune. "Let's go down to the water to watch."

They walked hand in hand through the tall beach grass and down to the shoreline. The tide was ebbing, leaving piles of seaweed and debris as it receded. Small bubbles escaped the sand as clams dove down deep. Tina dug her toes in, trying to catch one, laughing as she lost her balance and fell into Jacob's arms. He kept her from tumbling onto the wet sand, and she rewarded him with a sweet kiss on his cheek.

Once they reached the water, they walked along the edge, barefoot on the damp, hard-packed sand, dodging the lapping waves. Memorial Day might be right around the corner, but the waters off Onset beach would still be ice cold.

Tina and Jacob were enjoying the freedom that was Senior Week, a week to have fun and be carefree teens before Saturday's graduation flung them into adulthood. All-night bonfires on the beach, day trips into Boston, and sleeping in until noon would soon give way to summer jobs and college prep. But for now, their arms around each other, life felt perfect.

As the sun peeked over the horizon, turning the water pink and blue, they were almost to the marina. Reluctant to see the night end, they slowed. They would soon have to turn around and return to their friends to help clean up from the all-night senior party. Dawn gave way to a beautiful blue-sky morning. Tina couldn't imagine being happier than she was in this moment.

"What's that?" Jacob asked, pointing to a pile of debris a few feet ahead.

"What? Seaweed?" Tina asked, perplexed.

And then she saw what had captured Jacob's interest. The sun was glinting off of something in the wet tangle of the dusky-colored algae. It sparkled in the light, and as the water lapped over it, more of it was exposed. They wandered nearer to see what the ocean had deposited on the strand.

"It looks like a watch," Jacob said as they closed in on it.

Startled, they realized it was a watch and still attached to a wrist. Another wave pulled the mound of seaweed back into the water, exposing a hand. Their screams brought all their friends racing to them.

By the time the group reached them, Tina had realized there was an entire body wrapped in the debris. Then a lifetime of being a police officer's daughter kicked in.

"Everyone stay back!" she instructed firmly. "Jacob, call 911. Brent, Brian, keep everyone back. We don't want to disturb any evidence until the police get here."

She pulled out her phone and dialed her dad.

"We'd better ditch the beer before the cops get here," Denny warned. That was followed by a flurry of activity. Illegal beer and the non-sea variety of weed trumped a dead body. The group scattered to remove the evidence of their celebration. Jacob, Tina, and a few others who did not want them to wait alone, remained with the body until the police arrived.

Ten minutes passed, and a single patrol car pulled into the marina parking lot. Dispatch wasn't going to waste resources on a senior prank. Twenty minutes later, the lot filled with all manner of law enforcement, including Tina's dad.

Duxbridge Police Lieutenant Benedito – Bennie – Carvalho did not have jurisdiction here. He wasn't even on duty, but when his daughter called, he immediately drove to be with her. On his way, he made three phone calls. First, he phoned his police chief and gave him the few details he had. The second call was to the Wareham chief, who had jurisdiction of the crime scene. And finally, a call to his estranged wife, letting her know he'd be there to protect their eldest daughter.

The sun was well over the horizon, but Tina had not left the body. Everyone else had departed for the parking lot, even Jacob. *That's okay,* Tina thought. *Dead bodies are scary.* But she knew if the police were going to find out what happened, the evidence needed to be undisturbed. Patrol officers were busy taping off a large area, but no one was with the body. They were waiting for the coroner. So she stood watch until she felt her dad's hand on her shoulder.

"Good job," he said.

"Thanks," she replied, grateful he was there.

"I think the police can handle it now."

"I feel bad leaving him like this," Tina said, her voice steady and full of compassion.

"I understand."

"Do you know who he is?"

Bennie looked down. He'd been so focused on taking care of Tina, he'd only briefly glanced at the body. Now he took the scene in like a cop. He walked around, examining everything as he did. The body had not been in the water long. Water has a way of rapidly degrading skin tissue, and sea life makes quick work of eyes and extremities. This one showed no signs of such activity.

The body was male, early to mid-fifties, the watch on his wrist was expensive and obviously waterproof. It displayed the correct time, ticking away long after the man's heart had stopped. He was lying on his side, and most of the debris had washed away from his face. Going out with the tide. Bennie hoped the waves hadn't removed all the best evidence.

There was a deep gash on the back of his head that parted his thick dark hair, along with his skull. No blood left to speak of, not deep enough for brain matter. Finally, Bennie took a good look at his face. He recognized him immediately.

"I do recognize him, honey. I do." Bennie put his arm around Tina's shoulder and led her over to a young patrol officer.

"Why don't you give this man your statement, and then I can take you home. I'm going to go talk to the detectives."

Bennie left his daughter and walked the short distance to where two detectives were instructing several patrol officers to obtain initial statements and contact information from the witnesses.

"Get them on their way before we have a bunch of anxious parents to add to our crowd," said one of the detectives. A pale, balding, paunch-bellied man Bennie knew in passing.

The officers departed, leaving Bennie and the two detectives alone.

"Hi, I'm Lieutenant Carvalho from Duxbridge PD. My daughter was the one who found the body."

"Lieutenant, the Chief said you'd be here. Is your girl all right? She did a great job securing the scene until we arrived."

"She's a little shook up, but I'm real proud of her," Bennie replied, his chest swelling a bit at the acknowledgment. "I wanted to let you know I recognize the body. His name is Devon Friedrickson. He's the owner of Devo's off Route 44. He lives in Duxbridge."

Both detectives stared at him for a moment. Everyone knew Devon Friedrickson, the renowned chef who left big city life, successful restaurants in New York, New Orleans and Boston, for a quiet New England town. Hit with scandals and a few bad reviews, he sold all his restaurants and bought an old dairy farm in Duxbridge. He remodeled the large farmhouse into a lavish estate and then set his sights on a restaurant. He purchased the defunct Lobster House at auction and set about turning it into an upscale destination establishment serving his signature menus.

"Are you sure?" the younger, well-dressed detective asked him in hushed tones, knowing the death of an infamous celebrity could bring with it media and gawkers just as they were gearing up for tourist season. He groaned and silently wondered if he could request vacation time.

"Yes. We know him well at the station. He is - was - an interesting character. Made enemies easier than friends. If the coroner determines it to be suspicious, the list of suspects could be long. Very long." Bennie looked over toward Tina. "If you have all the information you need from my daughter, I'd like to get her home. It's been a long night for her." The detective nodded.

Bennie collected Tina and opened the car door for her. "Does Jacob need a ride?" he asked, trying not to sound too disapproving.

"He's going back with Gina and Eddie."

"Do I need to ask if they are in any way impaired?"

"They're fine, dad. I wouldn't let them drive if they weren't."

"That's my girl."

After Bennie dropped his daughter off with her mom, he drove directly to the house of the Duxbridge Chief of Police.

TWO

Maggie Stellino was sitting at the counter, sipping coffee and watching Juliet LaChapelle – Jules to her friends - package up a to-go coffee and muffin and hand it to a customer. A blue scarf kept Juliet's short bob of blond hair in place, a whimsical duck clip securing it, a nod to the improbably named café: The Duck. She was owner, chef, baker and hostess. Most mornings, business lined up out the door.

"Thank you, Don, have a great day!" Juliet said as the middle-aged man in a Red Sox cap took the coffee and bagged muffin from her.

"You too, Juliet. See you tomorrow," he replied. He opened the door, and the little bell above jingled. He held it wide for a smartly dressed woman, then went on his way, sipping his coffee and humming as he walked down the sidewalk.

Maggie began to jot a few notes into a spiral notebook as she scanned the cards in front of her. These were some of Juliet's favorite lunchtime recipes. Maggie was scaling them down from restaurant servings to family meal proportions. Next, she would test them several times and then select the best for her latest cookbook. Her third cookbook, it would feature comfort foods for busy families.

She loved working here in the early morning, arriving not long after Juliet, writing quietly at the lunch counter while Juliet and her assistant Carl prepped for the day. It was a much better atmosphere for working than her tiny converted gatehouse – with its efficient but equally tiny kitchen – behind her Aunt's house.

Each morning, Maggie would pour herself a cup of coffee from the first pot of the day and then take her favorite seat in the predawn hours. Soon wonderful smells would drift from the amazing kitchen behind the bakery counter. Soups and breads competed with cookies and muffins for best café smell. And as the sun rose and the café opened, all manner of people from Duxbridge flowed through the doors.

The entire café had a homey feel, with dark wood wainscoting paired with paint the color of butter and a charming assortment of mismatched wood tables and chairs. In the mornings, sun streamed through the large front windows, adorned with tiered yellow-checked cabin curtains and the Duck logo painted on the glass above.

The long vintage lunch counter and a tall bakery case sat at the back of the café. The wall behind the counter was lined with shelves filled with knick-knacks, photos, and gifts from customers who felt like family. Behind the bakery case, through double swinging doors, was the restaurant kitchen. Stainless steel counters and industrial appliances surrounded an ancient butcher-block island used for rolling out pastries and breads.

A side door near the lunch counter led to a small patio. Walled on three sides by flowering vines on lattice, it was a peaceful spot to enjoy a mug of coffee. As the weather warmed, Juliet added planters filled with annuals. It was terrific for people watching. Maggie had spent many an hour there during the warmer months, editing and re-editing her cookbooks.

The bell over the door chimed as a customer entered.

"*Kia ora,* Maggie," a tall, dark-haired man dressed in a denim jacket over a black tee and jeans greeted Maggie with a thick New Zealand accent. Her heart involuntarily skipped a beat. His gold-rimmed brown eyes captured her, and his smile lit up the room.

"Morning, Jake. Jules should be right out," Maggie informed him. "How's the remodel coming along?"

"Smoothly so far. But the buildings on this block are almost a hundred years old, so I expect to run into trouble at some point."

"Don't say that!" Juliet exclaimed as she popped out of the kitchen. "I can barely afford this expansion, to begin with." She handed him a stainless steel travel mug and a white bag. "Flat white and bagel with cream cheese. Come back for lunch. I'll make you a Sonoma chicken sandwich with a side of coleslaw.

"This is my favorite job. The employee benefits can't be beat," he said, flashing that smile again. "See you later, Maggie," he said with a nod. And with that, he was out the door.

Jake was Juliet's contractor. When the antique shop next door closed and the space came up for sale, Juliet decided it was the perfect time to expand. She had always wanted to own a venue large enough to host events, like small wedding receptions, parties and business conferences, and name it the Roost. This renovation would get her started on that goal.

"Jules, don't take this personally, but I sure hope your expansion takes a very long time."

Juliet laughed and handed Maggie a plate with a sesame bagel, a small ceramic container of cream cheese, and a few sliced strawberries on it.

"You spoil me," Maggie told her. Juliet went to help a customer, and Maggie returned to her notes. She was working on a French Market Chicken recipe, trying to do the math to transform Juliet's restaurant-sized quantities into workable portions for families. Proportions were tricky, which is why she would test each recipe after the initial breakdown.

Once she felt she had one that worked, she would put together a complete menu around it, including dessert.

Then she would test the entire menu on friends and family. And because her kitchen was the size of a postage stamp, Juliet was kind enough to let her prepare them at the café. Juliet, her wife Bria Rhys, and Maggie's brother Mike were her regular guinea pigs, often joined by other friends and family.

She would love to have them at her house, but since she had moved back to Duxbridge from New York City, she'd been living in her Aunt Carol's gatehouse. It had been repurposed as a cute one-bedroom cottage, decidedly inadequate for a dinner party, no matter how casual. Eventually, she'd buy a small house, but for now, she was content to be a tenant. Besides, her Aunt could use the extra income, and Maggie liked the company.

"Need a refill?" Juliet interrupted her thoughts.

"Yes, please." Maggie pushed her cup over. "It's quiet this morning."

"It has been," she agreed. "I haven't seen a lot of our regulars yet."

The bell over the door rang, and they both looked up to see Maggie's brother Mike breeze into the café. He was a Duxbridge police officer and was in uniform but looking more disheveled than usual.

"Morning, sis," he said as he strode over and sat next to her. "Morning, Jules."

"Coffee and a bear claw?" Juliet asked.

"Yes, and make it to-go, would you please?" Mike asked as he handed her his travel mug.

"I thought you were working days. You look like you've been out all night. Your uniform is filthy," Maggie observed.

"Haven't you heard? Big case. I've been over at Onset beach, helping work the crime scene. I'm heading out to get witness statements now."

"Onset? That's not Duxbridge jurisdiction. What's going on?"

Mike looked around. The café was empty, so he felt he could safely give them the details. He wasn't one to break protocol, but this was his sister, and he'd known Juliet his entire life, feeling she was more family than friend. He lowered his voice, "There was a murder, and he was from Duxbridge."

"A murder," Juliet gasped. "When was the last time we had a murder around here?"

"Right?" Mike continued, "The only one I can remember was when Old Man Barton pushed his brother down the stairs because he thought he was sleeping with his wife. Despite all of them being in their late seventies." Mike took a sip of his coffee. "But this one is going to be big. The deceased is practically a celebrity. It's Devon Friedrickson, and he washed up on the beach."

"Oh, my God," Maggie breathed. "Are you sure it was murder?"

"It looks like it. I think someone hit him in the head. Don't know if that killed him or if he drowned. The coroner will let us know later today."

"If it's murder, your suspect list is going to be long." Maggie shook her head, trying to absorb the information. She'd had her own run-ins with him.

"Wow, no kidding," Juliet agreed. "He treated everyone like crap. Did anyone like him?"

"Are you working with Wareham on this?" Being a cop's sister, Maggie was familiar with all the politics and administrative hassles when dealing with the various law enforcement agencies.

"Believe it or not, one of the teens who found the body was Lieutenant Carvalho's daughter."

"Tina?" Juliet looked alarmed. Tina worked for her on the weekends.

"Yeah, and she called Carvalho. When he realized who the deceased was, he convinced the Chief to ask

Wareham for jurisdiction. Wareham's Chief was more than happy to dump it on us. They have their hands full prepping for the summer season."

"And Bennie's got you running around doing his legwork?" Maggie asked, knowing that her brother was always first in line to request that duty.

"He handed it off to Joe Madigan. He didn't want there to be a conflict. This one's important, sis, and I'm not going to miss out," he said emphatically. "Helping solve a high-profile case will only advance my career, so I told Madigan I'd do whatever he needed."

Maggie tried not to sigh. She worried about her brother every day and wasn't happy he'd be in the middle of a potentially dangerous murder investigation. However, she would stay silent and supportive. She knew he had long-term goals that would lead him far away from police work and into politics. And it was true, being associated with a successful investigation would only boost his profile and hasten his political aspirations.

"What's your next step?" Juliet asked.

"I'm going to go talk with Tina, get her take on it. Hopefully, when I'm done with her statement, the warrant will be ready for Friedrickson's house. I'll join the crime scene crew there."

"I hope she's okay. What a horrible thing to discover." Juliet worried.

"From what I heard, she's her father's daughter. Took over the entire scene, wouldn't let anyone disturb the evidence. Made sure the party-goers dumped their contraband and stuck around for interviews."

"Good for her," Maggie said, impressed. She was sure she wouldn't have that kind of composure in a similar situation.

"Well, I've got to go. Don't go blabbing what I've told you." He stood up and gave his sister a quick kiss on the forehead.

"Be careful," she said as he walked to the door.

"Ten-four," he replied as he left.

"Wow," Juliet breathed, looking at Maggie.

Maggie knew they were thinking the same thing, Devon was a rat-bastard, but no one deserved this.

"I wonder…who?"

"Right?!" Juliet whispered. "I mean, who hasn't he ticked off since he arrived in Duxbridge?"

"Me, included." Maggie shook her head, feeling guilty because, with Devon dead, he would no longer be a thorn in her side.

"Me, too," Juliet said, getting up to refill her and Maggie's mugs.

"Wait? You? I don't believe it. You're the kindest person I know."

"Yeah, well, Devon sure knew how to push my buttons," Juliet explained. "He was demanding the de Lunas give him exclusivity so that no other local restaurants could buy specialty cheeses from their farm. Poor Bridie, she told him no, but he kept at her." Juliet frowned at the memory. "I finally gave him a piece of my mind one day when he came storming out to their place. I was there, delivering Bridie and Johnny a batch of a new pastry recipe I made using one of their specialty cheeses."

"Oh, boy," Maggie said, knowing that when Juliet went into mama tiger mode, no one was safe.

"Oh, yeah. It wasn't pretty. But he stopped pressuring them, and Bridie was grateful, so I have no regrets."

Maggie didn't bother mentioning her own run-in with him. Juliet was already very familiar with it. A few weeks ago, Devon's attorney served Maggie with papers. Devon was suing her, claiming many of the recipes in her first cookbook were his signature dishes, which was ludicrous. The entire theme of the cookbook was New York restaurant classics. She chose her favorite restaurant meals, went into her kitchen, and made her own versions. Devon's place wasn't even on her radar, except for the occasional night out with friends.

Nevertheless, his frivolous lawsuit meant she had to hire a lawyer and fork out a retainer she could hardly afford. She'd been seething about it ever since. But her very expensive lawyer assured her it would be settled quickly, so Maggie left it in her hands and focused on her newest cookbook. Recipe testing on friends was a great distraction.

"I sure hope Tina is all right," Juliet said, bringing Maggie out of her dark thoughts about the dead chef. "I know Mike said she was a pro. Still, that had to be horrible to see."

"It had to be. I know I wouldn't have been as calm in her shoes."

The little bell above the door chimed again, and Juliet left to attend to customers, leaving Maggie alone with her thoughts. There would be no more recipes today. All her energy was focused on who would murder Chef Devon.

Mike was not the only criminalist in the family. Maggie took great interest in even the inconsequential mysteries that came Mike's way on the job. The same mind that deconstructed dishes down to their smallest ingredients and recreated them was also a mind completely engrossed by criminals and the crimes they committed. She devoured mystery novels and true crime stories. Duxbridge didn't offer a lot of intrigues, but on the few occasions something beyond a petty theft occurred, Maggie had been known to entice Mike over for a home-cooked meal so she could get him to spill the juicy details and walk her through the persons of interest.

It wasn't exactly proper procedure, but in a small town where every home had a police scanner in the kitchen, those in charge would most likely turn a blind eye if they knew Mike and Maggie were sketching out crime scenes on napkins and digging up possible suspects. They would probably be impressed that on more than one occasion, Maggie's sharp mind would see a pattern that gave Mike a solid lead.

As happened when the bronze duck sculptures in the greenway were vandalized. The ducks, large enough for kids to climb on, were the centerpiece of the small park that sat in the town square. As old as the town, the square was surrounded on three sides by government buildings and on the fourth by the oldest church in the area. Countless families and high school seniors had their photos taken on those beloved waterfowl, and it was quite a shock to find them spray-painted in vivid fluorescent hues one morning.

An angry town demanded quick action. Unfortunately, there were no suspects and no leads. Mike sat dejected at dinner that night, telling Maggie that they would probably never know who had done it or why.

It was during that dinner that Maggie remembered a trip to Fellowes Hardware a few weeks earlier and seeing Roger Dawsey buying at least two dozen cans of spray paint. She overheard him telling hardware store owner, Gus Fellowes, that he was refinishing his patio furniture. She distinctly remembered that there were several cans of brightly colored fluorescent paints in the mix. At the time, she thought it odd, only because Mr. Dawsey didn't seem the whimsical type. When she mentioned it to Mike, he scoffed at the idea of the retired plumber vandalizing public property, much less spray-painting it like some delinquent teen.

"I'm not saying he did it," she defended herself. "Someone could have stolen it from his shed."

"Mags, it was probably some high school kids who bought the paint from the Walmart in Taunton, got drunk, and did something stupid."

"Could be. But it wouldn't hurt to talk to him," she prodded. "I mean, what better way to hide your criminal intentions than buying a ridiculous amount of spray paint in a variety of colors to hide the paint you actually wanted. Besides, who uses fluorescent paint on patio furniture?"

Mike relented, and the next day he went out to talk with Dawsey. The first thing he noticed was that the patio was full of almost brand-new rattan furniture, not a sign of any freshly painted pieces anywhere. He walked over to the shed and peeked in the open door. There was a shelf lined with a dozen or more cans of spray paint, but not one of them was florescent.

After Mike confronted Dawsey with all of this, he quickly confessed. Seemed he had been angry with the city council's decision to rezone his neighbors' large parcels for residential houses. Even though it was going to be a small development with five-acre lots, Dawsey believed it was the first step to being surrounded by fast food, gas stations and subdivisions.

"I ain't living in no suburbs of Boston," he hollered as he was handcuffed.

This time though, it wasn't vandalism. A murder was serious, and Maggie thought to herself that she had no business even speculating on who might have reason to kill Devon. But it was all too scintillating. He was a detestable human being, and the list of people who would not mourn his passing was inevitably long.

She got up and bussed her dishes, then closed her laptop and put it in its case. She stepped around the counter to bid goodbye to Juliet and Carl, gathered her belongings, and was about to step out the side door when a horrendous crash stopped her in her tracks.

THREE

Maggie, Carl and Juliet ran out of the café and toward the ruckus next door.

"Jake!" Juliet called out. Debris streamed from the open door, plaster particles dancing in the morning light. "Jake!" Juliet called again as she waved away the dust and stood in the doorway, letting her eyes adjust to the dimly lit interior.

"Do you see him?" Maggie asked, looking over her shoulder. Splintered wood and chunks of plaster filled the interior. Maggie's heart clenched, fearful Jake or his crew might be under it. She looked up. "Oh. My. Gosh. Jules, the ceiling!" Maggie pointed over Juliet's shoulder at what had been the ceiling. All that was left was a gaping hole.

"I'm going in," Carl said, pushing his broad, muscled frame past them. "Jake, buddy, you in here?" He gingerly stepped over wood and plaster.

"Stop!" Jake cautioned as he stepped into view from the back of the building. "It's not safe. I'll meet you out front."

Carl retreated to the sidewalk with Maggie and Juliet, and they waited impatiently for Jake.

"I hope everyone is okay," Juliet said, and then added with a sigh, "That all looks very expensive."

Maggie patted her shoulder. She hated to admit how glad she was to see Jake emerge unscathed. It was more than a mere feeling of relief.

"Well, that was a bit of excitement, wasn't it?" Jake said as he rounded the corner.

"What happened?" Juliet asked

"The ceiling fell," Jake replied matter-of-factly.

"I can see that," Juliet said flatly.

"No worries, she'll be right," Jake assured her. "I wasn't expecting everything to come down in a heap, but we were going to take it all down anyway. Just not all at once," he added with a smile.

"And you're okay?" Maggie asked, still shaken by what could have been.

" Good as gold. But we do have a bit of a mess to clean up. I'm just glad the crew wasn't here yet." He looked over at Juliet, who still had that stunned look. "Don't worry, Jules. We'll suss it out. Now, go take care of your customers. I'll handle this."

"Okay," Juliet said, though she didn't sound convinced. She and Carl returned to the café, and several onlookers followed them, not letting a little construction catastrophe interfere with their morning brew.

"I'm glad no one got hurt," Maggie said, giving him a warm smile.

"I'm glad to see you so concerned," Jake said with a twinkle in his eyes.

"I'm just worried about Jules. She already had a big shock today," Maggie teased. "Digging you out from under rubble would have added to her stress."

"Just what this town needs is another dead body, right?"

Startled, Maggie asked, "How…how did you hear about that?"

"It was all the talk at the lumber yard this morning. Murder is not an everyday occurrence."

"No, not at all. Mike and I were trying to remember the last one," Maggie said before catching herself, knowing she shouldn't divulge their conversation.

"Oh, so you get special police briefs, eh?"

"Nope. Never," she said with a grin. "What was the consensus at the lumber yard?"

"Mostly that the deceased had it coming. Although no one actually speculated who did the poor sap in," Jake added, looking to Maggie, hoping for a tidbit or two. Maggie wasn't falling for those dimples.

"Wear a hard hat," she said as she turned and walked down the street.

Jake watched her walk away until she disappeared around the corner, enjoying the view.

Maggie strolled downtown, making one quick stop at Fabiano's market to pick up a couple of jars of sun-dried tomatoes, so she could play with the recipe she had written that morning. Making her way through the narrow aisles of the little grocery, she couldn't stop thinking about Devon. Many people were not fond of him. But to kill him? She couldn't imagine that much hate.

Well, she could imagine it. She had felt it, that burning desire to eradicate everything and anything that reminded her of the man she once loved. She had wanted to destroy all that Brad owned, and he would have deserved it, the cheating, lying bastard. Nevertheless, other than throwing a vase of apology flowers at him, she had no desire to harm him. She only wished on him financial ruin and a miserable life with the skank from the local news station.

Though, in a fit of pique, she did call the skank's boss. She asked him if it was commonplace for his reporters to shag one-half of the couple they were interviewing for a story. A business spotlight piece that was supposed to launch their financial consulting company into the stratosphere but instead cratered it. By the time they dissolved their partnership and Brad bought her out, word had spread that he was the reason the dream team imploded, and clients left as quickly as she did.

In the wake of the split, dozens of people called, asking her to take them on and work her financial magic once again, but she declined. She needed a change, a new start...a new dream. She left New York and went home to Duxbridge to be around old friends and loving family, to regroup and revive. Then, one day, sitting in the Duck café, a lightning bolt struck, and she knew what she wanted to do. Three years later, she was happily writing cookbooks in the sleepy little village in which she had grown up.

Now, unpacking the groceries, she returned her focus to the day's recipe. She gathered all the ingredients she would need onto the broad rustic table that served as both a makeshift island and dining table. She had found it at a flea market and fell in love with its thick turned legs and scarred surface, a testament to its long history. She painted the legs a cheery red and oiled the solid oak top.

After patting a whole chicken dry, she skillfully quartered it, then seasoned it with salt and fresh ground pepper. Next, she turned her attention to the vegetables, chopping onions, celery, red peppers and carrots. Her large cast-iron skillet was heating up, and she poured a generous amount of oil into it. She quickly browned the chicken, removed it to a platter, and added the vegetables into the skillet. She reduced the heat and let them soften.

She turned the heat off under the boiling rice and set it aside to absorb all the water. Once the onions were translucent, she added crushed garlic. A few minutes later, in went the chicken broth, sun-dried tomatoes, and a sprinkling of red pepper flakes to spice things up. She returned the chicken to the pan and let everything braise while she cleaned up.

As she wiped down her chef's knife, her mind wandered back to thoughts of Devon. She should be making notes on how to simplify her current recipe, reducing the hour-plus cooking time to a simple thirty-minute dinner. Her brain had other ideas. *Washed up on the beach,* she thought. *Had he been at the marina or maybe out fishing?* His restaurant was closed on Mondays; he would have had the day off. Did he fish? He never struck her as someone who did anything leisurely. Running his restaurant consumed him. Downsizing and relocating to the quiet New England village had not dampened his drive. Or his temper. Anyone who had dined with regularity at Devo's had witnessed at least one outburst, usually directed at staff, but also the occasional guest who had not shown the proper respect for his cuisine.

Maggie shook her head. She did not envy the police. The list of suspects would be daunting. The timer went off, and Maggie returned her focus to her recipe. She jotted down notes and began a shopping list. She plated a serving of the chicken, placing a leg quarter on a mound of steaming rice and drizzling sauce over all of it. She enjoyed her lunch and her solitude.

Creating recipes had saved her. During her darkest moments, when her entire life plans were upended, the simple act of cooking gave her solace. And then, when she decided to try her hand at writing a cookbook, she was also ready to invite people back into her life. Cooking gave her that opportunity.

Then came the dinner parties, guests equipped with notebooks, tasting various dishes, and giving feedback. And suddenly, she felt purpose and direction. A cookbook author was born.

If she didn't keep her mind on this recipe, she'd be a washed-up cookbook author. She swept thoughts of murder from her mind and focused on spices, cooking times, and shortcuts. Once she had all her notes completed and a shopping list together, she deboned the chicken. She added it to the rice and sauce mixture before putting it in the refrigerator. Finally, she made an iced coffee and sat at her desk to plan the entire menu.

By mid-afternoon, she closed her computer, feeling accomplished. A few more days like this, and she would have a dozen menus to test out on her friends and family. She loved feeding people, and after a good meal, many would ask her if she had ever thought of opening her own restaurant. Her answer was always emphatically no.

Running a restaurant took a passion Maggie did not feel. She watched the long hours Juliet put in dealing with staffing issues, ungrateful customers, cranky vendors, and thought it would take away all the joy she felt in cooking. Juliet loved it and thrived on putting all the puzzle pieces together to create a homey dining experience.

On the other hand, Maggie thought, Devon appeared to thrive on creating chaos, with his staff, with his vendors and even with his customers. His food was divine, but the dining was never without some drama. Maggie wondered if many of his customers returned time and time again just for the show.

The day was too lovely to waste it all indoors, so Maggie set aside thoughts of recipes and murder and went outside to work in the garden. She had reclaimed a barren spot in her Aunt's backyard, adding raised beds, soaker hoses, and good soil. In the garden, she planted a variety of vegetables and herbs.

It was too early in the season to expect any produce, but her herbs were doing nicely, and the snap peas would be ready soon. She wandered between the beds and checked on the progress of the tomatoes, peppers and tomatillos. They were safely encased in water cages that Gus had recommended. She was so pleased with the results last year that she bestowed upon him six jars of various tomato sauces. As she peered into the water teepees, she was satisfied with the progress. Each small transplant had doubled in size over the past week.

She pulled a few weeds and turned on the soaker hose. After that, she went into the tiny shed next to her house – a building she was convinced was an outhouse in a previous era – and grabbed a wicker basket and clippers. Back in the garden, she harvested a bit from various herbs to dry and package. They would be available all summer, more than she could possibly use. Drying and storing the excess would keep her pantry stocked all winter.

She tossed the clippers back in the shed and took the basket of herbs into her cottage. She washed them and was setting them out to dry when her phone rang. Since she had no idea where she had left it this time, she made a mad scramble to find it as it rang a second and then a third time. A race to locate it before it rolled over to voicemail, she finally unearthed it from beneath the dishtowel on the far counter, just in time to say, "hello," and hear Juliet reply, "oh, I'm glad you answered."

"What's up?" Maggie asked, thinking Juliet sounded uncharacteristically serious.

"Maggie," Juliet replied in a low voice. "The cops were here, grabbing a quick break."

"Oh, was Mike with them?" Maggie asked.

"No, it was Pereira, Murphy, and a new guy I didn't recognize. I overheard them talking about the detectives having a good suspect in Devon's murder," Juliet whispered.

Maggie was confused because Juliet sounded frantic. "That's good, right?" she asked.

"Maggie, when I came out to refill their coffee, they shut up. Like, mid-sentence, and they wouldn't look at me when I refilled their cups. It was weird."

"Well, yeah, it is a bit, but you know they need to keep this stuff confidential. They probably realized they shouldn't be discussing it in public."

"Maybe." Juliet did not sound mollified. "There's something I should tell you." Maggie held her breath, knowing this was not going to be good. "I threatened Devon."

"What? When? What do you mean, 'threatened'?" Maggie asked, sure it was nothing.

"At the Farmer's market on Saturday. He was harassing Bridie again, and I'd just had it. I..I threatened him and told him to drop dead," She paused and whispered, "A whole bunch of people heard me," she sounded close to tears. "You don't think that makes me a suspect, do you?"

"Oh, don't be silly, Jules," Maggie reassured her. "Of course not. Trust me, you are not the first person to threaten that man. Unless you pulled out a knife and said, 'I'm going to kill you,' you're probably not even in the top ten of suspects. Relax."

"Okay," Juliet said, placated. "But, the cops sure were acting funny."

"Well, we don't get a lot of murders here. It's feasible they aren't clear on what's appropriate to discuss in a café and what's not."

"I suppose you're right," Juliet said. "But you'll let me know if Mike lets anything slip, won't you?"

"Of course," Maggie replied before disconnecting.

As Maggie patted the herbs gently, turning them over a couple of times to remove all the excess water, her mind was buzzing. A suspect? Already? She supposed that could be possible. Mike was always telling her criminals were rarely smart or clever in their crimes. If Devon's murder was committed in the heat of an argument, which seemed the most likely scenario, there might be an abundance of evidence to lead detectives to the perpetrator.

While she was glad they solved it quickly, she was a bit disappointed she wouldn't get to mull over sundry clues and scenarios any longer. She chastised herself for such selfish thoughts as she put the herbs on a drying rack.

Her phone rang again, and she saw Mike's photo pop up on the screen.

Oh, good, she thought. *He'll tell me what's going on.* She swiped on his photo and said hello.

"Sis, we need to talk. It's important. Meet me at our spot in fifteen minutes."

FOUR

Maggie drove through town, turning into Nemasket Park, and followed the curved, heavily wooded road until she reached the big iron gate that led into the Nemasket Cemetery. Then she slowed to a crawl, avoiding potholes and ruts in the tree-lined macadam that led to the family plot. Her brother was already there, sitting on a stone bench. Maggie eased her compact red Fiat onto the shoulder and got out.

"Is it weird our 'spot' is Gram's grave?"

Mike looked grim and did not respond to her attempt at dark humor. Maggie felt the chill of foreboding, and Juliet's concerns echoed in her head. She steeled herself and waited. Mike stood up and walked over to their grandmother's headstone. He swept away nonexistent debris from the curved top. Maggie couldn't take the silence any longer.

"Mike," she implored. "What's wrong?"

Mike turned to her and took in a deep breath. Maggie noticed he looked even more disheveled then at the café. He walked back to the bench and gestured for Maggie to sit. She complied, and he sat down next to her.

"Sis, I could lose my job for what I'm about to tell you," he began. "But..." He stopped and looked away for a moment before continuing. "We got a lucky break and recovered Friedrickson's cell phone at his house." Mike paused again. Maggie couldn't imagine what Mike was struggling to say, but she waited, dreading what he would risk his job to tell her. "You left a message, sis," he said quietly.

Realization hit Maggie, and she couldn't believe this was what had Mike unnerved. "That was weeks ago. He'd just had me served, and I was enraged," Maggie explained. "I hired a lawyer. I didn't bash him in the head."

"You threatened to kill him!"

"I used a colorful expletive our mother would not approve of and wished him dead. I was angry," Maggie repeated. "It's not like I said, stay out of the library, or I'll do you in with the candlestick," Maggie said, exasperated.

"Madigan talked to Friedrickson's attorney. He seemed pretty confident that they'd win the case against you. It sounded like it could bankrupt you."

Maggie was stunned by what she was hearing. Her brother could not be intimating she killed Devon. "Well, my attorney had a different interpretation. The words 'frivolous' and 'without merit' were used," Maggie said defensively. "You cannot seriously think I had anything to do with Devon's death," she finished adamantly.

Mike sat quietly for a moment, and Maggie suddenly felt nauseated. This could not be real.

"No," Mike finally replied. "I don't think you had anything to do with this. But as far as Madigan is concerned, you're the number one suspect, and he pulled me off the case."

"Wait. What?" How was this happening? "So the police are convinced I'm the one, and they aren't even letting you pursue any of the multitudes of people who had a grievance against the pretentious bastard? Based on a month-old voice message?"

"I don't know. I got bounced so fast, I don't know what other evidence they have, but they must have something else." Mike looked at her, his face serious. "Was there anything else? Did you threaten him in person, in front of witnesses?"

"No!" Maggie was quickly losing patience. "I didn't threaten him at all. This is ridiculous."

"Look, I'll find out what I can," Mike reassured her. "And I'm going to follow-up on other suspects...unofficially," he added when Maggie began to protest. "I have ways of relaying any information I find without it coming back to me. Trust me."

"I don't want you jeopardizing your job over this because I know I didn't do it. Truth will out."

"I know you didn't. But did you do something to piss off Madigan?" Mike asked, half-joking.

"I've met him all of once, when I brought lunch for the station," she replied. "See if I feed him again."

Mike leaned over and kissed her forehead. "Contact a criminal attorney, lay low, be prepared. I'll do what I can on my end." He got up, walked down the path, and disappeared beyond the heavy foliage.

Maggie should have been terrified. She should have gone straight home and called her attorney for advice. Instead, she jumped into her car and drove to the Duck. News this juicy must be shared with her best friend.

Besides, she knew it would help ease Juliet's own concerns about being a suspect. Even though her worry would no doubt shift to Maggie, it wasn't something Maggie could keep from her. Small town gossip would soon disseminate the information throughout the village, and the café would be second only to Fellowes Hardware for the gaggles to gather to apportion the latest developments.

She parked in the small parking lot in the alley behind the Duck. She entered through the kitchen door, not wanting to draw unwanted attention, in case her sudden status as suspect had already begun to leak. She carefully closed the screen door behind her to keep out the burgeoning summer bug population.

Juliet was checking on something in the oven and didn't turn around when she heard the door.

"Jimmy, can you put those vegetables in the cooler for me," she called out from the depths of the industrial oven as she poked at her cinnamon rolls.

"Not Jimmy," Maggie replied.

"Maggie!" Juliet exclaimed as she secured the oven door. "Do you want a fresh cinn -" she stopped as she turned and saw her. "What's happened?"

"I guess professional poker player will not be one of my careers," Maggie said with a laugh. She sat on a stool next to Juliet's island. "We need to talk," her tone serious. She patted the seat next to her.

Juliet sat, concern flooding her face.

"I have good news and some not so good news. You know the drill," Maggie tried to lighten the mood. Juliet reached over and put her hand over Maggie's.

"Good news first, get that right out of the way," Juliet said with a nervous laugh.

"I think I can confidently say you are not the number one suspect in Devon's murder." Maggie let that information settle for a moment.

"Well, that's a relief," Juliet said, suddenly very suspicious about what the not so good news could be. "Do we know who is?"

Maggie took a breath, steeling herself against the reality. "I am," she said, raising her hand.

Juliet gasped and went pale. "No!" she yelled, then lowered her voice to continue. "That's not possible. Who told you this insane information?"

Maggie looked around to make sure they would not be overheard. Mike was in a precarious enough position. He didn't need criminal activity added to it. "Mike," she whispered. "They pulled him from the investigation as soon as they honed in on me."

"This is absurd. Exactly what evidence do they have?"

"It's thin," Maggie began, grabbing Juliet's arm to lean in closer. "I don't want to talk about it here, can you come over after work? We can talk freely at my place."

"Absolutely. I'm almost done with tomorrow's prep, and it's been slow enough that Carl can take care of closing," Juliet reassured her, still huddled in close.

"Uh, oh, what mischief are you two planning?"

Maggie and Juliet started as Jake strode into the kitchen.

"Whoa, what's wrong?" Jake asked, seeing the worried look on Juliet's face. He came in close, and Maggie shivered when his arm brushed hers.

"The police think Maggie killed Devon Friedrickson. Can you believe it?" Juliet said in a hushed tone. Jake slipped his arms around both women as he listened. Maggie gave Juliet a cautionary look.

"Are you being straight up?" Jake asked, alarmed. He lowered his voice. "You didn't, did you?" he asked Maggie and then grinned at her defiant look.

"No, of course not," Maggie said indignantly.

"All good. I just wanted to make sure before I offered to assist you in proving your innocence."

"Well, I appreciate that," Maggie said, trying to ignore the sculpted arm holding her tightly. She was simultaneously comforted and flushed. "I'm not sure what you could do."

Jake leaned in closer, if that was possible. "I recently finished up a project at his house. I can confirm he had no shortages of people he's pissed off."

"We're going to meet up at Maggie's in about an hour. You should come," Juliet said, ignoring Maggie's stunned look.

"I'll be there. Should I bring a plate?" Jake asked as he released them.

"I've got food covered," Maggie said with a sigh. She wasn't sure what Juliet was up to but resigned herself to it.

"See you in an hour. We'll have a cuppa and get this sorted." He walked to the door, then turned back to Juliet. "Everything is locked up next door. I have to pick up some supplies and get a delivery scheduled. Then I'll be back at it tomorrow. *"Ka kite anō!"* And he was gone.

"What are you thinking?" Maggie asked when she was sure Jake was out of earshot.

"He likes you, in case you haven't noticed," Juliet said with a smile.

"And you thought my being investigated for murder was a good time for matchmaking?"

"No time like the present. You've been celibate long enough," Juliet goaded. "And a shared project is a great way to get to know one another."

"A shared project?!" Maggie was flabbergasted. "You consider proving my innocence a shared project?"

"Absolutely." Juliet was enjoying herself. "It's been three years, time to come out of mourning or self-flagellation or whatever it is you've been doing since you moved back."

"Well, my luck with men, Jake will turn out to be the killer."

An hour later, Maggie was fussing in her kitchen, serving up iced tea and homemade chocolate-chocolate chip cookies to Juliet and Jake sitting at her big table.

"I should have brought some of the leftover pastries, too," Juliet said as she bit into a cookie.

"Don't you take your remaining product over to the nursing home every day? Besides, it's better these don't stay around long," Maggie said with a laugh.

"I'm happy to take some off your hands," Jake chimed in, grabbing a second cookie from the plate. "So, what's this foolishness about you being a killer?"

Maggie sat down and stirred her tea absently. She knew she should be more worried about the accusation, but the absurdity of it kept her in denial.

"I left an angry voicemail – a month ago," she began defensively. "Somehow, that has made me a prime suspect. I'm finding it difficult to believe I'm the only one who had ever left Devon an angry message."

"Bollocks," Jake said as he set his glass down. "I witnessed several angry phone calls and as many angry visits while I was remodeling his patio and outdoor kitchen. He had his share of furious vendors, patrons and partners."

"Partners, as in business…or pleasure?" Juliet asked.

"Both. I had the impression he was quite the player," Jake replied. "It can't just be that message. Did Mike tell you anything else?"

"I didn't say Mike…"

"Oh, come on," Jake said, adding tea to her glass, then topping off his. "If it was my sister in trouble, rules be damned. Of course, he told you."

"Okay, but that does NOT leave this room," Maggie said adamantly. "The voicemail was all they had discovered before they pulled him from the case. He's going to try and find out more, but I do not want him risking his reputation over this. The boy has big dreams, and I'm not going to let him derail them because of me."

"Then we'll just have to go all Jessica Fletcher and go it alone," Juliet declared.

"Who?" Jake looked confused.

"Miss Marple, but in Maine," Maggie explained.

Jake rolled his eyes but said nothing.

"Can you think of any other evidence they might have?" Juliet probed.

"Just the lawsuit. But my lawyer was handling that. I couldn't be the only one Devon was suing. He seemed litigious to me." She looked over at Jake. He raised an eyebrow. "How did you manage to complete a job without raising his ire?"

"I'm just that good." This time it was Maggie who rolled her eyes. "Also, I have a standard arbitration clause in my contracts. Keeps things friendly."

"I don't want Mike to jeopardize his job, but I really need him to find out what else they have that has turned me into an alleged murderess."

"You need to contact a criminal lawyer, just in case," Juliet said with concern. She didn't say, just in case what, but they were all thinking the same thing. Just in case Madigan and a bunch of uniforms burst through the door, cuffed Maggie, and dragged her off to jail.

"Maybe I can find out what evidence they have," Jake proposed.

"How exactly would you do that?" Maggie quizzed him.

"Mates talk," he said with a smile. "Especially if there's a pint or two involved."

Maggie was not convinced, but desperate times and all. "When might this recon take place?" she asked, feeling that time was of the essence.

"Quite of few of Duxbridge's finest will be watching rugby later tonight at Duffy's. I suspect, besides discussing if Kieran White's injury is going to keep him out for the season, the hot topic will be murder."

"You might be on to something there. Just don't give away the game," Maggie cautioned.

"Don't worry, I'm a sly one," he reassured her with a wink.

Juliet grabbed another cookie and looked thoughtful. "Well, if we are all convinced Maggie is not a murder, who do we think it might be?"

"I hear you've got a pretty hot temper and were recently overheard threatening the victim on a cold spring morning," Maggie teased.

A phone buzzed, and everyone grabbed their cell to check if it was theirs. Juliet swiped hers open, ceasing the buzzing.

"Hi honey," she answered and walked out of the room, silently indicating she'd be right back.

"So, anyone jump to the front of the murder line for you?" Maggie asked Jake, pushing the cookie plate closer to him.

"There are a couple of folks. One I remember was some business partner in one of his out-of-state restaurants. He showed up one morning in a sweet electric red Mercedes. They had a heated argument that ended with him almost pushing Devon into the pool and Devon fending him off with the pool skimmer. I was about to intervene, but Mr. Red Mercedes left as quickly as he showed up. Fishtailed out of the driveway while Devon dove into the pool to do laps as if nothing had happened. Devon was a cold one with shark eyes. I doubt he lost many battles. Well, except for the last one."

Maggie thought Jake's description apt. Devon was indeed an ice-cold shark.

"What was the argument about?"

"I only caught a few words. Sounded like Mr. Red Mercedes believed Devon cheated him on the sale of one of the restaurants. I think he said French Quarter, but I was pretty far away."

"That's actually a good lead," Maggie said, impressed. "It wouldn't be difficult to track down who his investors were in any of his restaurants. See who was feeling aggrieved." Maggie grabbed a small spiral notebook from a pile she kept for recipes. She flipped the cover around and began to write a few notes on the lined page.

"And just who is going to track down these leads?"

"My schedule is flexible," Maggie replied without looking up from the pad.

"Are you taking the piss?" Jake sounded annoyed, and Maggie looked up sharply.

"Excuse me?"

"Sorry, I mean, are you serious? You're going to go poking around?"

"I was thinking about it. Mike is off the case, and I can't imagine if I'm the prime suspect, anyone else is going to do any deeper digging when they are convinced it's me."

"Yeah, nah," Jake shook his head. "That's not a good idea." Maggie stared at him. "I mean, I'm sure you're capable, but Maggie, this is murder."

"Any other good prospects?" she asked, ignoring his concern.

Juliet walked back into the kitchen. She looked at Maggie and then at Jake, understanding she'd walked into something interesting. "What'd I miss?"

"Jake thinks I'm rash and maybe a bit crazy."

"He's not wrong." Juliet smiled at him. "I'm going to have to bug out, that was Bria, and her client canceled. She was hoping we could spend some much needed time together."

"Definitely, go. Give her a hug for me," Maggie urged. Between Juliet's café hours and Bria's demanding design clients, time alone was a rare commodity. She didn't want them to waste a bonus afternoon.

"You'll call your attorney, right? Get a referral for a criminal lawyer?" It was more of a demand than a question. Maggie nodded and then hugged her friend, grateful for her concern.

"You two keep brainstorming on suspects, and we can confer at coffee in the a.m.," Juliet said as she hustled out the door, waving as she went.

"Now, who else created a stir at Devon's place while you were there?

FIVE

Jake absently stirred his tea as he thought about his weeks working at Friedrickson's. Maggie nibbled on a cookie and waited patiently. Finally, Jake set his spoon on his cookie plate.

"There were a couple of women that raised a ruckus," Jake began. He sipped his tea and continued. "Devon appeared to make a lot of promises that he didn't keep. At least, according to the women who stormed out, usually after breaking something expensive."

"Probably too much to think you'd know names."

"Yeah, nah," Jake shook his head. "Devon wasn't the type to introduce the chippy – carpenter - to his friends. I was there to work and be invisible. And I'm good at both."

"Well, it's a start. I can ask around at his restaurant, see if anyone can put names to those visitors."

"You aren't serious, are you? I mean about nosing around."

"Of course I am. If I learned anything over the last few years, it's that the only person looking out for my interests is me," Maggie said defiantly. "Everyone has an agenda. The detective wants a suspect, the media wants a good story, folks around town want someone to gossip about. I plan on being none of those things." She busied herself putting the remaining cookies into a plastic container she intended to send home with Jake. "The only one who is going to save me, Jake, is me. And I plan on doing just that." She slid the container of cookies over to him.

"I get it. It's your life on the line. But I'd like to help, if you'll let me," Jake said, looking at her with concern.

"I don't know," Maggie began. "This could get sticky. I wouldn't want your reputation to suffer by helping a murder suspect and affect your income."

"On the other hand, the notoriety I will achieve when I assist in proving your innocence will only enhance my prestige," he teased. He picked up the box of cookies. "Are these for me, are you hinting I should take my leave?"

Maggie laughed. "Yes, they are for you, and no, it wasn't a hint. I just needed to remove temptation," she said as she put her cookie plate in the sink. "I was going to ask if you'd like to stay for dinner. I'm serving leftovers." She walked to the refrigerator and pulled out the chicken and rice. "If you're going to help prove my innocence, the least I can do is feed you."

"I never turn down a free meal. What can I do to help?"

"If you want to grab plates," she pointed to the cabinet by the sink. "Silverware is on the counter in that basket." She popped the chicken into the large toaster oven on a rollaway cart. She set the temperature and timer. "Should be ready in about fifteen minutes."

"What, no microwave?"

"I had to make a choice. Take up space with a microwave with limited capabilities or use that space for a high-end toaster oven that can do it all: bake, air fry and toast. I won't have to heat up the cottage with my big oven all summer."

Jake looked around. "They sure did a nice job with turning it into living space. You could use a few more shelves, though."

"I keep thinking I'll go to IKEA in Stoughton and buy a nice wall unit, but then I think this is only temporary and make do with what I have." Jake frowned at her. "What, you have something against DIY shelving?"

"No, not at all. But you deserve custom-built."

Maggie wasn't sure what he meant by that, but it sounded nice. "Well, when I find a small house I like, maybe we can discuss that. Do you want wine or beer?"

"Beer would be great."

Maggie grabbed two bottles from the refrigerator and set them on the table. The oven timer chimed. She took the polka dot potholders off the hook on the wall and lifted the casserole dish out of the oven. Jake pushed a trivet toward her, and she set the chicken on it.

She pulled a large bowl from a shelf in the refrigerator and placed it next to the chicken.

"That looks tasty. What is it?"

"Summer squash salad. It has walnuts, shaved parmesan, tossed in a bit of lemon and olive oil."

"You sure do redefine leftovers," Jake said as he scooped some of the chicken and rice onto her plate and then onto his.

Maggie fussed a bit more, then sat down next to Jake. He was already digging into his meal. She loved watching people enjoy her food.

"This is really good."

"It's Jules' recipe. I'm working on making it family-friendly without losing any of the flavor. Something that can be whipped up on a busy weeknight."

Jake took a swig from his beer. "How did you go from being a big New York City financial guru to writing cookbooks?"

Maggie was surprised for a moment that he knew her history, but then she realized Jules had doubtless told him since she was intent on matchmaking.

"I was miserable, and cooking gave me solace and a purpose. Feeding people made me happy. And the more I thought about it, the more I realized that some of my favorite childhood memories came from sitting around the dinner table with Mike and my parents," she explained. She took a sip of her beer. "I think I write to recapture that feeling. And if I'm lucky, share it."

Jake was looking at her intently, his eyes soft and inviting. Suddenly she felt flush. Damn Jules and her witchy ways. Here she was a prime suspect in a grisly murder, and she was getting all hot and bothered by the carpenter.

"What about you? How'd you end up in a small New England borough?" she asked to distract herself from the inconvenient feelings.

"Oh, I was on a walkabout across the States, just about finishing up, when I went to visit my uncle up in Maine. He had a friend here who needed a bit of help with a job, and I needed the cash. One job led to another until I realized I liked it here in Duxbridge. So I started my own company, got my Green Card, and figured I'd stay on a bit longer."

Maggie found the idea of falling in love with a place and choosing to live there appealing. She had lived in New York because it was where her job dictated she live, and she returned to Duxbridge because it felt healing. She had never even entertained the idea of wandering the world looking for a place to call home. She found the idea romantic, or maybe what she found romantic was the man doing the wandering.

"I'm trying to figure out what could be so alluring to keep you in our small village."

Jake looked at her for a long moment before replying. "Oh, it has its charms."

Maggie looked away and tried not to blush. "Would you like some more," she said as she slid the dish of chicken and rice to him. He added another heaping serving to his plate, which pleased Maggie almost as much as his flirting. "Tell me about your home in New Zealand. Is it a small town like this?"

"Nah, it's out in the *wop* - the middle of nowhere - makes Duxbridge look metropolitan. But it's beautiful and a great place to grow up."

Maggie's phone rang, and she excused herself to answer it. She normally had a "no phones at meals" policy, but there was nothing normal about today. A chill went through her as she searched for her phone and wondered if it was Mike calling to warn her police were on their way to her house.

When she finally located it, the call had rolled over to voicemail. She looked at the Caller Id. It said: Blocked. *Stupid robocalls*, she thought as she rejoined Jake at the table.

"Sorry, where were we?" she asked as she sat down. Just then, her phone chimed with a voice message. She looked at Jake. "It's just a stupid robocall."

"You should listen," Jake said, suddenly alert.

"Okay," Maggie replied, equally on edge now. She pressed the message icon and listened as a low whisper of a female voice spoke, "Murderer."

Maggie sat frozen, looking at her phone, not understanding.

"Play it again," Jake said gently. Maggie once again pressed the message icon, and they listened.

"Well, this day just keeps getting better and better," Maggie finally said.

"You should tell your brother."

"No, I don't want him in the middle of this if something is happening at the department."

"Do you think, I mean, is it possible that something shady is going on there?"

"No, they're all a bunch of good people. I'm sure of it. However, Detective Madigan has made no secret of the fact he'd love to move on to the State Police. Solving a high-profile murder quickly would look great on his application." Maggie flipped her phone over several times, contemplating the message.

"Did you recognize the voice at all?"

"No," Maggie shook her head. "But I guess word has leaked."

Jake looked concerned but said nothing. They finished their dinner, and Jake cleared the dishes while Maggie made coffee.

"What's our next step?" Jake asked as he added cream to his mug.

"I was thinking I'd go talk to the staff at Devo's. Extend my condolences." Maggie sipped her coffee. "If anyone knows something, I'm betting it's his staff. They presumably knew Devon well, and as far as I know, Devon's life revolved around work. That makes the restaurant the logical place to begin. Maybe, if I'm lucky, someone will pass me a note identifying the killer, wrapped in his famous Papa Rellenas."

"I have never eaten at Devo's, but I have heard the food was extraordinary. How 'bout you wait until I'm done with work tomorrow and let me go with you? I'll buy you dinner."

Maggie smiled at him but didn't commit. "What time is rugby tonight?"

"Soon, so I should probably get going. Gotta change into my gear," he flashed that irresistible smile. "I can wrap up around three tomorrow, and we can decide our next steps."

"You really don't have - "

"Yes, I do," Jake cut her off, serious now. "I get you don't want to sit around and wait for the police to knock on your door, but this is perilous. So I suggest the buddy system."

Maggie knew he was right, and she would enjoy spending more time with him. But still, it felt like it was her fight, and waiting for someone, especially a man, to wade in and rescue her was intolerable. "We'll see," was all she said.

Jake knew enough to give her space. He took his leave with a promise to help Maggie in whatever way he could tomorrow. Maggie closed the door behind him and then finished cleaning the kitchen. As she wiped down the table, the notepad drew her attention.

She put down her towel and flipped the notebook open. She looked over the information Jake had provided. Grabbing her laptop, she opened it and pulled up a search engine. She typed in Devon's name plus New Orleans. The search results revealed the name of his restaurant, De Bistro; an article on it going up for sale; and another discussing the sale to new owners.

Maggie clicked on the link to the piece on Devon's decision to sell the property. She learned that Devon's company was the sole owner of the property after buying out his partners earlier in the year, but it did not specify who the partners had been.

She opened the link to the actual sale. No useful information there, not even the final sale figure, and no sign of the mysterious man Jake saw. Frustrated, Maggie refined her search: *Devon Friedrickson, De Bistro, dispute.* She clicked the search icon, and a second later, the top five links were to stories about a company called Winsight Investments. She opened the first one and read the article:

> CEO and the principal partner in Winsight Investments, Winston Eldridge, III, has cried foul in the most recent drama in the French Quarter restaurant scene. Accusing Chef Devon Friedrickson of defrauding his company of hundreds of thousands of dollars, Eldridge stated that

Friedrickson significantly undervalued the Friedrickson New Orleans property, De Bistro, during a recent buyout.

The article went on to explain that Winsight was one of two investors and detailed the legal proceedings, and quoted Devon's vigorous denial. There was also a photo of Eldridge and Devon standing in front of the restaurant in happier times. Maggie sent the article to her phone, intending to show the image to Jake. Hoping he could confirm this was the man he saw at Devon's house.

Having another litigant in town around the time of Devon's death would go a long way to providing at least a second likely suspect for Madigan. She closed her laptop and began formulating a plan for the next day. She jotted some notes in the notebook, then set the coffee pot up for the morning. She wouldn't be stopping by the Duck, so she would need to provide her own caffeine fix.

She got ready for bed, crawled under the covers, and closed her eyes, but her mind refused to follow. Why was Madigan laser-focused on her? She needed to know what other evidence he had and wondered how long before he arrived with a search warrant. Not that he'd find anything in her sparsely furnished abode.

She undoubtedly needed to commit to her new life here and buy a small house. Maybe one with an upstairs apartment she could rent out. That would mean getting her finances in order and finding a real estate agent who wouldn't pressure her into someplace unsuitable. Of course, if she had to defend herself from a murder charge, that would probably eat into her down payment.

She flipped over and pulled the comforter tighter around her, to no avail. She was back to wondering who had actually killed Devon and how. Did someone hit him with something or push him down, and he hit his head on a hard surface? One would be murder. The other might mean manslaughter. Did the head wound kill him, or did he drown when they dumped his body into the ocean? So many unanswered questions. She would have much more information if Mike hadn't been removed from the case.

She tossed again, aggressively molding her pillow into a new shape. Maybe Jake would have better luck at the pub and could extract a bit of pertinent information from his rugby mates. Grateful for his help, her mind wandered to his intense eyes and how fine he looked in his jeans. With those pleasant thoughts, she finally drifted off to sleep.

Wednesday morning, she was awake before her alarm, armed with a plan to prove her innocence. She showered and dressed, walking into the kitchen as the coffee maker finished brewing. She poured coffee into her travel mug and was out the door before the sun peaked over the horizon.

The restaurant business starts early, and Maggie wanted to talk with the prep staff at Devo's without fear of running into any police doing the same. She turned onto Main Street. The town was still quiet, just a few cars making their way to work. Shops were still dark, but she knew that wouldn't last long. At the Duck, Juliet and Carl would be popping pastries into the oven.

The lights flicked on at Dunkin Donuts as Maggie drove past. Cars would soon be lined up in the drive-thru. Maggie continued northeast out of town and then turned onto Route 44, heading east toward Plymouth. Dawn was breaking, and a deep mist hung over the cranberry bogs that lined the highway. Devo's sat equidistant between Duxbridge and Plymouth and only about forty minutes from Boston. A perfect location for locals, tourists, and city dwellers looking for an excellent meal.

Maggie pulled into the parking lot, dotted with a few cars, as the lights inside the kitchen flicked on, illuminating the shiny stainless steel through the bank of paned windows. As she walked up to the entrance, she could hear arguing. She rapped gently on the Employee Only door, and the heated voices went silent.

SIX

Maggie knocked again, firmer this time. She heard the deadbolt click, and the door opened a crack.

"We're not open," a petite brunette with a pixie cut said through the opening.

"Hi, I'm Maggie Stellino," Maggie said pleasantly. "I was a…," Maggie searched for a word that wouldn't be an outright lie. "…colleague of Chef Friedrickson. May I come in?"

"Who is it?" a voice asked from inside the kitchen.

"A friend of Chef's," Pixie Cut called back to him. She opened the door wider. "Come on in," she said without warmth and gestured for Maggie to enter.

The kitchen was gleaming and spotless, filled with natural light from all the windows. Trays of fresh vegetables sat on the counter near the prep sink. On the stainless steel table in the center, there were trays of frozen rolls, set out to thaw and raise before being placed in the wood fired oven that dwarfed the more conventional full-sized gas stove, with eight burners and three ovens.

"What can we do for you?" a young man, arms covered in tattoos, hair buzz cut, dressed neatly in a chef's coat and bib apron, asked.

"Honestly?" Maggie looked around. It appeared these were the only two working. "I was hoping to get some information about Chef Friedrickson. About his death."

"You a cop or something?" Pixie Cut asked suspiciously.

"I'm a cookbook author," Maggie replied matter-of-factly. "Are you the only prep staff on this morning?"

"No, kidding? Is there any money in that?" Buzz Cut asked.

"Some. It's complemented by my social media. I have cooking videos, some exclusive membership only content, and lots of photos of food."

"That's great," Buzz Cut said, extending his hand. "I'm Pacey, by the way. This is Celia."

Celia nodded but did not extend her hand. "There's usually three more on the morning crew, but no one knows if we are even going to open today, so they didn't show up."

"We're not sure if we will even be paid for our last pay period," Pacey added.

"That's why I want to go home," Celia snapped at him.

"I'm so sorry to hear that. Is there a general manager that can maintain things until the estate is settled?"

"There is, but he didn't show up yesterday, and no one knows what happened to him," Celia grumbled. "He probably ran off with our wages."

"I'm sure he didn't," Pacey said to her. "He's not answering his phone," he explained to Maggie. "I think some of us," he looked at Celia, "are worried he's met the same fate as Chef."

"We're all going to lose our jobs, so we might as well not be here," Celia pouted.

Maggie ignored her. She was intrigued by Pacey's revelation. "Do you think someone would want to hurt them?" she asked. "Or were there problems between the two of them?"

"Not that I know of; I didn't interact with Ricky much - that's the GM, Ricky Daniels. He'd come in just before the dining room opened and locked himself in his office. Chef was the one who handled the kitchen." Pacey seemed genuinely sad at his boss' passing.

"It sounds like you enjoyed working with Chef Friedrickson," Maggie said gently.

"I learned a lot from him."

Celia entwined her arm with his. "Pacey is going to be a great chef one day. Chef encouraged him a lot." Pacey beamed down on her, appreciative of her praise. He kissed the top of her head.

"I know a lot of folks found him abrasive, but he was always fair with me. Commending me when I met his expectations and explaining my mistakes so I could correct them," Pacey explained. "He wasn't the easiest man to work for, but I still can't imagine anyone wanting to kill him."

Maggie was surprised by the deep respect Celia and Pacey held for Devon. This was not a side she expected of him.

"He obviously felt your talent deserved to be nurtured, and he respected you," Maggie said sympathetically. "I'm truly sorry for your loss."

Pacey nodded, and Celia leaned in closer and squeezed his arm. "Were you writing a cookbook with him?"

"Not this one," Maggie obfuscated. "But his death is going to impact my work. I'd sure like to know who did this to him."

"Me, too," Pacey said angrily. "The police questioned all of us yesterday but didn't say if they had a suspect."

"Do you think it could have been one of the staff, I mean, someone who didn't have a positive experience like you had?"

"I don't know. He was definitely a taskmaster, but I think most of the staff understood he was that way so the restaurant would succeed. Customers expected a high level of food and service from him, and he expected his staff to rise to that level. Most of us have been here since it opened. We were used to his style." Pacey thought for a moment. "Although, a hostess quit on Sunday, I think. Celia, what was her name?"

"Janie," Celia replied. "She only lasted a month. She hated Chef. Luckily, Sandy will be back from maternity leave next week." She sighed deeply. "If the place is still open then."

"I'm sure once everyone gets over the shock, the investors will see to it that things get back to normal," Maggie reassured them.

"There weren't any investors," someone said as they pushed through the swinging doors from the dining area. "Who are you?" a tall, intense blonde woman asked. She was dressed in jeans and a flannel shirt over a grey tank.

"This is Maggie Stellino, a friend of Chef's," Pacey explained. Maggie didn't correct him. "Why are you here so early, Jo?"

Jo offered Maggie her hand. "I'm Joanne Sanchez, the sous-chef. I'm sorry for your loss," she said without warmth. She stripped off her flannel and walked to a row of chef coats hanging on hooks. She grabbed one that had JO neatly embroidered on one side and put it on, and buttoned it as she returned to the group. "There were no investors, just Chef, which is why I'm here now. If we plan on getting paid, we need to open on time and be on top of our game today. There will be a lot of gawkers enjoying the best food they've ever had, if I have anything to do with it." She walked over to the ovens and turned them on. "I've called in extra staff. If that loser Rick doesn't show up, I'm going to make sure everyone gets paid before we are forced to shut down." She stopped and looked around. "I am sorry about Chef, I really am, but we need to get to work, so if you'll excuse us."

"Of course," Maggie said. "Just one more question, was Sunday the last time any of you saw Chef?"

"I was supposed to meet him on Monday to check out a new produce vendor, but he never showed. I figured he got caught up in another meeting and lost track of time," Pacey explained. "It wouldn't have been the first time."

"Thank you, all. Would it be okay if I used the restroom before I leave?" Maggie asked, and Jo nodded.

Maggie slipped through the swinging doors and stood in the staging area, her mind racing. She didn't need to use the bathroom, but if her memory was correct, the office was down the same hallway as the restrooms. Before she could have second thoughts, she crossed the room to the bar. A neon sign on the wall said: Restrooms and had an arrow pointing down the hall. Maggie checked behind her and then followed the sign.

Jake walked into the Duck, expecting Juliet to greet him with his travel mug and a pastry. Instead, there was a line of about five people at the counter and no Juliet in sight. He maneuvered through the crowd, smiling and wishing them a good morning as he ducked into the kitchen.

Juliet was on the phone, looking distracted. "Maggie, where are you? This is my third message. Call or text me, or I'm calling Mike." She slipped the phone into her apron pocket and looked up to see Jake.

"Oh, thank goodness," she said when she saw him. "Maggie didn't show up this morning, and she's not answering calls or texts."

"That's unusual?" he asked, but he knew it was.

Juliet stepped in closer and lowered her voice. "What if the police arrested her? What if she's sitting in a cell right now, unable to contact us?"

"I'm sure Mike would know. Have you tried contacting him?"

"I texted him twice. Nothing," Juliet said frantically. "He's probably handling a call. It could be an hour or more before he can get back to me."

"I'm sure if Maggie was in police custody, he'd be with her, and he'd let you know," Jake reassured her.

"I guess," Juliet relented. "But I'm so worried. With everything going on…I mean, Jake, there's a murderer on the loose."

"I'll go check on her. If she's not at home, I think I know where she might be." Jake gave Jules a quick hug. "But I'm going to need sustenance."

She laughed and prepared his coffee and pastry to-go and handed it to him.

"Text me as soon as you know anything," she beseeched as he slipped out the back door.

Maggie had grabbed disposable latex gloves from her kitchen and tucked them in her bag before she left the house. Now she looked around before slipping them on and trying the knob on the door marked: Office. *No need to leave any suspicious evidence to encourage Madigan*, she thought. Sure she was alone, she opened the door and slid into the empty room. It was windowless, so she had to flip on the overhead light before shutting the door behind her.

The room was drab and sparsely furnished, with only a desk piled high with papers and a black metal filing cabinet. Both looked like they were picked up on the side of the road. Only the chairs seemed extravagant. The one behind the desk was an expensive, ergonomic beast on rollers, and in the corner opposite the desk, there was a vintage Art Deco leather armchair.

Maggie walked over to the desk and began to look through the papers. The various layers revealed the chaotic nature of Devo's financial health. Most of the vendor invoices were marked with red Past Due or Final

Notice stamps. Some had C.O.D. ONLY in bold black ink stamped on them. Maybe the staff's delayed pay had less to do with Devon's death and more to do with insolvency.

Maggie dug deeper, hoping to find a calendar or something that might indicate where Devon was or who he might have met with the night he died. All she unearthed were more past due invoices and creditor letters but no daily appointment book. She turned to the filing cabinet and pulled open the top drawer. It contained only a check ledger, deposit bags and a bank stamp. The bottom drawer held a half bottle of Scotch and two rocks glasses. Maggie shook her head at the reveal. Devo's was in trouble, and the general manager was missing. In her mind, that was more suspicious than the message she left for Devon.

Suddenly, Maggie heard voices in the hallway. She held her breath, stepping to the door and pressing her ear against it. She flipped off the lights and waited. The voices trailed off. She opened the door a crack and peeked out. The hallway was empty. She hurried out and quietly left by the nearest exit, breathing a sigh when it was unlocked. Stepping out into the bright light of full sunrise, she was surprised to see Jake leaning against her car, arms crossed, flashing that brilliant smile at her.

"Just couldn't wait for me, could you?"

"What are you doing here?"

"If you turn on your phone, you'll understand."

Maggie unlocked her car, opened the door, reached inside, and grabbed her phone. "Oops," was all she said as she scanned the texts and missed calls. Jules was worried. Chagrined, she sent a quick text:

> I'm fine. Jake is here now.
> Will stop by later and
> explain.

"So she sent you to check up on me? How'd you find me?" Maggie inquired.

"When you weren't at your house, I remembered you wanted to talk with the prep crew here. I have mad listening skills like that," he said with a laugh. "Did you find out anything interesting?"

"I did," Maggie said and looked around. "But maybe we shouldn't talk here."

"Let's go back to your place, and then we can take one car to snoop around some more."

Maggie blinked at him. "What do you mean?"

"Don't act all innocent. I'm sure you have a full day of sleuthing planned, and I mean to make sure you don't do it alone."

Maggie wanted to object. She didn't need a babysitter, she didn't need rescuing, and she was perfectly capable of taking care of herself. Then she mentally kicked herself. Here was a hunky Kiwi with irresistible dimples, offering to accompany her, and he was genuinely interested in unraveling the threads in which she was entangled. She would be an idiot to refuse his kind offer of assistance.

"Sounds like a plan," she agreed and hopped into her sporty Fiat. "We'll take my car. It's electric, better for the planet." She eyed his ancient Ford pickup and smiled before closing her door. She zipped out of the parking lot and headed back to the gatehouse.

As she retraced her path down Route 44, Maggie made mental notes of what she had discovered. She had been at the restaurant less than thirty minutes. Nevertheless, the time had been informative. Now there were solid leads to track down. And again, she had to wonder why the police were targeting her when a half-hour had gifted her with several viable suspects.

Pulling into the dirt drive that led to the gatehouse, she noticed Aunt Carol's car parked next to the big house at the front of the property. A three-story colonial, Carol Ann Stellino lived in the first two levels, while the third floor was a converted one-bedroom apartment she rented to various nieces and nephews as needed.

Maggie wondered why she would be home at this hour. Carol Ann was the mayor's chief of staff and should be fielding phone calls and extinguishing fires by this time in the morning. She hoped nothing was wrong and was about to text her when Jake drove into the driveway. He pulled up next to her, and she directed him where to park in the shade and out of the way.

"I could use another cup of coffee. How about you?" Maggie asked as she opened the front door.

"Sure," he replied as he followed her in and closed the door behind him. "Any more of those delicious cookies?"

Maggie laughed as she tossed her purse onto the couch. "I sent them all home with you."

She set about making coffee, and Jake came into her tiny kitchen, making it feel microscopic. He set his travel mug next to the sink and then leaned against the counter and watched as she added water and coffee to the coffeepot.

"So, what'd you find out this morning?"

Maggie leaned against the table opposite him. He looked comfortable in her kitchen, she thought, right at home. That made her inexplicably happy.

"It was revealing. First of all, it looks like Devo's was cash-strapped. And get this, his general manager is missing! The staff hasn't been paid in weeks, and bills were piled up and past due. According to the morning crew, Devon was the sole owner, no partners, so he'd be feeling the stress of the financial crunch."

"When did the manager disappear?"

"Same time as Devon," Maggie explained. "No one has seen him this week. Before that, he spent all his time locked up in the office. And according to Pacey, a hostess hated Devon and quit on Sunday in a flourish."

"Pacey?"

"One of the prep crew. He really admired Devon and is understandably torn up by his death," Maggie said thoughtfully. "It's funny to hear the staff speak of him fondly. I guess I expected them to all despise him for being an all-around jackass. But it sounded like he was a good, if prickly, teacher."

The coffee pot chimed. Jake grabbed his mug and rinsed it out in the sink.

"Oh, shoot, I left my mug in the car. Be right back," Maggie exclaimed and started to dash out the door. She stopped, remembering she wanted Jake to look at the photo of the investor on her phone. She swiped to the photo and slid her phone over to Jake. "Take a look at him and see if he looks familiar." Then she ducked outside and grabbed her mug from her car. As she closed the door, she saw Aunt Carol striding with purpose across the lawn toward her. Maggie waved, but she did not return the gesture.

"Aunt Carol, is everything okay?" Maggie inquired when she was closer.

"Why didn't you tell me?" she gasped as she reached her.

SEVEN

"Tell you what? What's going on?" Maggie asked, not grasping her aunt's concern.

"That you are a suspect in a murder investigation!" Carol Ann exclaimed. "We have to get you a lawyer, and Mike needs to talk to those idiots in the department if they believe you could murder anyone!"

Oh, the joys of living in a small town, Maggie thought. "Aunt Carol, it will be okay, really," Maggie reassured her. "How did you find out?" Maggie worried how far the information had circulated.

"I was at Miss Kitty's looking at a new armoire for the office, she picked it up at an auction this weekend, and you were all anyone was talking about there," Carol Ann said with equal parts annoyance and concern. "I was completely blindsided and told them they were all crazy, saying nonsense like that about you."

Dammit, if they were talking about it at Miss Kitty's Antiques, it was most likely all over town by now. Maggie was discouraged by the thought. She put her arms around her Aunt and hugged her close.

"It's early in the investigation. I'm sure there are a lot of suspects the police are looking at," Maggie lied. "Don't let the town gossip get you all worked up."

Carol Ann returned her hug. "As long as you're doing all right," she said. "But I want you to get a lawyer. Today." Maggie nodded, and Aunt Carol gave her a quick kiss and returned to her house.

Maggie watched her leave, trying to process what this would all mean. She was sure that before dinner, the entire town would think she was a killer. That thought chilled her to the bone.

"Hey, where are you?"

Startled, Maggie jumped and turned to see Jake standing at the front door.

"You must have been far away. I called your name twice." He walked over to her and took the mug. "What deep thoughts were you thinking?" he asked as he led her back into the house.

"Seems the entire town knows I'm the most likely suspect in Devon's murder. My Aunt Carol heard about it downtown."

"Oh, boy," Jake said, worried for her. He rinsed out her mug and filled it with coffee. "I suppose the good news is the real killer might let their guard down. That could make it easier to flush them out."

Maggie took the travel mug from him and smiled. "I hadn't thought of that. It's a possibility."

"I am not just another pretty face," he teased. He picked up her phone off the counter and handed it to her. "I didn't recognize that guy," he said as they walked out the front door.

"That's too bad," Maggie said, trying not to be disappointed. "He's one of the New Orleans' investors." She opened the car door and slid into the driver's seat.

Jake folded himself into the passenger seat of her car and pulled the door closed. "Definitely not the guy I saw in the Mercedes. He was very tall and dark-haired, not short, bald and rotund."

Maggie noted that Aunt Carol's car was now gone. She hoped her current situation did not make her Aunt's job difficult. She was sure the mayor would not be pleased that his right-hand woman had a family member in trouble with the law. As she pushed the button to start the car and began to back out, she was more determined than ever to clear her name. The last thing she wanted was for her dilemma to reflect badly on her Aunt or her brother…or her parents.

"Oh my God," Maggie blurted out, putting the car into park. She rested her head on the steering wheel.

"What?"

"My parents," Maggie sighed and lifted her head up, resisting the urge to bang it against the steering wheel a few times. "Aunt Carol is going to call and tell them."

"Isn't it better they hear it from you instead of the gossip at the Duck or Fellowes?"

"They are on a three-month RV tour of the south. I was hoping to have all of this resolved before they returned," Maggie sighed and continued to back out of the driveway. "Then it would just be a funny story we told around the Thanksgiving table."

"Well, buck up. At least they won't be surprised if you call them for bail money," Jake joked. "So where are we off to now, chief?"

"I thought we'd head to the scene of the crime. Or at least where they found the deceased."

"Won't the cops find it suspicious if you show up and start looking around?"

"They released the scene late yesterday," Maggie explained as she turned onto Main. "Wareham was anxious to get its beach back and erase any sign of this tawdry mess. Don't want to upset the tourists after all."

The morning fog had burned off, and the air was warm and humid. Maggie reached up and pressed the switch to open the sunroof. The cool breeze whipped the curls around her face. Impatiently, she grabbed her sunglasses off the console and shoved them onto her head, to act as a headband to tame her wild hair.

"Hey, how was the pub last night? Did you learn anything?"

"I learned that police work is slow and meticulous. Every cop show I've ever watched has lied to me," Jake chuckled. "I feel so deceived. Our cops are waiting on all kinds of lab tests and forensics to come back. They figured they would all have a busy day today as those results came in."

"I'm sure they don't want to screw this up, so they're going by the book. Probably why no one has shown up at my door to question me. Yet." Maggie didn't want to follow that thought too far.

"One of them did say they found Devon's keys, wallet and phone at his house, which they all thought was odd."

"Hmmm…" Maggie made a mental note to see what Mike thought about that. It did seem unlikely Devon would leave all that behind if he was meeting someone and going out for the evening.

Traffic in town was light, so they made their way quickly to I-495. Maggie eased onto the interstate, maneuvered into the left lane, and sped down the road, weaving around slower vehicles without ever taking her foot off the accelerator.

"Hey, Mario Andretti," Jake said as he pressed his hand against the dash to brace himself. "I'd like to get there in one piece."

Maggie laughed as she sped up to pass a semi, then pulled in front of it so she could make the Onset exit. She slowed the car as the road curved around before dumping them off onto the two-lane highway. She merged onto Depot Street and headed east to Onset Beach.

"Maybe next time, I should drive," Jake said, sitting back in his seat now that her speed had slowed. "Where did you learn to drive? The Autobahn?"

"You know, you didn't have to come along," Maggie teased. She turned onto Onset Avenue, and the salty smell of the ocean was thick in the air. The strong briny odor said it was low tide.

The beach parking lot was only half-full. The big crowds wouldn't arrive for another couple of weeks. Plenty of time for the stench of murder to dissipate. Maggie pulled into a parking space near the beach. She and Jake grabbed their coffee and set out to explore the crime scene.

"I don't think there is much point spending too much time where they found the body," Maggie said as they walked on the sand toward the water. The police still had yellow crime scene tape around it, but Maggie doubted the crime techs had missed anything. "I'm more interested in following the beach over to the marina, where the boats are moored."

"Looking for anything in particular?"

"I want to get a feel for what Devon might have been doing. Was he fishing? Was he out on his boat?" Maggie elaborated. "Was he meeting someone on the dock? Or did he wash ashore after falling off one of the comedy cruises, and no one missed him?"

Down at the water's edge, Maggie turned around and looked back at the yellow tape. Jake was beside her. He pulled out his cell phone and looked up the tide charts.

"High tide was at two twenty-three Tuesday morning. So if he washed onto shore, it would have to have been sometime around then, dumping him at the strandline."

"Right, otherwise he'd have floated back out to sea as the water ebbed."

"Do you know how long he was dead before they found him?" Jake asked as he pocketed his phone.

"No, and I'm afraid to ask Mike too many questions. I don't want to put him in a bad spot."

"I could ask him, I mean if that wouldn't be overstepping. I could be the secret relay between the two of you." He winked at her, and Maggie almost forgot the dire straits that brought them to the beach.

"That's sweet, but I'm not sure how much he'll actually know now that he's been reassigned."

"Oh, come on, you know he's working his contacts to get any information he can," Jake said as he took her elbow to guide her away from a breaking wave. "At least that's what I would do if I were in a similar situation. He's not going to abandon you, and I'd bet anything he's working hard to clear your name."

"I'm sure you're right," Maggie said, turning toward the marina. "All the more reason for me to find who killed Devon because if anyone found out Mike was trying to help me, it could jeopardize his future. And I'm not going to let that happen."

Low tide allowed them to walk under the dock leading to the marina. From the water's edge, Maggie looked out at the tethered boats. Since none of them were secured with yellow crime scene tape, she had to assume Devon didn't have anything moored there.

"Do you know if Devon had a boat?" Maggie asked Jake as they walked to the boardwalk access.

"He did. He asked me if I knew anyone who could refinish the deck."

"He didn't by any chance say where it was docked? Because it doesn't look like it was here." Maggie waved her hand toward the moored watercraft. "I'd expect, even if they were waiting on a warrant, if his boat were here, it would be cordoned off."

"Agreed," Jake said as he grabbed her hand to help her step onto the dock from the sand.

Regardless, they walked the entire length of the landing, inspecting each boat along the way. At the end of the dock, Maggie looked back at the police tape on the beach.

"I'm no expert, but I'm betting if he fell from the wharf, he would have washed up that way," she pointed in the opposite direction of the tape. Look at the way the buoy is pulling away from its mooring."

Jake nodded his head in agreement and followed Maggie as she walked to the parking lot.

"So my working theory is, he was out on a boat. I was hoping it was his boat and whoever did it brought it back here to dock, and the police would be all over it. That would clear me pretty quickly."

"Now, why is that?"

"I can't drive a boat - much less dock one. I'd probably end up running it all the way up the boardwalk and into the marina. And there are plenty of people who could vouch for that."

"Not to mention, unless you had somehow cleverly planned all of this ahead of time, your prints would be all over the boat. I mean, Devon would probably have been suspicious if you donned latex gloves before boarding."

"Exactly," Maggie said, playing along. "However, I suppose I could have worn elbow-length satin gloves and joined him for a moonlit dinner. You know, the person who was suing me, that I had just left a message so vile for him I'm now the prime suspect."

"If I had to guess, they still haven't determined how he landed on the beach. But I wonder if they've located his boat?"

"I bet they have. I'm sure they found payment information when they searched his house," Maggie speculated. "It shouldn't be that difficult for us to find it. I believe there are only three marinas relatively close to his house. I don't think he'd use one further away, do you?"

"Makes sense. Should we go exploring?" Jake asked as they reached the car.

"Absolutely."

They jumped back into the car, and Maggie drove along the coastline. They checked the next two marinas near Onset, and both were police-free. Maggie was discouraged but continued up Route 6 to Mattapoisett. The marina there catered to a wealthier clientele, and she held out hope that it would be Devon's choice.

As they entered the parking lot, they could see the boats were much bigger, with a lot of brightwork to be maintained and polished. The marina boasted an upscale seafood restaurant and an upscale lobster shack, both busy readying for the upcoming summer season. People bustled about washing windows, painting trim, and sweeping around the buildings. This was a destination, not just a place to launch your boat.

Maggie and Jake exited the car and walked down the dock, past boats that looked like they'd never seen sea air, a few yachts, and one vintage wooden cabin cruiser wrapped like a present in police tape.

"I guess we found it," Jake said as they walked toward it.

"Do you see anyone on duty?" Maggie asked cautiously.

Just then, a uniformed officer emerged from the cabin and strode the length of the mahogany deck. Maggie ducked behind Jake's impressive six-foot frame, hoping it would be enough to conceal her. She breathed easier when she realized he wasn't a Duxbridge cop. *Probably someone from Mattapoisett or Wareham,"* she thought. Regardless, she felt it best to keep her distance. Detective Madigan didn't need any additional ammunition.

"Let's get out of here," Maggie whispered.

Jake deftly turned around, keeping himself between Maggie and the view of the officer on deck. Once back in the car, they scanned what they could of the remaining boats, looking for any other areas cordoned off by tape.

"Well, if they have the crime scene, then I should be eliminated quickly enough," Maggie stated as she started the car. "Maybe they'll even let Mike back on the investigation." On that hopeful note, she spun out of the parking lot and steered them back to Duxbridge.

"We should stop in at the Duck and let Jules know you're okay," Jake said as they picked up speed on the highway. "I know she's worried about all of this, and she would be relieved to know you are presumably in the clear."

Twenty minutes later, after stopping at Maggie's so Jake could get his truck, the red Fiat pulled in front of the Duck, and Maggie skillfully paralleled parked in a spot by the front door, Jake just behind her. She and Jake got out, and when Jake opened the café door, fragrant smells wafted toward them.

"I don't know about you, but I'm starved," Jake said as he held the door open for her.

Maggie nodded in agreement and stepped inside. Juliet was behind the bakery counter.

"Maggie!" she cried when she looked up. She rushed around the counter and to both of them. "Is everything okay?" she asked in hushed tones, not wanting to add fuel to the town's efficient gossip machine.

"Yes," Maggie answered, matching her tone. "Do you have time to take a break and have lunch with us?"

"I'll make time. Let's eat behind the kitchen."

The three of them went back to the kitchen, and Juliet filled dishes with lamb stew and biscuits, and they ducked out back to the picnic table designated for employees.

"This is a good idea. First time I've had to sit down today. It's been exceptionally busy," Juliet said as she took her place at the table. "Which is a good thing, by the way, since otherwise, I would have been frantic about what was going on with you."

"Message received. No more running off without conferring with you first."

"Did you find out anything?"

"Nothing definitive, but some interesting financial info," Maggie replied before taking a bite of her stew. "Oh, this is wonderful. We did locate Devon's boat, or at least a boat taped off with a cop stationed at it."

"Was it at Mattapoisett?" Juliet asked.

EIGHT

Maggie was excited. "Yes!" she replied. "How did you know?"

"Two dispatchers were in here today grabbing coffee and pastries to take back to the station, and I overheard them discussing Devon's boat, docked at Mattapoisett."

"What did they say? Did the police find evidence of the murder there?"

"No," Juliet explained. "According to what I heard, the deck was being refinished, and witnesses said the boat hadn't left its mooring in weeks. The work crews were there when the police arrived and had no idea anything had happened to Devon."

Maggie looked at Jake, deflated. He reached over the table and patted her hand reassuringly.

"Well, that's unfortunate," Maggie sighed. "I was hoping if they found the murder scene, it would easily prove I wasn't involved."

"Oh, honey," Juliet intoned, "I keep hoping this is all some bizarre mix-up."

"I just wish I knew why the police are so fixated on me. We are missing something important."

They finished their meal in silence, everyone fretting over Maggie's predicament. Finally, Jake pushed away his empty bowl with a satisfied sigh.

"Jules, that was excellent," he said as he stood up. "I need to get back to work. Maggie, as soon as you know your next move, you call me." Maggie nodded. "Promise?" Jake prodded.

"Yes, I promise. I'm not sure where we go from here, though," she said, trying not to sound dejected.

"I don't understand why the police don't just interview you and let you clear your name," Juliet said, frustrated.

"Because I'm the sister of a very good cop," Maggie said with a genuine smile. "And they know the only answer they would get from me would be, 'I'll wait until my lawyer arrives to answer that,' and then I'd clam up. According to my brother, dumb suspects make a cop's job easier. I don't plan on being one of those." Maggie stood up and gathered the empty bowls and plates. "I should get back to work myself." She took the dishes into the kitchen.

"I'll keep an eye on her," Jake told Juliet before Juliet followed Maggie.

Back at home, Maggie puttered around the house and tried to focus on the adaptations for her current recipe. She jotted notes on a pad and pulled out the original recipe, making more notes in the margins. She stopped, chewed on her pen, and stared out the front window. Her work seemed trivial right now. Finally, she picked up her phone and tapped out a text.

> Hey little brother, want to
> come over for dinner
> tonight? New recipe

She didn't wait for a reply. Instead, she began to prepare her newest adaptation of the French Market Chicken she'd made the day before. Only this time, her version simplified it while keeping all the original flavors. She used chicken breasts cut into cubes instead of a roasting chicken. She streamlined it further with frozen vegetables and chicken broth to shorten the cooking time. She wrote furiously as she calculated the proportions she would need for a family of four. She checked the refrigerator and cupboards to inventory ingredients.

Once she was sure she had everything and had a reasonable thirty-minute adaptation of the meal she made the day before, she went to her desk to go through her notes for her next recipe. She tried to stay busy while waiting to hear from Mike and keep her mind from going to dark places. She opened her dessert file and pulled out Juliet's recipe for Blueberry Coffeecake, which made enough for fifty and began to do the reductions for a more reasonable serving size.

Finally, her phone buzzed, and she picked it up to read Mike's reply.

What time?

She replied with the time, relieved to be seeing him, and then turned back to her calculations with a lighter heart. She reflected on how lucky she was to have a sibling as smart, funny, and loyal as her brother. An hour later, she popped the coffee cake into the oven and began preparing the main course. She was fluffing the rice as Mike breezed through her front door.

"Smells great," he said as he walked into the kitchen and hugged her. "I heard you were busy today."

"Who ratted me out?" Maggie asked as she pulled plates from the cupboard.

"Jules, of course. I stopped by for a refill, and she told me you and Jake made quite the twosome."

"Jake was trying to keep Jules from calling in the cavalry because I didn't show up for coffee this morning." Maggie piled Mike's plate high with rice and then topped it with a generous helping of the chicken mixture. She handed it to him. "He has been handy to have around lately. What do you want to drink?"

"Beer if you've got it. Been a helluva day."

Maggie pulled a bottle of craft beer from the refrigerator. "Glass?" Mike shook his head and took the bottle from her. Maggie fixed her plate and took a quick look in the oven before joining Mike at the table. "Blueberry coffee cake for dessert."

"So tell me what you and Jake found out today," Mike said between bites.

"Probably nothing you didn't already know. Devon was in some financial straits, his general manager is missing, his hostess quit a few days earlier in a snit, and while were plenty of people who had grievances with him, there were a few who genuinely respected him." Maggie moved food around her plate. She wasn't quite happy with the recipe yet, but couldn't put her finger on why.

"How did you find out he was in financial trouble?" Mike asked suspiciously.

"I have my ways," Maggie evaded. "Gossip has it that police found his boat, and it was not the crime scene. Is that true?"

"Yes, 'gossip' is that whatever happened, it did not happen on his boat. Or on the dock at the marina. The currents were wrong for where his body washed up. 'Gossip' indicates they have not found the crime scene and without it will have difficulty resolving this." Mike sipped his beer, looking glum. "Finding his phone, keys and wallet at his house leads everyone to believe he knew his killer and they probably met him there."

"Till seems odd that he would leave his phone and wallet behind." She stood and did a quick check on the dessert. "I'm sorry they kicked you off the case," Maggie said as she sat down again, feeling guilty as hell.

"It's not that," Mike reassured her. "It just, without a crime scene, we can't clear your name."

"Well, it's not like they've announced it publically," Maggie countered. "I mean, people can speculate all they want. It's not going to land me in jail if they do. You haven't heard the coroner's findings, have you?"

"I have. Defensive wounds on both hands and right arm. He was stabbed a couple of times, but those wounds were only superficial. The wound on his head was fatal. He did not drown and was likely dead when he hit the water. They found glass fragments buried in his head wound. In addition, there were slivers of rope fiber and fiberglass under his nails. It was embedded in the skin under his nails, and luckily, he washed ashore before the water degraded it. They weren't so lucky with any DNA evidence."

"Boy, you've got some loyal sources, don't you?" Maggie was impressed her brother could garner substantial information while writing parking tickets and investigating vandal calls. "Any idea why they are so obsessed with me? I mean, if he was killed elsewhere and hauled out to sea on a boat, how was I supposed to do that? I'm not a weakling, but dragging a dead body onto a boat and dumping it seems…improbable."

Mike couldn't meet her eyes; instead, he stared at the bottle in front of him. He finished off the beer, set the bottle down, and inhaled deeply.

"I believe they think I helped you."

The room went wavy for a minute, and Maggie found it difficult to breathe. It was a good thing she was sitting. Otherwise, she would have probably been on the ground. When she finally regained her composure, she found she was angry.

"What could possibly make Madigan think this?" Maggie asked incredulously. "None of this can be based on a single angry voicemail."

"I wish I knew. Madigan is playing this close to the vest," Mike said, getting up to recycle his bottle. "None of my sources have an inkling. But I'm going to do a bit of investigation on my own."

"You will absolutely not put your career in jeopardy over this," Maggie said in her best big sister voice. "I did not do this. You did not do this. Eventually, the truth will out."

Mike said nothing but grabbed their plates and put them in the sink. Then he kissed Maggie on top of her head.

"You're right. It will all work out." However, he didn't sound convinced. "I have to get going. Dinner was great. Sorry to leave you with clean-up." And before she could object, he had grabbed his jacket and was out the front door.

Despondent, Maggie pulled the coffeecake out of the oven and set it to cool, then cleaned the kitchen. Once she was done, she sat at her desk, intending to make adjustments to the recipe. Unfortunately, her mind had other ideas. All she could think about was the precarious situation in which she and her brother now found themselves. It had the feeling of a slow-motion crash with no way out. And none of it made a lick of sense.

A knock at her front door startled her from diving deeper into the rabbit hole. Her heart clenched. What if it was Madigan and his team coming to finally take her into custody? She got up, looked out the sidelight, and breathed a sigh of relief to see Jules and Bria standing there, holding up bottles of wine.

Maggie threw open the door and exclaimed, "What's this?!"

"We bring cheer in the form of wine and chocolate," Juliet said as they pushed past Maggie. "We figured you could use some company."

Bria walked over to the kitchen, opened a cabinet, and grabbed the wine glasses. She was tall, exotic, and looked stunning in an oversized sweater and jeans. She was also one of the sweetest, kindest, and most talented people Maggie had ever met. Which was a good thing because Maggie only wanted the best for her friend, and Bria sure seemed to be a perfect fit. Calm to Juliet's frenetic vitality. Adventurous to Juliet's single-minded focus on the café, they complemented each other in ways that brought out the best in both. Maggie might not be envious of Bria's model good looks, but she definitely longed for what Jules and Bria had together.

"Jules tells me you're in a bit of a sitch," Bria said as she opened the first bottle of wine.

"I guess you could call it that," Maggie said as she reached for the wine Bria poured for her. She then caught them up on the latest developments as Juliet unwrapped an absolutely decadent bar of imported chocolate.

"Wait, so now they think Mike is an accomplice?" Juliet was stunned by the revelation.

"Are they daft over there or just incompetent?" Bria asked as she broke off a large section of chocolate.

"I honestly don't know," Maggie replied as she took the half Bria split apart for her. "It's like Devon left them a note or something that said, 'If anything happens to me, it was the crazy cookbook lady who did it.' He hated me enough to do it, too," Maggie said with a grim laugh.

"Well, I know how we can have the last laugh," Juliet said as she finished off her glass and poured another. "Let's go to the funeral. It's going to be the event of the season. Filled with gawkers and haters alike."

"That sounds like a grand time," Bria said as she held up her glass. "I say we go and toast his evil ass."

They all laughed and clinked their glasses. Then Juliet turned serious.

"Tell me you have an attorney. And I mean a criminal lawyer, not the one who is handling that frivolous lawsuit of Devon's."

"I do. My attorney gave me a good referral," Maggie assured her. "I've spoken with the new lawyer on the phone, and he made it clear he was my first phone call if this advances beyond wild speculation. So I'm all set."

"Okay, then. I've got bail money stashed in a coffee can in the café kitchen," Juliet laughed. "So I'm your second phone call."

They made a plan for the funeral as they finished their wine. Then Bria and Juliet said their goodnights, leaving the unopened bottle of wine and three bars of chocolate for Maggie.

"Emergency rations," Juliet said as she walked out the door.

Maggie locked up and went to bed before the glow of friendship and good wine wore off, and she was back to obsessing over Devon's death.

She made one call before turning off the lights.

"Hey Jake, sorry for calling so late," Maggie said as she tried to hear him over the din in the background. "Where are you?"

"Pub. Rugby night," he shouted into the phone. "Let me step outside." Maggie waited a moment, and the noise ceased. "Oh, that's better," Jake continued. "Is everything okay?"

"Yes, it's all good," Maggie reassured him. "I wanted to ask a favor, though."

"Anything."

"Devon's funeral is Friday morning. I was wondering if you'd go with me…us…Bria and Jules and me. I thought we could compare notes on the mourners."

"Wouldn't miss it. What time?"

She gave him the details and wished his team good luck.

Maggie was relieved he agreed. She thought the person responsible for Devon's death could be at the funeral. She planned on doing what the cops would be doing, watching the mourners closely, looking for suspects. Many she would know: the local vendors;

restaurant owners; and residents. She might even know some of the New York City restaurateurs and chefs from her days researching the first cookbook. With Jake sitting next to her, she could quiz him on anyone he may have seen at the house.

She would have loved to ask Mike, to hear his thoughts on the myriad of mourners. Unfortunately, she felt they shouldn't be seen together at an event where law enforcement would be in attendance.

With a solid plan for the funeral, Maggie pulled up the covers, turned out the light, and willed herself to sleep. She couldn't save her own ass if she wasn't well-rested, she reasoned.

The next morning, after a quick shower, Maggie made her way to the Duck. Despite her current dilemma, she still had work to do and deadlines to meet. She felt explaining to her publisher that she needed an extension because she was under investigation for murder wasn't a good career move. She let herself in through the kitchen and waved to Carl as he pulled a hot tray of croissants from the oven.

"I hope there are some chocolate ones on that tray," she said as she glided through the swinging doors into the dining room. "Morning, Jules!" she said, watching Jules fill the display case with fruit-filled turnovers.

"Morning, honey," Juliet said with a smile as Maggie looked over her shoulder into the case.

"Yum, are those new on the menu?" she asked.

"Yes, Bria and I were reminiscing about favorite childhood food memories the other day, and I remembered making turnovers with my mom. I couldn't believe I'd forgotten until that moment, so I had to make some," Juliet said as she popped her head out of the case. "Incredibly easy and so flaky. Want one?"

Maggie grabbed a plate, and Juliet slid one onto it. Then she headed back into the kitchen to continue morning prep. Maggie poured herself a cup of coffee and settled into her favorite spot. Juliet would be opening the doors soon, but for now, it was peaceful and quiet in the café.

Maggie pulled notebooks, pens and her laptop out of her vintage leather messenger bag and set them on the counter. She dug through one of the many pockets until she found Juliet's recipe cards. She rifled through them, finally locating the one she wanted to work on next, Butternut Squash Pasta She studied it for a minute and then began making notes in the margins, reducing amounts so she could make a smaller portion. Once she had those calculations finished, she would make her shopping list.

She opened up her laptop to type out her first draft of the smaller recipe, wondering if Jake would be willing to accept another dinner as a thank-you for accompanying her to the funeral. She was enjoying his company, a bit too much, she feared.

Juliet unlocked the front doors, and the bell rang. "*Kia ora*, ladies!"

NINE

Jake held the door open for a young mom and her twin boys. As Juliet waited on them, Jake walked over to Maggie.

"How are you this morning?"

"I managed to get some sleep, so I'm functional," Maggie said. She held up her coffee cup. "But I'm going to need a few more of these."

Jake looked over at the long line Juliet was now managing. He grabbed Maggie's cup. "Looks like if I'm going to get to work, I'm going to have to serve myself this morning."

He walked behind the counter, gracefully maneuvering around Juliet, and refilled Maggie's cup before filling his insulated mug. He kissed Juliet on the cheek. "Put this on my tab."

"Here, take a turnover, too," she said as she handed him a small white bag. "I hope you like cherry."

Jake smiled and grabbed the bag. He placed Maggie's cup back on its saucer without spilling a drop. "I've got to get over to the Roost and get the crew going, but let's talk later about the funeral," he whispered to her before dodging the crowd by exiting through the patio door.

The Duck was filling up. Early risers occupied tables, discussing business, reading the morning news, and sipping coffee while they waited for their omelets or eggs and bacon. The place was filled with happy chatter as those waiting for takeout greeted those who were seated. Most of them were regulars that Maggie knew by name.

Behind the counter was orchestrated chaos, Juliet taking orders, Carl refilling the quickly emptying case from trays of fresh-out-of-the-oven pastries. Amber, one of Juliet's part-time servers, went into the kitchen and came out carrying food, weaving through the tables, dropping off hot plates of breakfast meals, and refilling coffee before returning to the kitchen to repeat the process. Maggie sipped her coffee and watched it all. She tried not to think of how many of them thought she was a murderer.

Grateful no one was staring or pointing, she went back to her work. However, concentration was elusive. Her mind continued to wander back to all the things she didn't yet know about Devon's death. She reminded herself again that explaining a missed deadline to her publisher would be unpleasant. Her self-motivational efforts were ineffective, and after her third cup of coffee did nothing for her concentration, she abandoned any pretense of working.

She opened up a browser on her computer and thought about exploring some of the unanswered questions she had from yesterday's revelations. Then she realized there were too many curious eyes around her. It would be better to poke around the internet at home. She packed her things, bussed her dishes, and said a quick goodbye to Juliet before slipping out the kitchen door.

Back at the gatehouse, Maggie dropped her lightweight cotton jacket on the sofa and walked to the table, where she dispatched her bag. She grabbed a bottle of kefir from the refrigerator, opened it, and took a sip before sitting in front of the computer.

Launching a browser, she typed in Devo's, and the page quickly filled with results. The first one she wanted to explore was the restaurant website. Clicking on the About tab, she skimmed through the information until she found a photo and bio of Ricky Daniels.

Ricky Daniels came to Devo's with a strong background in both restaurant development and management, having successfully launched popular restaurants in New York City and New Orleans. He relocated to Duxbridge from New Orleans to work with Chef Devon Friedrickson on making Devo's a destination dining experience.

Further searches online brought up a modicum of information, mostly a few press releases, as Daniels joined and then left several restaurants. No whiff of scandal, no legal actions against him, and unfortunately, no home address.

Maggie went to her bookshelf and pulled out a small red phonebook. Fondly known as the CB, its cover read: *Duxbridge Census Book*. The Chamber of Commerce published it for as long as she could remember. It listed not only names, addresses and phone numbers but also where people worked, how many children they had, and to which organizations they belonged. Some people even listed their favorite activities and charities. It was like social media, only on paper.

Even with the advent of online resources, Duxbridge continued the tradition, privacy be damned. The business section was filled with fun tidbits about owners and staff. You couldn't expect to be successful in Duxbridge if you didn't have at least a two-by-two listing on the business pages.

Of course, you could opt out of your listing, but that would cause more talk than anything that might be listed about you in the book. In her school years, it was a great way for her and her friends to find out all they could about their latest crushes, where they lived, where their people were, and how many siblings they had. *Silly memories*, she thought, as she turned the pages of this year's book until she reached the Ds. She had no idea if Daniels lived in Duxbridge, but it wouldn't hurt to look.

She ran her finger down the D names until she came to Daniels. There was an entire clan listed, some she recognized, most she didn't. Then, almost at the bottom of the page, there was a hopeful entry: Daniels, R. The only details were an address - no mobile phone, no landline, no spouse, kids, or even a job - it had to be him. Newcomers often balked at the Census Book the first year or so but soon realized it was all part of the charm of Duxbridge and showed up in full detail a few years after relocating to the village.

Maggie snapped a photo of the page and went back to the computer. She pulled up the address on the map. It was in a newer development comprised of condos and townhomes. Maggie sat and stared at the map for a long while. She knew she shouldn't, but she wanted to drive over there and see if Mr. Daniels was at home and find out why he stopped showing up for work. She hesitated because she promised Jules, Mike and Jake, no more foolish expeditions without backup.

Instead, she decided to search for Devon's house. He wasn't listed in the CB, so she searched online to see if she could locate it. Discovering the location wasn't difficult. Devon had purchased an old Victorian mansion on a defunct dairy farm on the outskirts of town. She found several big write-ups in the Duxbridge Gazette. Hugh Tulley, the editor and publisher, interviewed Devon on multiple occasions, including when he purchased the house and when the build-out was happening at Devo's.

While the articles didn't list the exact address, Maggie knew from its description where it was located.

Again, her desire to go exploring competed with her promise to everyone. She busied herself with searching Devon's restaurant reviews.

While all his restaurants were well liked for their culinary offerings, many reviewers had deducted stars for onsite drama. In particular, Devo's had a glut of three- and four-star reviews mentioning confrontations with Devon or Devon berating the staff. It made sense to Maggie, as far as she knew, he was at Devo's every night. When he owned multiple venues, he most likely rotated between them, limiting his nasty interactions.

None of this was helping Maggie clear her name. Frustrated, she picked up a pad and made a quick shopping list. Then she grabbed her jacket, bag and keys and headed out the door. She motored out of the driveway and turned down Oak, winding her way down the tree-lined street. Instead of turning right and driving to the large grocery store at the edge of town, she made a sharp left and headed across town to Daniels' condo complex. Midday traffic was light, so she found herself turning into the new development before she could question her bad decisions.

Tucked into a wooded lot were rows of Colonial-style townhomes and a large condo complex. Red brick with black trim and black shutters, the condos were unremarkable. The townhomes on the other hand, had white columned entrances, dormers, and white shingle siding with cobblestone walkways leading to each door. Narrow roads separated the rows of townhomes, creating a neighborhood feeling.

Unsurprisingly, Daniels' address was one of the condos. *Perfect for a bachelor who worked long hours to make a utilitarian choice*, Maggie thought, The two-story condo complex wrapped around an interior courtyard and each condo had either a patio or a balcony facing into it, offering privacy from the parking lots and storage units. A large pond was within walking distance, surrounded by pines and sporting a small fishing dock.

The complex consisted of four buildings, and the entrances to each were between the buildings, away from the street. Maggie looked at her phone to confirm the building and condo she was looking for, before walking over to one of the entrances. On the wall by the door was an intercom with several rows of buttons. Maggie scanned them, looking for Daniels' name and unit number.

Once she located it, she pressed the buzzer. No answer. She pressed it again. If he was ignoring her, she would try annoying him into answering. Still no response. She was about to leave when someone walked down the hallway and approached the door.

A tall, muscled gentleman in running gear was engrossed in his phone as he hurriedly opened the glass door. He held it for her for a moment before continuing down the sidewalk and then jogging down one of the many walking trails. Maggie didn't hesitate and slid into the lobby as the door closed behind her.

She had to wonder how many burglaries and assaults happened because someone was polite enough to hold open a locked door. Since she had no intention of burglary or assault, she took the stairs up to the second-story condo without guilt. As she reached the top of the stairs, there were two doors to her left and two doors to her right.

The numbers on each one were large enough for her to read, so she could see Daniels' door to her right. The floor felt abandoned. No music or television emanating from units. No cozy cooking smells filled the hall. Maggie assumed everyone must be at work.

She walked down the thickly carpeted hallway and knocked on Daniels' solid, four-panel wood door. Silence. Maggie looked around furtively and then pressed her ear to the door, in the vain effort to ascertain if anyone was lurking behind the peephole. She knew finding him home was a long shot, but she was disappointed anyway. She trudged back downstairs and out to her car. She sat for a moment, contemplating her options. On the off chance he had returned to work, Maggie called the restaurant and asked to speak to the general manager. She was told he was not there.

So, he wasn't at the restaurant, and he wasn't at home, Unless, of course, he had met the same fate as Devon, and was lying dead on his living room floor. Maggie put her car in gear and drove out of the development.

Once on the road, she knew where she was headed next.

Mike sat on the stone bench by his grandmother's grave. He looked up as a car slowed and stopped next to his cruiser. Tina exited the vehicle. Her hair pulled back into a long ponytail. She was dressed in denim shorts and a white t-shirt, her flip-flops slapping against her feet as she walked over to Mike.

"Hey, Tina," Mike greeted her.

"Hi," she said, sitting next to him.

"Thanks for meeting me here," he said, looking uncomfortable. "I'm not sure we should be doing this, but I appreciate your offer to help."

"Totally," Tina said as she dug through her bag to fish out her phone. "I think it's lousy that they took you off the case. We both know your sister did not kill a man and dump him in the ocean." She swiped through her phone. "I have no idea what Detective Madigan is thinking. My dad feels the same way." She stopped swiping and handed the phone to Mike. "But he's in charge, so all my dad can do is follow his lead."

Mike swiped through several photos. "This is good stuff."

"Yeah, I went through the files on Madigan's desk when no one was around yesterday. I snapped every page before I took my dad to lunch."

Mike pulled out a small flash drive, plugged it into Tina's phone, and downloaded all the photos.

"I've been asking my dad what he knows. He's reluctant to tell me stuff, doesn't want what happened to ruin my summer. I'm surprised he hasn't made me see a counselor to make sure I'm not traumatized."

"Well, you did find a dead body."

"I know, and I suppose it should bother me, but I didn't know him, and you know what it's like for police. It's a puzzle to be solved. And I know I'm just a cop's daughter, but I was hearing about cases with my snack cups. I feel like a LEO."

Mike laughed and handed her the phone. "Well, I don't want you to risk getting in trouble by helping me. If anyone found out, your dad would kick my butt from here to Gloucester and then have me fired before grounding you until you were twenty-one."

"I'll be careful, but it's not suspicious at all, me asking him all kinds of questions. I mean, how often do we have a dead semi-celebrity as a case?"

Mike's phone buzzed, and he pulled it out and read the text message. "What the actual f...," he stopped himself, remembering he was in the presence of his boss' daughter. "I've got to deal with this. Thanks again for all of this. I'm sure it will help."

"No problem, but you have to promise to keep me in the loop, okay?"

"Will do," Mike said as they walked back to her car. Tina got in and drove off, much too fast, with music blaring. Mike sat in his cruiser and made a call.

Maggie pulled up to the long driveway that led to Devon's house. The farm had long ago returned to a more natural state of meadows and woods. Creating more of an estate vibe befitting the old Victorian mansion that was its centerpiece. A variety of trees that created a tapestry of colors in the fall, lined the driveway. A stone wall separated the road from the property, two stone pillars and a tall, ornate iron gate kept out strangers.

From the roadside, Maggie couldn't see anything beyond the gabled roof of the house. She drove past the property and turned right at the crossroad. With a bit of distance from the tall wall and a powerful set of binoculars, she was able to get a good look at the mansion. It was crawling with patrol cars, several sedans, and the crime scene van.

Maggie's heart skipped a beat. Could this be the murder scene? If so, it would quickly clear her of the crime. She had never stepped foot onto Devon's property. There would be no physical evidence of her there. She strained to see if she recognized any of the officers. She almost screamed when her phone rang. She looked over to the passenger seat where she'd tossed it and saw Mike's photo pop up. She scrambled to answer, hoping he had good news.

"Hey, little brother," she sang into the speaker.

"What the hell do you think you're doing?"

"What do you mean?" Maggie suddenly worried her brother was working the scene at the mansion and had seen her car. "Where are you?"

"I'm at the cemetery," he said, exasperated. "The question is, why are you at Devon's house?"

"How do you know that? And I'm not at his house. I'm parked down the road from the place," she added defensively.

"Bob saw your car, and he figured you were up to no good, so he texted me. Get out of there now, and we'll talk about this when I get off duty."

"Okay, okay," she relented. "Come over for dinner. I'm trying out another recipe."

She disconnected and took the long way to the grocery store, avoiding driving past Devon's house again.

A few hours later, savory smells of roasting butternut squash and spicy Italian sausage filled her house. Maggie put out two place settings on seashell-adorned placemats. Then she returned to the stove and put the finishing touches on the dinner. She was tossing the squash and sausage mixture with the pasta just as Mike strolled through the door.

"It smells great, sis!"

TEN

Maggie shaved fresh Parmesan over the steaming pasta.

"I hope you're hungry. There appears to be enough to feed a large family," she said as she set the pasta bowl on the table.

"You know I'll take any leftovers," Mike replied enthusiastically. He grabbed the water pitcher from the refrigerator and filled his glass. "Water or something else?" he asked, the pitcher poised over her glass.

"Water is fine," Maggie replied as she dished out a serving of pasta on her brother's plate.

Mike pulled out his chair, took off his duty belt, and draped it over the back before sitting down. "I will be glad to get home tonight," he said wearily.

"Long day?"

"Tedious. While everyone else is busy on Friedrickson's case, I'm stuck running around town on vandalism, traffic and noise complaints." He stopped to taste his dinner. "Oh, sis, this is really good. Don't get me wrong, I enjoy my job, but it's like I'm being frozen out."

"I am so sorry...about all of this. It's not fair to you. I wish I knew why Madigan has singled me out. From all I'm learning, Devon had no shortage of suspicious people around him."

Mike stopped eating; the fork paused halfway between his plate and his mouth. "What exactly have you been doing? This is no joke. I thought we talked about this. You shouldn't be poking around."

"Well, I'm not going to sit around and wait for your buddies to decide to arrest me," she said sharply.

"Look, I know it's stressful, but I've got this. Trust me."

"What does that mean?" Maggie eyed him suspiciously.

"It means…I have a good source, and by tomorrow I'll be up to speed on the entire case."

Maggie said nothing but held his gaze. Mike knew that look. He held out for as long as he could but finally relented.

"Tina Carvalho has been feeding me information," Mike held up his hand to stave off Maggie's protests. "Today, she managed to get me Madigan's entire case file. I have tomorrow off, and I'm going to spend the day reviewing it."

"How could you get Tina involved in this?" Maggie snapped. "Carvalho will kill you if he finds out."

"It's not like I could stop her. First, she called me, said she had found the autopsy report on her dad's desk, and gave me those details. Then today, she asked to meet. She'd slipped into Madigan's office and photographed the files on his desk."

"Michael Robert Stellino, that girl has had a crush on you since the day you put on that uniform, don't tell me you're taking advantage of that?"

"You know I'd never do that. I've been very careful," Mike protested. "Honestly, sis, she's worried about you. She can't believe you're a suspect - and neither can the Lieutenant - and she is determined to help. I figured better she comes to me than do something foolish," he paused, looking sternly at Maggie, "like going out and hunting down a murderer on her own."

Maggie poured more water into her glass and took a sip. She trusted her brother and knew he was looking after both her and Tina. Nevertheless, if anyone found out, he had those files and how he got them, she knew his political aspirations would be toast. And not the good kind with butter and jam.

"You should know, I'm going to Devon's funeral tomorrow with Jules, Bria and Jake."

"I don't think that's a good idea. Madigan will be looking for any suspicious behavior from you."

Maggie waved off his objection. "It would be more suspicious if I didn't go. Half the town will be there, all of the foodies for sure. How would it look if I stayed away? It would look like I knew I was under suspicion, and Madigan's first thought would be that you tipped me off." She forcefully stabbed bowtie pasta onto her fork and then pointed it at Mike. "So I am going, and I'm going to be very interested in who else is there."

"Fine," Mike sighed. "Take notes, and we can compare our findings tomorrow night. But seriously, sis, don't do anything to bring attention to yourself."

Later, after Mike had left with an armload of leftovers and the kitchen was cleaned, Maggie pulled out her clothes for the funeral and hung them on her wrought iron valet. Then she made a quick phone call to Jake to coordinate the morning before crawling into bed. Though she tried, sleep did not come quickly. Her mind churned with worries about the chances Tina and Mike were taking and the constant fear of suddenly being dragged down to the police station for questioning. After an hour of useless worrying, she finally drifted off to a fitful sleep.

The following morning, Maggie made her usual foray to the Duck. She had abandoned her casual work attire of jeans and t-shirt for a sleeveless sheath dress in dark navy, accessorized with a necklace of varying sizes of silver discs and matching silver earrings. Her plan was to keep to her regular writing schedule for the morning, but she wasn't sure how successful she would be.

After pouring her first cup of coffee, she peeked around the kitchen door to see Juliet and Carl busy taking baking trays from the ovens and transferring hot pastries to large cooling racks. Maggie found that reassuring, the comfort of routine. She poured a touch of cream into her mug, settled into her usual seat, and pulled a notebook out of her handbag, flipping it open.

Her morning goal was to map out the theme of the cookbook. She scribbled a few ideas onto the page. In her mind, it was about foods that reminded her of home, but she needed to expand that to include her readers' idea of home. That challenge still eluded her but solving the puzzles was what made writing fun.

Juliet slid a hot cinnamon bun in front of her, the icing oozing down the sides.

"Mmmm, that smells heavenly," Maggie said as she breathed in the spicy warmth. "And I'm starved."

"You look lovely," Juliet said. "I don't think I've seen that dress before."

"Thanks. It's a remnant from my old life. I have so many business and evening clothes that I rarely have the occasion to wear any longer. I should give serious thought to donating most of them."

"Bria is bringing my clothes when she meets us later, and I'll change here."

"I invited Jake," Maggie said casually. "I told him to meet us here, and we could all go over together. Just a group of friends attending the funeral of a fellow villager."

"Uh-huh," was all Juliet said before she went to unlock the front doors.

Two hours later, Jake strolled in, dressed in a charcoal grey suit and black shirt. He had forgone the tie, and to

Maggie's eyes, looked sexy as hell. She tried not to stare. Or drool.

"*Kia ora*," he said by way of greeting. "Don't you look lovely this morning."

"You clean up nicely, too," she managed to say nonchalantly.

"Thanks," he replied as he sidled up to her. "Have I got some news for you."

Just then, Bria breezed through the door, looking stunning in black slacks and a navy blue cashmere sweater. She waved as she made her way to the kitchen, a dress bag draped over her arm. Jake and Maggie waved back then Maggie returned her attention to Jake.

"Don't keep me in suspense." She gave him a warm smile, happy he was on 'team clear Maggie's name.'

Jake leaned in close, keeping his voice low. "When I was at the hardware store this morning, the gossip mill was in full swing. Seems Devo's was behind on payment for many of the tradespeople who worked on the reno. Rumor has it there are quite a few liens on the business. And a lot of angry people with access to a lot of deadly tools."

"Isn't that interesting. Any of them planning on attending the service today?"

"I believe so. It sounds like the entire town will be there. Gus was planning on closing the store for the rest of the morning," Jake said with a grin. He looked around at the almost empty café. "Looks like Jules could do the same. I need some coffee. Can I refill yours?"

"I'm good, thanks."

Jake walked behind the counter and poured himself a mug.

"I'm beginning to wonder who didn't want to kill Devon," Maggie said when Jake sat down next to her. "The suspect list gets longer the more we look into it. I wish Madigan saw it that way."

"Does Mike have any new insights?"

"No, but he's working on it," Maggie replied. "Unfortunately, since it appears the entire town knows the police have me in their sights," she sighed, thinking of her Aunt Carol, "I can't wait for the murmurings to begin when we arrive at the funeral home."

"Life in a small town," Jake agreed.

Maggie realized, sitting there, wearing a dress and heels for the first time in months, that life in a small town suited her. She didn't miss the revolving closet of suits, dresses and heels, the endless meetings with choleric clients, and the ubiquitous cocktail parties and social events that were her former life. It surprised her because moving to New York City was her big dream when she was working her way through college.

She pictured a glamorous life in the fast-paced world of finance, playing in the big leagues, respected by clients and colleagues alike. Once in New York, she quickly worked her way up and soon realized it was not the life she had pictured. Her world was populated with cutthroat, self-centered, overworked colleagues, whose morals were highly questionable. Their allegiance was less to those they worked with than to some mythical ladder that led to more and more success.

Of course, her perspective could be clouded by her evil, cheating ex. No, here in Duxbridge, she had found a balance that was missing in her days in New York. Like Dorothy, she had realized there really was no place like home. And besides, if she needed an evening of excitement, Boston was forty minutes away with all the bars and ballet a girl could want.

Bria and Juliet came out of the kitchen, Juliet looking sleek in a sleeveless black silk sweater over a pinstriped black pencil skirt. She had a matching jacket folded over her arm.

"Are we ready to do this?" she asked Maggie as she joined her and Jake at the counter.

"I'm not sure if I'm ready for all the stares," Maggie sighed, suddenly thinking this was a particularly stupid idea.

"You need to summon your inner Barbara Stanwyck," Juliet encouraged her.

"Who?" Jake asked, confused.

"We need to have a femme fatale classic movie night," Maggie said as they walked to the front door. "Introduce you to the women of Film Noir. Start with *Double Indemnity* and then *The Postman Always Rings Twice*, maybe *Gilda*."

"Don't forget the *Maltese Falcon*, oh, and *The Lady from Shanghai*," Bria added.

"I know the *Maltese Falcon*. I'm from New Zealand, not Mars." Jake laughed as he held the door open for them, and they proceeded to the sidewalk.

Keohane's Funeral Home was only two blocks away, and the morning was sunny and warm, so they decided to walk. With all the people attending, they would probably have parked a block away anyhow. They chatted about movies and favorite snack foods to avoid talking about murder and death while they strolled.

Bria and Juliet walked ahead of Maggie and Jake, Jake staying close to Maggie, giving her protective looks along the way. With her friends surrounding her, Maggie felt less apprehensive as they neared the chapel. It had a separate entrance off the parking lot, so people didn't have to walk through the entire funeral home. Mourners were streaming in, and the café gang fell in line to join them.

"Let's sit in the back row," Maggie whispered to Jake, grabbing his hand to lead him to an open pew. Juliet and Bria followed.

They settled in and commenced people-watching. Maggie opened up the memorial folder they were each handed at the entrance. She scanned the unfamiliar list of speakers. Then flipped to the back page and read the obituary. She was surprised to see that along with his parents and sibling, there was a woman, Vivian Larkspur, identified as his fiancée. She leaned over to Jake and showed him the obituary.

"Do you know her?" Maggie pointed to the name.

Jake read the name and shook his head. "Not by name. Maybe if I see her," he whispered. "I am surprised, though, because quite a few women were coming and going when I worked for him. He didn't seem like the commitment type."

Maggie found that very interesting. A womanizer with a woman claiming to be his life partner. Definitely, someone Maggie would like to speak with after the service. She looked around, craning to see past the people still filing down the aisles to find a seat. The front row was roped off, Maggie assumed for family. Those seats were still empty.

"Isn't that Mario Petrocelli?" Juliet nudged Maggie and discreetly indicated the robust man with a graying ponytail walking toward the front of the chapel. "The owner of Molto's in New York?"

"Oh, it sure is," Maggie whispered back in admiration. "One of the few things I miss about living there. His risotto is other-worldly."

"Hey," Jake nudged Maggie. "Guy in the black turtleneck, walking two rows in front of us," he nodded his head in the direction of the man. "That's Mr. Red Mercedes. The business partner Devon was arguing with at the house."

Maggie could only see the back of him as he slowly made his way down the aisle. He was tall, slender, and had jet-black hair. She wished he would turn down one of the rows so she could get a better look at him. She leaned over to Juliet.

"Any idea who the guy in the black turtleneck might be?"

Juliet looked for a moment and shook her head. "Maybe when I can see his face."

Maggie continued to scan the crowd, glancing back at Mr. Red Mercedes every few seconds to see if he had picked a row yet. She knew most of the townspeople who had shown up: Gus Fellowes; the de Lunas; Hugh Tulley; and by the looks of it, every restaurant owner in the village.

"There are Pacey and Celia, from Devo's," Maggie quietly pointed out. "I don't see Joanne, though. She's the sous-chef. She was all business when I met her. Maybe she's not the sentimental type."

The crowd began to thin as the seats filled. Mr. Red Mercedes finally chose a row, and Maggie got a good look at him. He had sharp, chiseled features, high cheekbones, and intense dark eyes, but she didn't recognize him. She pulled out her phone and opened up a search tab. She typed in: Devon Friedrickson business partner. A second later, the page filled with responses. She tapped the images tab so she could quickly scan for him. It didn't take long to find him.

She clicked on the photo of a smiling Mr. Red Mercedes and Devon, shoulder to shoulder. The article headline read: *Sean Park Lee and Devon Friedrickson Go to Court*. Maggie skimmed the article and learned that Lee had also invested in Devon's restaurant in New Orleans, and at some point, Devon bought him out. As with Winston Eldridge, Lee had accused Devon of undervaluing the restaurant and then turning around and selling it for a hefty profit. From what she could find, it sounded like it was still in litigation at the time of Devon's murder.

Maggie passed her phone over to Jake and let him read it.

"Yup, that's the guy," he said as he passed the phone back to her.

At that moment, a hush fell over the crowded chapel.

ELEVEN

Maggie hurriedly put her phone back in her bag and looked up to see the family file in from the front of the chapel to the reserved row. The funeral directors followed with a white satin-draped casket. They parked it in front of the large photo of Devon. Maggie wished she had gotten a better look at the younger woman who entered with the family. She was dressed head-to-toe in black, including a small stylish hat with a short black tulle veil. It contrasted nicely with her bleached blonde hair, which cascaded down like a waterfall over her shoulders.

Maggie wanted to retrieve her phone and do a quick search on Vivian Larkspur, but the service was starting, and she didn't want to be conspicuous in her lack of sorrow for the departed. Instead, she sat quietly, hands folded in her lap, and observed the mourners as the service droned on. Finally, the minister concluded without anyone standing up and screaming, "I did it, I murdered him," or worse, turning to her and shouting, "Why is that murderer here?"

John Keohane walked up and thanked the minister and then turned to the chapel and said the dreaded phrase, "Would anyone like to come up and say a few words?"

The silence was deafening, so Keohane quickly wrapped things up, and he and his team escorted the casket down the aisle. The family stood up and followed solemnly. Maggie watched and waited as they drew closer, hoping to get a good look at Vivian as she passed.

Instead, as Vivian approached and saw Maggie, she sucked in her breath and scowled at her. Maggie felt the rebuke as strongly as if she'd been slapped. She prayed no one else noticed. Jules grabbed her hand and squeezed it reassuringly as they waited for the family to exit through the double doors.

Jake put a protective arm around Maggie and whispered, "I guess the detective has shared his suspicions with the family."

Row by row, the crowd exited the chapel in an orderly fashion, but Maggie could not wait. She whispered to Jules and Bria to follow her to the outside aisle, and they quickly left by the side entrance. The last thing Maggie wanted to confront was the family receiving line. Once outside, Maggie finally began to breathe again.

"What the hell was that?" Bria asked as they snaked their way through the alley and back onto the street.

"That was the look of a woman who wanted me dead - or at least in jail," Maggie said grimly.

"For a moment there, I thought she was going to lift her veil and yell out 'murderer' while pointing at you," Jake joked.

"You and me both," Maggie agreed. "I'm starved. Anyone else? I may need to eat my feelings with some serious stress food."

"I'll have Carl get some burgers and fries going for us," Juliet said as she texted him. "That should get us started. After that, we can eat our way through the leftover morning pastries."

"Did we learn anything from the crowd?" Bria asked. "I'd like to think I sat through that farce for a reason."

"I definitely gleaned a few good pieces of information, and right after lunch, I'm going to do some serious research," Maggie said. She wanted to know more about Vivian and Mr. Red Mercedes, Sean Park

Lee. She hoped that the notes Mike had obtained would shed some light on why Vivian had given her the evil eye at the funeral. And she wanted to know more about Mr. Lee. *Why, when you were in litigation with someone, would you show up at their funeral*, Maggie wondered, then did a mental head-slap. Devon was suing her, and she went to his funeral. Still, Sean Park Lee intrigued her.

They arrived at the Duck and entered the back door into the kitchen just as Carl finished adding fries to their plates. They grabbed plates and took them to the patio, ditching their jackets as the sun beat down on the picnic table, and sat down to eat.

"I need to get the umbrella out soon, or this area is going to be unbearable in the afternoon," Juliet said as she sat next to Bria. Carl appeared with a condiment caddy and placed it in the center of the table. "How's the lunch rush?" Juliet asked him.

"Still pretty slow, but I'm betting it'll pick up now that the funeral is over."

"I suppose that depends on how good the luncheon reception was," Juliet replied. "I'll be in once we've finished here and give you your break."

"No rush. Amber and I have things covered," Carl said before returning to the kitchen.

"I don't know what I do without him," Juliet said as she poured ketchup on her burger. "He's great in the kitchen and manages the café like a pro. I need to think of something nice to do for his first anniversary."

"It's been a year already? Time flies," Maggie mused. "And yet, it feels like he's always been here."

"I never worry when he's prepping meals. I know every dish is going to be perfect before it hits the table." Juliet bit into her burger, and approval spread across her face. "He's really the only reason I felt able to expand next door."

"Speaking of," Jake interjected. "We should go over the next stages of the plans today. We finally have the interior gutted, a bit ahead of schedule due to the ceiling's early exit. I'd like to walk you through the layout, if you have time."

"I'll change clothes when we're done here, and if it's still slow, I can meet you over there."

"I need to run home and change, too. How about we meet at three?" Jake said before finishing the last bite of his burger.

"If I wouldn't be imposing, I'd love to see your ideas," Maggie said.

Bria raised her hand to be included, unable to chime in because she had just popped a handful of fries into her mouth.

"Okay, it's settled. We'll all meet at the Roost at three," Jake said as he sprinkled malt vinegar on his remaining fries. "We'd be further along if I didn't have to keep interrupting my days to help clear Maggie of murder charges." He winked at Maggie as he scooped a handful of fries into his mouth.

"I'd sure like to know what that Vivian woman knows," Bria said. "I swear I've seen her before. I just can't remember where."

"Well, if something summons her to mind, let me know," Maggie said. "I'll be -"

"Hello, everyone. Don't you all look spiffy," Miss Kitty interrupted as she swept through the kitchen door into the patio area with dramatic flair. "Back from the funeral, I assume."

She was smartly dressed in linen slacks and an embroidered silk blouse, adorned with a triplet of seed pearl strands. Her short-cropped hair was unnaturally red, complementing her ivory complexion, which sported nary a wrinkle, despite the fact she would shortly be celebrating her seventieth year. Her antique store could always be counted upon to have the unique item you didn't realize you needed and the advice you knew you did. Warm, funny, beautiful and kind, everyone in town knew her, and she knew everyone.

"Hi, Miss Kitty," Juliet stood up to greet her. "Have a seat. Can I have Carl bring something for you?" Miss Kitty slipped in next to Jake.

"I would love an ice tea, dear," Miss Kitty replied, and Juliet went into the kitchen. "How was the funeral? Tell me everything."

"I'm surprised you didn't attend," Jake remarked. "It seemed like everyone else in town did."

"I'll let you in on a secret, Jake," Miss Kitty whispered conspiratorially. "Devon Friedrickson was a son-of-a-bitch, and he owed me a hefty sum of money. I was afraid if they asked us to talk about the deceased, I wouldn't be able to hold back," she said, tapping Jake lightly on the shoulder and laughing heartily. "I know, I'm horrible, but I'm sure there were quite a few people in attendance who felt similarly."

Bria, Jake and Maggie shared knowing glances as Juliet returned with a tall glass of iced tea, a lemon wedge garnishing the lip. "What'd I miss?" she asked as she sat down.

"We were about to tell Miss Kitty how uneventful Devon's service was," Maggie replied. "No outbursts, no one confessing to his murder, no illegitimate heirs suddenly appearing. I mean, it was practically solemn."

"You should know, dear, I don't believe a word of what anyone is saying about you." Miss Kitty reached across the table and patted Maggie's hand. "Murder isn't your style. You'd ruin him financially and make him watch while you did it," Miss Kitty declared and winked at Maggie.

"Thank you, although I cringe thinking about the sordid things people must be saying."

"People like to gossip, but we all know that between your brother and Detective Madigan, your name will be cleared in no time."

Maggie hoped Miss Kitty was right, even though she did not feel as confident. All the same, it felt good to hear her declare her loyalty.

"Are you sure you wouldn't like something to eat," Juliet asked, as Miss Kitty squeezed the lemon into her tea. "Carl just sliced up some very nice roast beef. He could make you a toasted sandwich with his amazing avocado spread."

"Maybe I'll grab one to take back to the store when I leave." She sipped her tea before continuing. "Tell me how the renovations are coming next door."

"Zipping along," Juliet said. "We were just going to head over there in a bit to walk through the next steps. Want to come with us?"

"I would love to because I would like to talk over a business proposition with you, Jules."

Maggie and Juliet exchanged startled looks.

"Meet us at three," Juliet instructed without missing a beat. "I can't wait to hear what you're thinking."

"Can I walk with you back to the store?" Maggie asked. "I'm heading that way anyway."

Dishes were gathered as everyone prepared to leave. Bria helped Juliet take everything into the kitchen. Miss Kitty followed behind to get her to-go order.

"How are you really doing?" Jake asked Maggie. "Still shook by the bereaved's unspoken rebuke?"

"I think I'm fine. Maybe it will sink in later how serious this all is, but I know I didn't kill Devon. The rest is an ugly inconvenience. I suppose I'm in denial, assuming the truth will just come out."

"It will. I'm sure of it."

After saying their goodbyes, Jake left for home, and Maggie joined Miss Kitty and walked with her back to the antique store. They exchanged pleasantries along the way. Miss Kitty asked about Maggie's parents and were they enjoying their trip, and Maggie asked her about business. They parted ways at the door to the shop, and Maggie continued to her cottage.

After changing into jeans and a t-shirt, Maggie sat down at her laptop and tried to focus on work. That lasted about two minutes until her mind drifted to Vivian and Mr. Red Mercedes. She wondered how well they knew each other, thinking dark thoughts about them, imagining them conspiring to rid themselves of Devon. But, no matter how she turned that over in her mind, she couldn't make it work. Why would they?

It couldn't be for his money because, from all indications, he was deep in debt. Love? Maggie had serious doubts that Vivian and Devon were actually engaged, so if she and Sean Park Lee wanted to be together, why not just leave? From everything Jake had told her, it was unlikely Devon would have cared much.

Maggie typed Vivian Larkspur and Sean Park Lee into her browser to see if, by chance, they would come up together anywhere. Lo and behold, they did. Maggie clicked on the link, and it took her to a charity event five years earlier, on Long Island. To her disappointment, it was only a photo of Devon, Sean, Vivian, and a few other folks, mingling at the event. That was the only connection her search provided. She knew that didn't mean much, but without better resources, like her brother looking into it, that was the best she'd be able to do today.

Maggie's phone began to chime. She slid her finger over the front of it to dismiss the alarm and closed her laptop. Time to meet everyone at the Roost. She grabbed her jacket and locked the front door behind her.

It was a pleasant spring walk back downtown. Maggie was pleased to see all the cherry trees in full bloom, along with plenty of daffodils and waldsteinia creeping along nicely with waxy yellow blossoms. Soon the peonies and azaleas in front of her Aunt's house would bloom. A few more warm days, and it would be safe to take the water cages off her tomatoes and peppers, as New England summers warmed up quickly.

As she rounded the corner, she could see Bria, Juliet and Miss Kitty waiting for her at the entrance to the Roost. "Waiting for me?" she asked brightly, as she joined them.

"Of course, wouldn't want to start without you," Juliet replied. She pushed the door open and called inside, "Jake? Safe for us to come in?"

Jake appeared from the back room and strode across the main floor, now cleared of all the ceiling debris. "Sure, come on in." He looked up and added with a laugh, "I don't think anything else can fall down."

They all followed Juliet inside, the tall front windows lighting up the entire room. It was an expansive, open space, perfect for receptions or large meetings. There were two squared arched openings at the rear, which led to the back half of the structure. A paneled glass door on the right opened to the stairwell leading upstairs. The stairwell also had a separate outside door, giving direct access to the upstairs.

"Oh, Jules, this is going to be perfect," Miss Kitty exclaimed. "Now, let me tell you my idea," she said, looking into the gaping hole above them.

TWELVE

Everyone stopped and turned to Miss Kitty. She walked around the perimeter, looking at the gaping hole the entire time. Finally, she stopped in the middle of the room, having commanded everyone's attention.

"Jules, the second door out front leads directly upstairs, correct?"

"Well, it opens into a narrow lobby, and that door," Juliet pointed to the side door on the far wall, "and the stairs to the second floor."

"Perfect, perfect," Miss Kitty mused. "Here's what I'm thinking. The upstairs would be a perfect Bed and Breakfast." She turned to Jake. "It could accommodate two large suites and two bathrooms, couldn't it?" she asked him. "Maybe even a sitting area at the top of the stairs?"

"Sure, I think the square footage could be divided that way." Jake was excited as he added, "If we make the bathrooms a Jack and Jill style, then you could conceivably have four separate rooms that share the two bathrooms when needed."

"Exactly my thoughts. And a nice sitting room with a couple of couches and overstuffed chairs to sit and read or chat with other guests. And then breakfast would be included at the Duck," Miss Kitty finished with a flourish. She turned to Juliet. "This is terribly exciting, don't you agree? There are so few places in town for guests to stay. Everything is out by the interstate and part of some big chain, cold and impersonal. This would be a pleasant alternative for folks."

"Wait, wait, wait," Juliet protested. "I admit it's a great idea, but I can barely afford the downstairs remodeling. And where would I find the time to run a B&B on top of everything else?"

"Oh, darling, I wasn't suggesting you take this on all yourself," Miss Kitty reassured her. "I was thinking we could be partners. Or if that's still too much, I could lease the space from you and pay for the remodel in lieu of rent for a while."

Juliet looked first at Bria and then at Maggie and shrugged. "I'm intrigued, Miss Kitty. My only plan for the second floor was storage and maybe a dressing area and extra bathroom for party guests." She turned to Jake. "What do you think?"

"I can write up an estimate of what the remodel would cost for you both to discuss. You can see if it's doable."

"Bria, what do you think? Would you be onboard with yet another project?"

"Hey, as long as I get the design contract, I'll support whatever you decide," she replied with a wink and a laugh.

"Well, Miss Kitty, you've completely upended my entire plan, but I agree, this could be a wonderful addition," Juliet said as she reached out her hand. "Let's be partners!"

"Excellent!" Miss Kitty grabbed Juliet's hand with both of hers.

"Let's get back to the business at hand, and let me walk you through the downstairs," Jake said. "Then I can get the crew back here to begin the rough in plumbing, and I'll start working on your upstairs estimate."

As Jake, Juliet and Bria walked through the archway to the back half of the building, Miss Kitty gently tugged on Maggie's arm to hold her back.

"I had an interesting visitor in the shop this afternoon," Miss Kitty began conspiratorially. "He said his name was Sean Park Lee, and he used to be Devon's business partner."

"He told you that?" Maggie asked, astonished.

"Well, he didn't pop in the shop and say, 'Good afternoon, I was Devon's business partner,' silly," Miss Kitty laughed. "He wanted to know if I had a particular style of secretary, early American. It's a bit too high-end for my tiny shop, but I gave him a couple of good leads for antique dealers closer to Boston..." Maggie nodded, wondering how any of this pertained to Sean Park Lee disclosing his personal business to her but confident Miss Kitty would reveal all eventually, in her own way.

"...I offered to call a few for him, but he was content with dealer names and addresses. Anyway, I noticed he was dressed rather formally for a day of antiquing, so I asked him what else brought him to town. He said he was in town for Devon's funeral. I asked him how he knew him, and he explained he was a former business partner." Miss Kitty leaned in and continued with a dramatic flair, "But the way he said it, he did not sound grief-stricken. I wanted to ask him more, but a group came in, more out-of-towners from the funeral. I'm sorry for Devon, but I sold five large items between lunch time and when I left to come here, all folks who attended the funeral."

"What made him standout from the other mourners?" Maggie asked, trusting Miss Kitty's well-honed radar.

Miss Kitty laughed. "I wish I could tell you it was some extraordinary detective skills or a sixth-sense that piqued my interest. But alas, it was only my listening skills. He took a phone call, and I overheard him tell the other person he was staying in town to tie up a few loose ends. He wanted to ensure that Devon hadn't 'screwed him over' again. Call me crazy, but that doesn't sound like an affable partnership."

Maggie had to agree. "Any idea where he might be staying?" she asked.

"No," Miss Kitty replied and then pivoted. "Now see, if we had a proper B&B in town, I could have asked him where he was staying and then recommended this place," she finished with a laugh and a sweep of her hand.

"What are you two plotting over there?" Juliet called out from across the room.

Miss Kitty took Maggie by the elbow and led her to the group. "I was explaining to Maggie how nice it would have been to have a B&B to recommend to all the funeral tourists who came into my shop today."

Jake showed them around the gutted back half of the building, pointing out the plans for the European-style bathroom with two private stalls and a larger lounge area with sinks and seating. To Maggie, it all looked like one big empty space, but she could tell Jules was excited as Jake pointed out the small office space and coat check area. She did enjoy watching him work. Their final stop was at the far side of the space, closest to the Duck.

"This area," Jake explained, "will be the staging area for food and waitstaff. The door to your kitchen will be here." He waved at the blank wall. "And there will be built-in storage on this wall and a long counter. We should decide if you want a built-in island buffet here or if you want free standing so you can add or eliminate utility carts as needed."

"Would it be possible to have several buffet carts on wheels?" Juliet responded. "I like the idea of configuring them as needed." Jake nodded.

"Now, the only thing left to decide is if we are going to build a bar," Jake said as he led them back to the front room. "I was thinking along this wall." He pointed to the wall that adjoined the Duck.

Juliet sighed. "Let's plan on it. But I'm running into some issues with the liquor license."

"What?!" Miss Kitty exclaimed. "Don't tell me that busybody, Rosella Doucette, is giving you a hard time."

"Hmmm," Juliet replied. "I'm not sure she likes my lifestyle, the old bat."

"Well," Miss Kitty said indignantly, "she is not one to be casting any stones, let me tell you. Four husbands and a gambling addiction…you let me handle this. You'll have your license in record time." Miss Kitty hugged Jules. "This all looks lovely, dear. I should get back to the shop. Let's talk soon about the B&B." She turned and gave everyone a vibrant smiled. "Good to see you all."

And with that, she was gone, taking a bit of the sun with her.

"She is a force to be reckoned with, isn't she?" Jake said with admiration.

"Yes, she is," Maggie affirmed.

Back in her own kitchen, Maggie had trouble finding her motivation for the next recipe. Instead, she texted her brother with another dinner invitation, knowing he would want to hear about the funeral. She hoped he would share what he had gleaned from his illicit evidence gathering.

> Little bro, trade you funeral
> gossip and leftovers for any
> new info you have

When he responded in the affirmative, she got busy putting together various leftovers. By the time he arrived, she had quite the spread and that good feeling she had when she knew no food would go to waste. She threw together a simple salad and sliced up a loaf of Italian bread to complete the meal. Mike breezed through the door just as she was filling water glasses.

"Free food, my favorite," Mike said as he dropped his jacket on the couch.

"Hello, to you, too," Maggie laughed. "Do you want a beer?"

"No," he replied as he gave her a quick hug and then pulled out his chair. "I have to work tonight."

"Night shift? I thought this was your day off."

"Covering for Wolinski, she went into labor today."

"Oh good," Maggie said as she sat down. "For a minute, I thought you were being punished because your sister is a killer."

"Alleged," Mike reminded her. "How was the funeral?"

Maggie passed him the leftover chicken and rice. "As you would expect for a man loathed by many, sweeping platitudes and feigned grief, topped with a dollop of morbid curiosity." Maggie dished out salad, then grabbed a slice of bread and buttered it.

"No one confessed to the murder, then?"

"Nope, but boy, did Devon's girlfriend give me a look that would have curdled milk. Madigan must have really filled her head with all kinds of suspicions about me," Maggie said with a sigh.

Mike put down his butter knife and stared at Maggie for a moment. "Well, that's interesting."

"Not the word I would use," Maggie countered.

"No, I mean, I read the reports last night, and the only mention of Vivian is as the 'alleged' fiancée."

"So?"

"So, it's not likely that Madigan would share information with her, but if he were, it would mean he had at least interviewed her. And there's nothing in the reports to indicate he's done more than get her general information."

"Well, regardless, she made her feelings clear," Maggie replied, but now she wondered what elicited that reaction. If it wasn't Madigan, what spurred Vivian's animus? "Did the reports give you any cogent information on real suspects?"

"It was sparse on any facts or leads. Until they locate the crime scene, there isn't much to go on except to investigate a bunch of angry associates, of which there seems to be no shortage."

"Then why fixate on me?"

"That's the thing, sis," Mike replied between bites. "Other than the voice message and removing me from the case, there's not much to indicate Madigan is focusing on you. He spoke with Friedrickson's attorney again, and she intimated that he was trying to get you to settle to avoid court. I think you were right, there wasn't much of a case, and the point was to intimidate you into settling. And if what you're saying about his financial situation is correct, you're probably not the only one he had his eye on for that."

"I guess that's good, but it sure doesn't explain why half the town is gossiping about me."

"It probably has more to do with me being reassigned than anything else. That is what makes you look guilty," he said with a wink. "Despite your known homicidal tendencies."

Maggie stuck her tongue out at him. "It sounds like, despite the risk Tina took, Madigan's files didn't reveal much. Anything in there about you and I dumping the body together?"

"Nope. I have to wonder if he's keeping anything he suspects about you or me unofficial. That way, it's less likely to leak. I mean more than it has already," he added as Maggie began to protest. "There are a lot of people in the department who are looking out for us and think Madigan is way off base for his suspicions. He could have any details about us locked away from prying eyes. If only to avoid gossip and criticism."

Maggie told him about Sean Park Lee and Miss Kitty and then regaled him with Miss Kitty's plans to expand Juliet's remodeling project. He laughed as she described how deftly Miss Kitty commandeered the entire upstairs and had Jake doing her bidding in seconds.

Maggie sent Mike out on the nightshift with a large container of the blueberry coffeecake from the night before. She had lost her appetite once she realized that despite her original relief that Madigan's notes had revealed few facts to connect her in Devon's death, the idea of a secret file meant she, and Mike, were not in the clear yet. She wrapped up the remainder of the coffeecake. It would make an excellent breakfast in the morning.

By the time Maggie had cleaned up the kitchen and crawled into bed, she was despondent. She had really hoped the funeral would shed some light on suspects, but nobody screamed vengeful murderer to her. It was all very respectful and dignified. She had to admit, she was a bit disappointed. Drama would have been much more fun.

The next morning, after another night of tossing and turning, Maggie was slow to start her day. She spent the first few minutes staring at the ceiling, wondering how her life had come to this, before stumbling into the kitchen for coffee. As it was Saturday, no one was expecting her at the Duck. She usually spent the day cleaning, gardening and running errands. As she sipped her coffee, she wondered if some retail therapy might do her good. Clear out the cobwebs.

She opened her laptop and perused the latest news headlines, then poured herself a second cup of coffee. Back at her laptop, she typed Sean Park Lee into the search bar. She pressed enter and received a page of results. There was an article stating he was in the top one hundred bachelors in NYC – number 47. There was also a business journal piece on his expanding company, a neighborhood Korean newspaper story on "local boy makes good," and a small bio on his company website. Maggie grabbed her notepad and a pen and then clicked on the company bio first.

> Sean Park Lee was born in Chicago and attended the University of Illinois – Chicago as an Air Force ROTC, and after that, he spent four years serving his country in the Air Force and was honorably discharged. He began SPL Investments soon afterward and has led it to exponential growth in a short time.

Maggie was impressed. She opened the link to his bachelor status. A short puff piece on his business acumen, a couple of quotes from him on how much he loved his mother, and several beefcake photos, one with his shirt unbuttoned and showing off well-defined abs - typical stuff. The Korean newspaper told the sweet story of a young man who excelled in school, performed volunteer work, and credited his parents for his success.

Then Maggie searched through the links on Lee's business. The entirety of the information she could find pointed to a shrewd and honest executive. The only legal entanglement was with Chef Devon.

By the time Maggie had read through everything, she had doubts the he had been involved in the murder. Still, his presence in Duxbridge and Jake's account of the encounter at Devon's house gnawed at her. She was wishing she had braved the reception yesterday so she could have talked to him.

Her phone buzzed, and Juliet's face popped up on the screen. Maggie tapped on the speaker icon. "Good morning, Jules. What's up?"

"Maggie," Juliet said in a hushed tone that immediately put Maggie on edge. "You're not going to believe who is sitting here having breakfast."

THIRTEEN

Maggie's heart clenched. Her mind went to dark places. But, even in her wildest imagination, could she conjure what Jules said next.

"It's Bradley...YOUR Bradley!"

It was a good thing Maggie was sitting down. Rage competed with confusion at the sheer audacity of his presence in her café, making her dizzy.

"He's not MY Bradley," she retorted. "And what the hell is he doing there?"

"At the moment, eating a ham and gruyere omelet," Juliet replied.

"Oh, very funny. I'm on my way."

"Are you sure you want to see him?" Juliet asked.

"My guess is, he's on his way here for reasons I absolutely cannot comprehend," Maggie explained. "If I bump into him at the Duck, there's less likely to be a scene, and I can keep the interaction short."

"Okay. Should I hide the knives?"

"Har, har," Maggie answered before disconnecting.

She quickly dressed, dabbed on a touch of makeup, and fluffed her curls. She looked in the mirror and sighed. It would have to do. She had no need to be spectacular as some kind of revenge. She was completely over the cheating bastard, and she couldn't imagine why he was in her hometown. But she was annoyed. She jumped in her car and sped off to the Duck.

Parking in the back, Maggie slipped into the kitchen so she could scope out the situation unseen. Juliet met her at the door.

"He still here?" Maggie asked.

"Uh-huh," Juliet whispered. "Enjoying his breakfast."

"Did he mention why he was here?"

"He was pleasant but not particularly talkative. I'm surprised he was brave enough to order food and trust I wasn't going to poison it," Juliet sneered.

"Now, now," Maggie cooed sarcastically. "It's been three years. He's not worth losing your five-star rating. He's broke and miserable. That's enough."

They both suppressed their laughter as they looked toward the dining room.

"Do you need a cup of coffee to bolster you before you confront him?"

"Why don't you bring one to the table if he invites me to sit down," Maggie suggested. "Maybe one of your chocolate croissants, that way, I'll have something to bite into in case I want to say something awful to him."

Maggie went out the kitchen door and walked around to the patio entrance. She strolled in and over to Bradley. He was seated facing the front door, so he was surprised when she sidled up to his table.

"Hi Bradley, what brings you to Duxbridge?" she asked, cutting to the chase.

Bradley looked taken aback. "I was hoping to see you," he replied smoothly.

"Well, here I am."

Bradley stood up and pulled out the chair next to Maggie. "Here, sit down. Let me buy you breakfast."

"Thank you, but I don't want breakfast," she replied and sat down.

Bradley returned to his seat, and Juliet placed a mug of coffee and a chocolate croissant in front of Maggie. She topped off Bradley's cup and disappeared into the kitchen.

There was a long, awkward silence as Maggie waited for Bradley to screw up his courage and tell her why he was here. She felt no obligation to ease his discomfort. He took a bite of his omelet and savored it. Maggie's impatience grew, but still, she did not speak. Instead, she leaned back, crossed her legs, sipped her coffee, and continued to wait. Finally, Bradley put down his fork and reached across the table.

"Maggie, I was a complete idiot and what I did was inexcusable," he paused to gauge her reaction. Maggie's face remained dispassionate.

The little bell over the door dinged, and a familiar voice called out, "*Kia ora!*"

Jake strode in and stopped when he saw Maggie sitting with Bradley. She smiled at him before turning her attention back to Bradley. Jake walked up to the counter and raised an eyebrow at Juliet. Juliet rolled her eyes and indicated she would explain later, then nodded to a counter seat where Jake could eavesdrop. He sat, and she brought him a flat white and blueberry turnover.

Maggie picked up her croissant and bit into it while watching Bradley, wondering what the hell he was doing here.

"I was thinking...hoping, really, that you and I could talk. We had such a good thing going before I screwed it up, and I wanted to try again, see if we could rekindle the magic." Maggie almost choked on her croissant. She grabbed her coffee and took a sip while he continued. "I know...I know I would have a lot to prove...to make you understand I've changed..."

Maggie held up her hand to stop him. "Bradley, I hope you enjoy your omelet." She stood and picked up her coffee and croissant. "But I can assure you, there is nothing you could do to make me ever want to return to my old life," she said without acrimony. "Have a safe drive back to New York."

Maggie turned, took a deep, calming breath, walked over to the counter, and sat next to Jake. He turned to look at her, question in his eyes but said nothing. Juliet came over to her and topped off her coffee, giving her a warm, knowing look. Maggie found comfort in the concern of her friends. She sipped her coffee and willed Bradley to beat a hasty retreat. Her wish was granted as he paid his bill, and the bell over the door signaled his departure.

Jake waited until he was sure he was gone and then finally spoke. "Well, that was anticlimactic. I was hoping you'd go after him with a butter knife."

"So you know who that was?" Maggie asked, surprised.

"I overheard enough of the conversation to suss out the situation. I'm assuming that was your big city ex."

"Uh-huh," was all Maggie said and took a bite of her croissant. "Jules, these are excellent, as usual."

"Yeah, yeah, enough about my excellent baking skills, spill," Juliet said as she crossed her arms and leaned on the counter in anticipation.

"Not much to tell. He apologized for being a horse's ass and asked me if I'd consider picking up where we left off. I said no. He left." Maggie shrugged her shoulders like it was no big deal, but actually, she was feeling pretty proud of herself for how she handled the situation.

"I can't believe he had the nerve to show his face around here. He's lucky Mike didn't see him."

"I take it the split wasn't friendly," Jake speculated.

"A tale as old as time. Guy blows up relationship and business because he can't keep his hands off the local news reporter," Maggie said sarcastically.

"I would have gone for the butcher's knife," Jake replied.

Maggie smiled at him, and he gave her that dazzling smile that began in his deep brown eyes and radiating to his, oh, so tantalizing lips. That thought made her blush, so she quickly turned her attention to her coffee, adding more cream before sipping it.

"I think fate and karma delivered the message in record time," Maggie mused from behind her coffee mug. "Although," she continued, "I do wonder, after three years, what made him decide to attempt a reconciliation?"

"Well, if you hadn't kicked him to the curb so quickly, you could have asked him," Juliet laughed.

"I'm happy to let it remain a mystery."

Jake let out a hearty laugh, and Juliet snickered as she left to attend to a customer.

"You are not going to believe who I just ran into," Mike proclaimed as he came in through the side door.

"Brad," Maggie said flatly.

"He was here?" Mike was incredulous. "You mean that cheating, lower-than-pond-scum narcissist actually came to the café?"

"Oh, better than that, mate," Jake said with a laugh. "He tried to hit your sister up for another go-round."

"You wouldn't -" Mike began.

"It didn't even cross my mind," Maggie interjected.

"Good."

"Morning, Mike. What can I get started for you?" Juliet said, rejoining the group.

Mike handed her his travel mug. "Coffee and bagel with cream cheese would be great."

"Toasted?" Juliet asked. Mike nodded.

Juliet went to the kitchen for his order. Mike leaned into Maggie and whispered, "We need to talk."

"Kitchen," Maggie replied and walked behind the counter and through the swinging doors. Mike and Jake followed. Juliet looked up when they entered, concern flooding her face.

"What's going on?" she whispered as they joined her.

"Well, I was going to share some important information with Maggie, but I wasn't expecting an audience."

"You know I'm just going to tell them when you leave," Maggie reasoned with him. "Jules is like a member of the family, and Jake..." she paused, not wanting to reveal he had been helping her investigate. "...Jake has made sure I stay out of trouble," she finished vaguely. Mike raised an eyebrow but said nothing.

"Let's go out to the patio," Juliet suggested as she handed Mike his mug. He took it and followed Maggie and Bria. Juliet joined them at the picnic table after making sure Nancy, another of her part-time staff, was taking the next order out to the dining room.

"Okay, what I tell you goes no further than us," Mike began when they were all there. "It turns out that Vivian woman is telling anyone in the department, who will listen, that she is sure Maggie killed Devon. And that she found that voice message and made sure we knew about it."

"That evil witch," Juliet gasped.

"Why would she say that?" Maggie asked, dismayed.

"I have no idea. But you can be sure if she's telling everyone, she told Madigan."

"Which would explain why Maggie's the prime suspect," Juliet reasoned.

"Yes and no," Mike countered. "There was no official mention of Maggie in any of the reports I've seen. If Madigan knows, and I'm sure he does, he has not entered any information officially."

"Why would he do that?" Jake asked.

"It could be for a couple of reasons. He could be treating Vivian as a confidential informant. That means he'd keep anything she told him in a locked file only he and the Chief would be able to access. Or he's making sure no one knows, so they won't be tempted to tell me about Vivian's accusations and how Madigan is following up on them." He sipped his coffee and then continued. "It could simply be he doesn't believe her and wants to keep it out of the official records in order to protect Maggie from false accusations."

"I'm definitely rooting for that theory," Maggie chimed in.

"Me too, sis. Me, too," Mike said. "Well, I've got to get back on duty. We're all pulling extra hours while this investigation is ongoing. Of course, that means I'm on traffic duty for the graduations today," he said with resignation. "I'll be glad when we get you cleared, so that I can go back to regular duty." He gave her a quick kiss and then walked over to his patrol car and drove off.

"Now about that ex…" Jake began. Maggie rolled her eyes. "He seriously thought you'd go back to him?"

"He was never one for critical thinking skills," Maggie replied.

"He's lucky you didn't dump your coffee on him," Juliet said.

"I'd prefer to hit him with a chair, but I figured I should be the adult," Maggie laughed.

"You know, I have tools to make him disappear," Jake said with a wink.

Maggie looked at him for a long moment. Glad Brad's visit seemed to disturb him.

"How about we don't discuss disposing of my ex," she replied, looking around. "Lest someone overhears, and the police decide you're the one who helped me do-in Devon." She realized how that sounded and quickly added, "Allegedly."

They all laughed uncomfortably. It was surreal but at the same time, terrifying that Maggie would ever be accused of such a horrendous crime. Maggie handed her coffee mug to Juliet.

"I'm going home to get some work done and try to forget about this entire morning."

"If Brad shows up at your house, call us for backup," Juliet called out as Maggie walked toward her car.

"He won't, and I will," Maggie replied.

Back at home, to keep from obsessing about Devon or wondering what the hell was wrong with Brad, Maggie busied herself with cleaning. Since the space was small and her furnishings sparse, it didn't take long. She then went out to the garden, did a bit of weeding, and made sure everything had enough water to get through the heat of the day. After that, she showered and sat down to get a bit of writing done. She stared at the French Market Chicken recipe for a while and still could not put her finger on what it needed to give it that extra something she knew it was missing.

Finally, she went back out to the garden, snipped some Spanish Lavender, and hung it to dry. Once it was dry, she would crush it and add it to her Herbs de Provence, convinced that was what would take the dish to the next level. With that problem solved, Maggie decided she should eat something. Running strictly on caffeine and sugar was probably a bad idea.

She opened the refrigerator and realized that Mike had cleaned her out of leftovers. She did not feel like cooking. What she was in the mood for was one of Tony's meatball grinders. Before she left for an early dinner, she made a call to a corporate lawyer friend from her days in New York.

"Hey Mitch, it's Maggie Stellino," she began. She explained the situation to him, starting with Devon's death and the inexplicable fact she was a suspect. She asked him if he might be able to answer some legal issues surrounding Chef Friedrickson's restaurants.

"Are you talking about the restaurant sale in New Orleans?" Mitch asked.

"I am. Do you know about the lawsuits around it?"

"Talk of the town, since it involves Winston Eldridge and Winsight Investments, it's pretty big news."

"Do you know any of the details?"

"From what I've heard, it's going to be a tough case to win. The plaintiff alleges that Friedrickson devalued the property to his investors before buying out their shares. I doubt he could have done it alone. He probably paid off a few people to falsify the appraisals and alter the accounts. But unless he used those numbers for tax purposes and then different numbers to secure a loan or sell the property, it technically isn't a crime," Mitch explained. "A civil lawsuit was the only recourse the partners had. But from a legal standpoint, they entered into a contract, and it was their responsibility to obtain their own appraisal and have an accountant examine the books."

"Well, that could piss off a few folks." She had flipped open a notebook and was taking notes while Mitch spoke.

"Without a doubt. But since the investors didn't lose any of their initial investment and were only looking at a potential profit when Friedrickson sold the business for a higher price, damages would be iffy, even if they did manage to win the case. Nothing about it is a slam-dunk."

"I'm surprised they went to the trouble to pursue it."

"From my understanding, this is about reputation. Eldridge and Lee are not as worried about money as the idea they were scammed. Friedrickson had become a pariah to investors, and the rumor mill says his girlfriend was the one who made the introductions, so her reputation is sullied, as well."

"What a mess. Devon sure left a lot of destruction in his wake."

"I hope that doesn't include you, Maggie," Mitch said. "If you need a good recommendation for a criminal attorney, you let me know."

Maggie thanked him for everything and disconnected. She tucked away the notepad, grabbed her bag, and walked down to Tony's to order a grinder for dinner. To her surprise, Jake was standing at the counter.

"Hey, stranger."

FOURTEEN

Maggie ordered her sandwich and waited with Jake.

"What, no kitchen duty tonight?" Jake teased.

"Cook's night off."

"Do you want to take our subs over to the park and eat together?" he asked as he picked up his order.

"That sounds lovely."

They walked to the park that was next to a small stream, an offshoot of the Nemasket River, and sat at a table under the canopy of a tall maple. They unwrapped their subs and dug in.

"I like Tony's," Jake said between bites. "I usually grab dinner there a couple nights a week. They have a killer lasagna."

"Can't beat them for a meatball grinder," Maggie agreed. "I don't mean to pry, but do you know how to cook?"

"Oh, I can make the basics," Jake began. "I can fry eggs, make a quick pasta, grill almost anything, but that's about it. I can't bake, so Jules is a lifesaver with her breads and pastries."

"Well, I'll make you a deal," Maggie said. "As soon as this murder nightmare is over, as a thank you for your help, I'll give you some cooking lessons, if you like."

"Choice!"

"I take it that means yes." Maggie laughed.

"It does indeed."

Maggie filled Jake in on her conversation with her lawyer friend.

"I'm not sure it is a motive for murder, but if something happened in the heat of the moment, maybe,"

Maggie mused. "I sure would like to talk with Sean Park Lee about it. Pose it as I am someone who also had legal troubles with Devon."

"That seems risky. What if he is the murderer? You could be next if he thinks you know too much," Jake cautioned.

"I'll be careful," Maggie promised.

Jake did not argue. They finished their dinner with more pleasant conversation about living in Duxbridge and its quirky residents.

"You said you might buy a house. Have you been looking?" Jake asked.

"It's more nebulous sometime-in-the-future talk. I have no idea what the market is even doing these days. I do know it must have a fabulous kitchen."

"Of course," Jake laughed. "Anything else?"

"Lots of bedrooms and bathrooms. Oh, and a big dining area so I can feed everyone," Maggie added. "How about you, are you looking?"

"I keep my eye out for something choice, for sure a reno. I'm up for the hard *yakka*." Jake crunched his bag and stood. "I have to get going, my landlord's porch railing. It's *munted*, and I need to fix it. She's eighty, and I want to make sure she makes it to eighty-one." He tossed the bag into the trashcan. "You call me before you get into any trouble, eh," he said as he walked away.

Maggie smiled at him and nodded. She watched him walk away as she wrapped the remainder of her grinder and put it into the bag. It would make a great late-night snack.

She wasn't ready to go home, so she decided to walk downtown and stop in at some shops before they closed for the evening. She started at Blackstone's Kitchenware, browsing the specialty spices and the various gadgets. She looked up to see two women whispering. She recognized them, so she smiled and nodded. Instead of returning her smile, they looked embarrassed and went in the opposite direction. Soon after that, she walked across the street and popped into the Tables to Teacups Flea Market to wander through several booths.

She wasn't searching for anything specific but hoping a bit of retail therapy would clear her mind. She was deep into a booth with vintage cookware when she heard whispers a few stalls away. She didn't even bother to look up. She already knew the whispers were about her. She cursed small town life and made a beeline for the door. She escaped down the street to the safe harbor of Miss Kitty's Antiques.

The cat-shaped bell over the door jingled as she entered. Miss Kitty was helping an older, well-dressed woman that Maggie did not recognize. She was holding a mint green hobnail ruffled Fenton vase while trying to decide between it and a delicate, white ruffle vase with floral designs sitting on the table. After a brief exchange with Miss Kitty, she decided on both. Miss Kitty ran her credit card at the antique mercantile case that served as her checkout counter. Then she wrapped both vases and added them to a paper bag with twisted twine handles and a Miss Kitty's Antiques logo on one side.

She escorted her to the door, and after she left, Miss Kitty turned the sign from open to closed and locked the door.

"You look like you've had a day, dear. Let's have some tea."

Maggie could have used something stronger but agreed. Miss Kitty set two cups down on a quaint table in the back room and poured Earl Grey into them from an impossibly dainty china teapot. She added a plate of French galettes before sitting across from an exhausted Maggie.

Maggie sipped her tea and relaxed into the chair, letting the negativity of the past hour slip away. She snagged a cookie off the plate and nibbled it.

"Oh, these are delicious, Miss Kitty. Did you bake them?"

"I did. I convinced the baker at my favorite patisserie in Paris to share his recipe. It took a bit of flirting, but I managed to pry it out of him," she replied with a wink. She bit into a cookie and continued, "It does take French butter to get the right flavor, but I have Fabiano's order me a case once a year. It freezes well, and then I have it on hand when I'm in the mood to bake."

Maggie nabbed another cookie and wondered what it would take to extract the recipe from her.

"Tell me about your day, dear."

And Maggie did because Miss Kitty was incredibly easy to talk to, always sympathetic, forgiving and frank. She told her about Brad, her frustration with being a murder suspect, and her worry about involving Mike, and now Jake, in the foolishness. She finished by lamenting how everyone was gossiping as if she had been found guilty.

"Well, don't let the busybodies get you down. The moment you're exonerated, they'll all be claiming they never believed for a moment that you were ever involved. As for Brad," she smiled, "it sounds like the universe has rendered its verdict." She added more tea to Maggie's cup.

Maggie felt the weight of the day lift. Miss Kitty always had a way of putting things into perspective.

"Speaking of Devon's...mishap," Miss Kitty continued. "That nice-looking business associate of his was in here again this morning."

"You mean Sean Park Lee?"

"That's him. I'm telling you if I were ten years younger…" Miss Kitty winked and sipped her tea.

Maggie was startled to learn he was still in town but excited she might yet have a chance to speak with him. "Was he looking for more antiques?"

"Matter-of-fact, he was. He bought a sterling silver cigarette case he had admired yesterday."

"Oh, the one with the pretty filigree engraving?"

"Yes. And he was definitely the right buyer for that piece. You know, I believe every antique is looking for its perfect match."

Indeed, Maggie did. It was one of the traits that made Miss Kitty so endearing.

"Did he say if he was staying around for a while?" Maggie asked, knowing Miss Kitty had a way of getting people to reveal these things without hesitation.

"He is. He planned to peruse a few antique shops between here and Bourne. He asked about a nice place for dinner. I told him to go to the Hideaway. That he couldn't go wrong with their bacon-wrapped scallops and the rustic berry tart for dessert." Maggie readily agreed. It was no Michelin star establishment, but for local flavor, it was a great choice. "I also told him that Jules made the best breakfast in town. Miles ahead of whatever he was eating at the hotel he was camped out at on 495."

Maggie smiled, knowing that before the conversation was over with Sean Park Lee, Miss Kitty knew where he was staying and for how long and would happily share that information with her. She waited, and before long, Miss Kitty revealed that he was staying through mid-week on some type of business matter. She said he was staying at the Marriot in the complex of hotels near exit four.

"You know, after talking with him, Maggie dear," Miss Kitty said. "I don't think he could have had anything to do with the murder. He seems like such a nice man." She paused and then added, "Although Devon could probably drive anyone to homicide." She flashed a wicked grin at Maggie, and Maggie couldn't help but smile back. Miss Kitty was a good judge of character. She had an uncanny knack for reading people, and Maggie trusted her evaluations.

"Speaking of Devon," Maggie tried to sound casual but could tell from Miss Kitty's arched eyebrow. She was having none of it. "I'm wondering if you ever met his fiancée, Vivian Larkspur? She's an event planner."

"I have," her voice dripped with disapproval. "She came in on Thursday and asked if I could give her an appraisal on a few items. She sure didn't seem all that broken up, I mean, for someone who had just lost the love of her life." She sat back in her chair. "That was the first time I met her, but boy, howdy have I heard some stories. Did you know she refused to be in the CB? Not even a business listing!"

That was only the beginning of her indiscretions, according to Miss Kitty. "Willodene Rogers tried to engage her business for her parents' fiftieth-anniversary party, and Vivian told her she didn't plan small events like that. Made Willodene feel like a Duxbridge shindig was beneath her." Miss Kitty shook her head. "She was a piece of work. Refused to use local vendors for her events. They had to come in from Boston or New York. She flew some fancy sommelier in from New York to handle a yacht party last summer."

Maggie perked up at "yacht."

"How did you find that out?"

"The Miller twins worked with the caterer as servers. They talked for days about serving on the yacht as it sailed to Martha's Vineyard and back. I understand it was immense."

"Wow, sounds exciting. Does her event company own it?" Maggie asked, hopefully.

"Oh, I doubt it, it sounded like it belonged to the client, and they used it to summer around the islands. I think then they went back to wherever it is they lived. New York or DC, I can't remember."

Maggie was disappointed but not surprised. If Vivian's company had access to a yacht, the police would have already searched it. However, she decided she would make a point of running into Tim Miller, one of the twins, next time she was at Fabiano's. He was a clerk there.

Miss Kitty also relayed the local scuttlebutt that Devon had a bevy of women. While no one actually believed Vivian was his fiancée, they agreed if she was, she did not know of his dalliances or did not care.

While all the gossip was titillating, it didn't offer much insight into Vivian's motive for incriminating Maggie. It was probably too much to hope for an epiphany over tea and cookies. Maggie and Miss Kitty continued to chat amiably for a few more minutes before Maggie took her leave. She thanked Miss Kitty for the tea and sympathy.

Miss Kitty unlocked the door, and before she opened it, she asked, "Have there been any developments that don't implicate you?"

"Not that I know of," Maggie replied and hugged her.

"Don't worry, it'll be okay," Miss Kitty whispered.

Maggie walked out onto a quiet street of closed shops. Duxbridge rolled up the sidewalks early, even on weekends, leaving nightlife to the pubs and sports bars, so Maggie walked home. She was determined to get some work accomplished.

At home, she added flavored seltzer to an ice-filled glass, opened her laptop, and settled in to map out the first few chapters of the cookbook. A knock on the door immediately interrupted her efforts. Her heart lurched, once again worried this was the moment of reckoning. A quick look through the front window revealed it was not a S.W.A.T. team but instead Jake. He did a small finger wave. She smiled and walked over to open the door.

"Hate to be a bother, but I thought you'd want to hear this tonight," he said as he followed her into the kitchen.

"Never a bother." She caught herself before she accidentally babbled on about always being glad to see him at her door. "Do you want something to drink?"

"Yeah, nah."

Maggie blinked at him. "I'm sorry. Is that a yes or a no?"

He smiled that room-lightening smile at her, and her heart clenched again, but for an entirely different reason.

"No, thank you, I'm *chocka*. Been at the pub, doing a bit of detective work…" He caught her look. "And maybe had a pint," he laughed. "Anyway, the talk of the night was Vivian's behavior at the reception. She made quite the scene, screaming about how the police still hadn't arrested you, that you had killed the love of her life. Sounded like she was quite dramatic about it, having an absolute *mare*."

"Oh, my God," Maggie sighed. "That explains my shopping excursion today. Everyone in town must know by now." She sat down, trying to keep the anxiety at bay. It was one thing to know she was under suspicion, an entirely different animal hearing she was publically accused by the grieving girlfriend. There had to be plainclothes officers there who heard it all. Did that mean Mike knew? And if he did, why hadn't he told her? Why didn't he prepare her for what awaited her out in the world?

"I didn't mean to upset you. I thought you should know," Jake said, worry in his voice. "She sounds like a real piece of work."

"I was willing to give her the benefit of the doubt before, but now I'm furious," Maggie seethed. "I'm going to be her worst nightmare."

"Not without me, you aren't. Especially if everyone knows now, it could look suspicious if you start following Vivian or confronting her," Jake warned. "Together, we'll play it smart, okay? Okay?" he repeated.

Maggie reluctantly agreed, but deep down, she knew he was right and was grateful for Jake's concern and willingness to assist. She told him about her experience downtown, how she took shelter at Miss Kitty's, and Miss Kitty's assessment of Vivian.

"I'm going to do some serious homework on her tonight, make a few phone calls tomorrow. I want to know everything about this Vivian Larkspur before she gets me strip-searched."

"It will be all right, we'll figure this out, and as soon as they find the murderer, everyone will swear they never believed for a second you could murder anyone."

"That's what Miss Kitty said," Maggie laughed. "I'm sure it's true, but the sooner, the better."

After Jake left, Maggie made a pot of coffee and sat down with her computer. She opened the search engine and typed in Vivian's name. The top result was an article on Vivian's father. He had been a prestigious hedge fund manager until he was convicted of defrauding his investors and the government, leaving his family broke and disgraced.

The next article was a People magazine profile of Vivian, a true comeback story. A socialite, photographed with the rich and famous, who then lost everything because of the shameful behavior of her father. She used her contacts and rode the wave of sympathy to create a successful event-planning business, organizing parties for her former pals.

Socialite to party planner, for Maggie, it seemed less like a success story and more a humiliating endeavor for a woman who had few life skills. Nevertheless, she looked happy in the photo spread, and the parties were stylish. Maggie was impressed with Vivian's business acumen. As humbling as it must have been, she found a way to make a tidy profit off her former social circle.

The remainder of the search results were all about her events. Photos and write-ups of lavish events all around New York, and recently, a brief announcement about her move to Duxbridge. Quotes from Vivian and her staff fended off disbelief regarding her departure from New York, painting it as an opportunity to expand to Boston and the Islands. It seemed a less than stellar career move to Maggie, but she didn't judge, considering she made a similar choice.

She poured another cup of coffee, ignored the late hour, and searched once again for any mention of an engagement.

FIFTEEN

Despite an extensive search, Maggie found no additional photos of Vivian and Devon, no engagement announcement, and no wedding date. Absolutely no results showing them together in Duxbridge, either as a happy couple or in any business endeavor. Maggie felt that did not bode well for Vivian's fiancée story.

Her business, though, appeared not to suffer from the relocation. The most recent articles were for fancy gatherings in Hyannis, on Martha's Vineyard, and even Nantucket. The social media page for her business, Elegant Events by V, was filled with flattering photos of the rich and famous, tagged for all to see. Smaller events garnered no more than a photo or two.

And that was it. That was all Maggie could find. Discouraged because, besides the aura of a charmed childhood to broke socialite, Vivian, for all appearances, was successful and happy, with no apparent reason to murder Devon or continually accuse Maggie.

Maggie was sure Mike could easily dig up any dirt with his resources, but she didn't want him chastising her for prying into police business. Again. She took a deep breath and dialed Jake.

"I know it's late, but are you up for some surveillance?" If they took his truck, Maggie figured it would be less conspicuous, and the cops wouldn't rat her out to her brother again.

Jake was more than happy to be her chauffeur. "I'll be there in ten."

Maggie wasn't sure what she expected to accomplish, only that she needed to know what Vivian was doing at

Devon's house. It could be they would get there, and all the drapes would be closed, but Maggie held out hope of catching her with an illicit lover or burying the murder weapon. Mostly, she could no longer stand the continued inaction, not with Vivian disparaging her all around town.

"*Ahiahi*," Jake called out as he strode through her door. "What mischief are we up to tonight?"

Maggie grabbed her bag, and the jacket draped over the chair. "I want to drive by Devon's house to satisfy my curiosity. See if Vivian has any guests, or maybe she's committing some crime."

"I'm happy to spy on the leading suspect in Devon's death. I take it I'm driving because my ute is less recognizable than your car?"

"What? It couldn't be I enjoy your company?" Maggie slipped on her coat and walked to the door. "You genuinely believe Vivian could have murdered Devon?" She was surprised to see a beat-up dark blue Wrangler Jeep instead of Jake's work truck.

"I'm leaning toward it, mostly because she is so quick to implicate you."

"I don't know. I'm not as sure. Although I suppose she could have hired a hitman. I think she's covering for someone. Maybe a secret lover?"

Just as Maggie reached for the door to open it, her phone rang. She pulled it out of her bag and saw Mike's face on the screen. She took a deep breath and answered.

"Hey, sis, what are you up to? Can you chat for a moment?"

"Sure," Maggie replied while all the hairs on her arms stood up.

"I found out some news, and I wanted you to hear it from me first," Mike began, and Maggie held her breath. "Bob was at Devon's funeral and the luncheon afterward, observing the mourners."

"Funny, I didn't see him. I guess that was the point," Maggie mused. "If you're calling to tell me that Vivian made a scene and accused me of killing Devon, I'm already aware. I spent a bit of time downtown today, and it wasn't pleasant."

"Oh, I'm sorry. I didn't hear about it until this afternoon, and this was the first moment I had to call you. Hold on a bit longer and stay out of trouble, don't let the rumor mill wear you down."

"It's okay," Maggie reassured him. "Miss Kitty reminded me that once this is all sorted out, everyone will be contrite and swear they never believed the gossip."

"She's not wrong. Lay low, okay? Let the department handle it. I'm doing what I can on my end."

Maggie didn't commit one way or the other to her brother. She would never lie to him, but she could obfuscate with the best of them. She reminded him to be safe and disconnected. Jake gave her an inquisitive look as she dropped her phone back into her bag.

"Let's go," was all she said.

They drove in silence out to Devon's estate. The moon was rising above the heavy canopy as they cruised past the house. It looked like every light in the house was lit, and not a curtain was drawn in any room. As the trees parted and the driveway was revealed, Maggie gasped, and her heart sank. So much for Miss Kitty's intuition, she thought.

In the driveway was a red Mercedes. Maggie directed Jake to the macadam near the fallow cranberry bog, where they would be hidden a bit by the dip in the road and low brush. Jake parked the Jeep and turned off the ignition.

"This is an interesting development," he whispered.

Maggie leaned in and whispered back, "Isn't it?" "Got to wonder why someone who has active litigation against her dead fiancée would be socializing."

"That's a bit sus," Jake agreed, "I bet it's not to pay his respects. Maybe they decided it would be quicker to get what they both wanted if Devon was no longer around."

"But what does she want? If not Devon, then his business? His estate? Maybe she didn't know how bad his financial situation was?"

"I -" Jake began, and then Sean Park Lee stepped out the door and walked briskly to his car. He sped off and proceeded down the road, heading in the direction of Duxbridge. "What do you think? Should we follow him?" Jake asked.

"He is staying in town for the next few days. If we decide to invade his privacy, we know where to find him," Maggie reasoned. "I want to see what Vivian is up to this evening."

Jake reached across Maggie, and his touch sent a zing through her. He opened the glove box and grabbed a black case.

"Then we'll probably need these." He opened the case and pulled out a large pair of binoculars.

"I like the way you think," Maggie said as she took them from him.

Vivian made an animated phone call, waving her hand as she paced past the large French doors in what looked to be a study or den.

"Does that look like an urn?" Maggie asked as she passed the binoculars over to Jake. "There on the corner of the desk?"

Jake observed for a moment and replied, "Yes, and those are sympathy cards strewn across it. Not to be judgmental, but it doesn't appear she cares much about any of it."

Vivian disconnected her call and disappeared into the interior of the house. A few moments later, a dark sedan emerged from the detached garage and sped down the driveway, kicking up rocks as it stopped to let a car speed by on the narrow country road. She turned and headed past them.

Jake quickly covered Maggie's body with his own and whispered in her ear, "In case she looks over here, all she'll see is a couple having a little fun in a secluded spot."

Maggie enjoyed the weight of his body and the warmth of his breath on her neck. Once he was sure Vivian had passed, Jake moved back to his seat and started the Jeep. He left his lights off until he reached the main road. He turned and sped down the street until they saw what they believed were her taillights. He kept his distance until the car turned onto Route 44. With heavier traffic, Jake closed the distance between the vehicles.

"Where do you think she's going?"

"Taunton, from the looks of it," Maggie replied.

She secretly hoped Vivian was going back to the scene of the crime, but they were headed inland, so the chances were slim. Maggie's hopes were completely dashed when Vivian pulled the sedan into the parking lot of a small liquor store on the edge of Taunton and went inside.

Jake parked across the street, in between streetlights, and they waited. Less than five minutes later, Vivian reappeared with a bottle peeking out of a brown bag and a fistful of scratch tickets. She maneuvered herself back into the car and reversed out of the parking lot.

"Just a fun Saturday night at the packie," Maggie mused. They followed her until it was evident she was returning to Devon's. They gave up the chase, and Jake took Maggie to her house.

"I wonder where Vivian actually lives," Maggie pondered. "You know, when she's not squatting at Devon's."

"I was curious about that, myself. When I worked at Devon's a few months ago, she did not live there. I'm certain of that. Quite a few women were coming and going during that time."

"I really, really, want to know more about her. Maybe then I can figure out why she seems determined to pin Devon's murder on me."

"I can think of one reason," Jake replied. Maggie looked at him expectantly, noticing the end-of-day stubble casting a shadow on his strong jaw line. "To throw suspicion on you and away from her."

"I've thought that, too. And if Devon's boat had been the crime scene, I would have put my money on it. I suppose she could own a boat, but if she did, I think Mike would have mentioned it. I'll ask him tomorrow. If she did and they've already searched it, then we are back where we started. No crime scene, no evidence to acquit me."

"Don't lose hope," Jake said as she got out. He stayed until she was safely inside, and she watched him back out of the driveway before turning off the outside light.

Inside, Maggie could not quiet her mind. She texted Mike and asked him if Vivian owned a boat. She staved off any recriminations by explaining she was just curious.

While Maggie waited for a reply, she prepped for the morning. Putting her laptop and recipe cards in her messenger bag, she tried to focus her mind on anything but Vivian. It was hopeless. Since she had gleaned as much as she could from the internet, she decided there had to be another way to uncover more information on the mysterious Vivian Larkspur. By the time she crawled under the covers, she had a plan.

Heavy fog hung in the air as Sunday dawned. Maggie had a restless night, and looking out on the dreary day did not improve her morning mood. She dragged herself out of bed and prayed a shower would adjust her outlook.

After she poured her first cup of coffee, she sent Bria a text, asking her if she would like to meet her at the Duck for brunch. She had a plan, but it needed an accomplice, and she hoped Bria would be willing. She topped off her mug and looked over the headlines on her tablet.

Her phone dinged with a message from Bria, happy to meet with her. She tried not to worry that she hadn't heard back from Mike. Perhaps because he was trying to find her answers, at least that is what she told herself.

By the time she left for downtown, the fog had lifted, and the sun was bright and the air warm and humid. She arrived at the Duck to find it almost empty. In the kitchen, she found Juliet sitting with a cup of tea.

"Slow day?"

"Yesterday was graduation. I think everyone is recovering or doing family things. I'm grateful because I'm short-staffed. I gave my seniors the weekend off."

"What are you going to do when they leave in the fall?"

"I don't even want to think about it. With any luck, I'll find a couple of sophomores to train and hope they stay until they graduate - the cycle of life at the café. Tina is going to be very difficult to replace. She's smart, dedicated, and a hard worker," Juliet sighed. "I could confidently leave her in charge when I needed time off. She has a bright future, whatever she chooses to do."

Bria walked through the back door, letting the screen bang behind her. "Morning!" She made a beeline for the coffee. "Can I get you a cup, Maggie?" she called from the front.

"Sure," Maggie called back. "Would it be okay if we sat at the picnic table?"

Juliet nodded and finished putting bacon and toast on a plate of scrambled eggs. Maggie held the screen door, and Juliet carried the dishes out. Bria followed with three mugs of coffee.

"Yum," Bria said, kissing Jules on the cheek. "You spoil me."

"Are you sure you don't want something, Maggie?"

"Just coffee, for now. I may snag a muffin in a bit."

They sat at the table. Bria dug into her eggs, and Juliet sipped coffee while Maggie caught them up on the latest details.

"You mean that bottle-blonde had the nerve to accuse you in front of an entire room of mourners? Rude," Bria said between bites.

"I know. I'm feeling a bit maligned," Maggie joked. "Then, last night, Jake and I saw Sean Park Lee at Devon's house with Vivian. I'm assuming they were wrapping up the final stages of framing me."

"Well, damn," Juliet said. "I was hoping that Sean guy wasn't tangled up in all of this." She put her coffee down and looked at Maggie. "You and Jake?! Did the two of you decide to go for a drive down a lonely country road and -"

"No," Maggie interrupted her. "I asked him to go with me to Devon's. You know, because you didn't want me roaming around on my own."

"Oh, good, my plan is working," Juliet said with a wink.

"Other than Sean Park Lee's visit and an animated phone call, staking out Vivian didn't reveal much." Maggie sipped her coffee and then came to the point. "I want to know more about this woman. Her business, her contacts, what brought her to Duxbridge. I need to understand why she's made me a target."

"I'd be happy to talk with my clients, see if any of them have used her services," Bria volunteered.

"I appreciate that. That would be great. I have another idea, though, if you're willing. I was wondering if you would call her business and ask her staff for references for a party. Explain you have a client working on a big charity event in Hyannis, and you are tasked with finding an event planner for her. Maybe float the idea of a yacht party. See if the company owns one or has a relationship with a rental company."

"Oh, I see what you're getting at. You want to know if she had access to a boat."

"Yes. And I want to know what kind of reputation she has…you know, is she miserable to work with, does she pay her bills, do clients like her?" Maggie stole a glance at Jules and wondered how she felt about her asking Bria to be involved in this.

"I'm more than willing to talk with them," Bria said, excited with the intrigue. "I could even do a sit-down with Vivian."

The bell in the café chimed, and Juliet gave Maggie a concerned look as she went inside.

"While I appreciate that, I don't think that's a good idea. I believe Vivian is unstable at the moment, and it would be too easy to connect you to me. I don't want you even peripherally involved. I'm not sure what she is capable of right now."

Bria didn't argue. Instead, she began to embellish the story of the charity event, obviously enjoying herself. She and Maggie fleshed out the details and mapped out a game plan until they had a solid back-story and a good idea of the questions Bria would ask.

"Thanks for this," Maggie said and then looked toward the kitchen. "I hope Jules isn't upset I asked you to do this."

"I don't know how she could be. All I'm doing is making a couple of phone calls."

Maggie wasn't so sure. She was about to go inside and talk with her when Juliet bustled through the door, the screen slapping behind her.

"You will never believe who just sat down."

"If you say Brad again, I'm sneaking out, and you're going to give him food poisoning."

SIXTEEN

The trio bustled into the kitchen. Juliet grabbed two plates of omelets from Carl and leaned her backside against the swinging doors. "I'd be happy to, but it's not Brad. It's Sean Park Lee.

"You're kidding."

"Nope, looking at a menu now." Juliet pushed through the door and set off to deliver the plates.

"Huh," Maggie mused to Bria, "I think I'll go out the side door." She followed Juliet out of the kitchen, crossing the dining room to exit through the patio, passing Sean Park Lee along the way. She wished she was bold enough to initiate a conversation, but what would she say, "Hi, I saw you at the funeral, and I've been cyber-stalking you?"

To her surprise, when she walked past him, he looked up from his menu and asked, "Ms. Stellino?" stopping her in her tracks. He closed his menu, set it down, and stood. "I'm sorry to be so forward," he continued, his voice soft and deep. "I am Sean Park Lee. I am – was – a business partner of Chef Friedrickson." When she didn't respond, he continued. "I saw you at the funeral, and I know this is...unusual...but I was hoping we could talk. Miss Kitty spoke highly of you, and I was going to stop at her shop after breakfast and ask her if she could put me in contact with you."

Maggie's radar was humming. He was handsome, that was a given, and smelled heavenly, but he also had the air of the financiers she knew too well. The expensive, tailored suit, the vintage chronograph watch layered with a woven leather and gold bracelet, and the imported

Italian loafers, all put her on guard. She tried not to let his polite demeanor cloud her judgment. She had ample experience with the type, and she was not to be easily charmed.

"You and Miss Kitty were discussing me? That's…interesting." Maggie said coolly.

"I confess, I sought her counsel on a sensitive matter," Sean admitted. "It seems like she knows everyone and everything around here."

Maggie smiled despite her hesitation. "You are perceptive. She does, in fact, know most of the folks in Duxbridge," Maggie agreed.

"Could I buy you brunch? Please?" Sean asked as he indicated the empty chair. "I understand you have no reason to be inclined, but - "

"I would be happy to join you," Maggie interjected, ignoring Juliet's subtle look of disapproval while she assisted a customer at the bakery case. Maggie had an agenda and was confident she could handle Sean Park Lee, having dealt with people like him for years. She wanted to know what he knew, and here he was. She'd be a fool to pass up the opportunity, so Maggie sat in the chair he offered her.

Juliet set a mug of coffee in front of her, giving her a questioning look. Maggie did not meet her eyes, instead, remained hyper-focused on the menu. Once she and Sean ordered, Juliet returned to the kitchen, but Maggie could feel her reproach even from there. She turned her attention to Sean and waited for him to tell her why he had invited her to sit with him.

Sean sipped his coffee and then spoke. "Again, I know this is unusual, and you have no reason to indulge me here, but I'm concerned about something I heard after the memorial. I wanted to discuss it with you. I think we can help each other."

"Okay, you have my attention."

Sean put his mug down and smiled at her. "I can provide references if you like," he joked.

Maggie wanted to laugh with him but remained impassive. Until she understood his motives, she would remain cautious. For all she knew, he was here to gather intel for Vivian to use in her campaign against her.

"How well did you know Chef Friedrickson?"

Maggie appreciated his directness. "Mostly by reputation. We didn't necessarily run in the same social circles. I've dined at Devo's several times and saw him there." She sipped her coffee before continuing, watching him. "We were sparring over a legal matter through our lawyers. But I don't think I had spoken to him more than on one or two occasions."

She didn't feel the need to elaborate on the legal matters. She was curious, though, if Vivian knew about the lawsuit and if she shared that information with him. She wasn't ready to inquire about that. Yet. Instead, she asked, "How long were you and Devon partners?"

"Not long. I met him through Vivian Larkspur," Sean began. "I'm assuming you read in the obituary that she was his fiancée?" Maggie nodded, and he continued. "She and I have known each other since college. Chef served as the celebrity caterer at several of her more elegant events. It was a good arrangement. Gave her cachet and helped him network."

Their brunch arrived, and Sean thanked Carl as he slid the plates into place. He seemed relieved for a chance to regroup. While Maggie had been listening intently, she kept her business manner in place, letting him know she had yet to decide if she trusted him or not. She sipped her coffee and then cut into her Belgian waffle, forking up the piece, along with fresh blueberries, sliced strawberries, and the crème fraiche topping. She was willing to give Sean the time he needed to wind back to how they could help each other.

Once he had taken several bites of his omelet, Sean continued. "This is excellent," he said as he put his fork down. He paused, choosing his words carefully. "I trusted Vivian. She convinced me and another investor that Chef's New Orleans restaurant would be an excellent way to segue into hospitality ventures. She touted his track record as proof it couldn't fail." He took another bite before continuing. "It was successful – not an exceedingly profitable investment – but respectable." He sipped his coffee.

"I take it, it didn't end amicably."

"No, it didn't. Devon inexplicably decided to screw us over, and like you, we were sparring through our attorneys. I held out hope that Vivian was unaware of his deception, but I have my doubts she is the friend I thought she was," he paused and looked directly at Maggie. "Because of my suspicions, my belief that Vivian is not who I had always thought her to be, I wanted you to know what I know." Maggie suspected what was coming next. "At the memorial luncheon, she very publically accused you of murdering Chef Devon," he stopped to gauge her reaction. She remained placid, and he nodded. "Since you don't seem shocked by that revelation, I'll assume small-town gossip is in full force."

"That and my brother is a cop." Sean seemed genuinely surprised by that. Maggie was left to wonder if Vivian was aware her accusations involved a member of the Duxbridge police family. "You don't believe her claims?"

"Let's just say, my recent interactions with Vivian have made me question many of her motives. I'm not ready to declare her a co-conspirator in Chef's fraud, but I find her behavior toward you suspicious."

"Beyond her public declarations of my crimes?"

"Last night, I stopped by to extend my condolences and express how shocked I was at the circumstances surrounding Devon's death. She was quick to share her belief that you were involved in his murder. I pressed her on it, but all she would say was the police were handling it." That sent chills through Maggie. It had to mean Madigan was following up on her accusations. "I wanted you to know what she was capable of, so you could protect yourself.

"She is certainly messing with my life," Maggie said, scowling at her waffle, before putting her fork down. She had lost her appetite.

"There is something…" Sean searched for a word before giving up with a shrug, "…hinky – for lack of a better word – about all of this. I can't articulate it. It's a gut thing. I will tell you this, I don't believe for a moment she was Chef's fiancée. And I have to wonder why she would lie about that. Moreover, what is the advantage of casting aspersions toward you? Accusing someone of murder is pretty damn serious. She's up to no good."

Maggie sat back for a moment, contemplating what he was saying and weighing his motives against her own. Her instincts were to trust him. He had nothing to gain that she could see by telling her all of this. But she needed to know more before she was going to jump on the Sean-train. Charming manipulator was practically a prerequisite for high-risk investors.

Maggie leaned across the table and whispered, "What, you don't think I could off Devon?" She sat back, smiling, and sipped her coffee.

He smiled, too. "What I think," Sean said, serious now, "is that someone I thought was a trusted friend is willing to drive over anyone to get what she wants. And right now, you appear to be directly in her path."

"Tell me more about your investment with Devon and her involvement."

"Our senior year in college, Vivian's father was convicted of defrauding his investors and tax evasion. Completely bankrupted the family. It was a very public humiliation, and I admired how she managed it, head held high. She had to drop out but created a successful life for herself. We stayed in touch over the years, and when I moved to New York, she kindly showed me around the city. Introduced me to some very influential people." He paused to grab another bite of his eggs. Maggie could see his relationship with Vivian brought up complicated emotions. He sipped his coffee before resuming. "When she introduced me to Chef, I was probably less diligent than I might have been with another investment. His other properties were flourishing, and he had solid name recognition."

"And you trusted Vivian."

"I did," he said sadly.

"And then things went south?"

"You could say that. He doctored property documents, used deceptive practices to devalue the restaurant, and then offered to buy out the investors. We didn't discover, until after he sold the business and property for a hefty profit, that we had been deceived." He paused and absently stirred his coffee before continuing. "Reputation is everything in my line of work. He made us look like schmucks. We couldn't let that stand, so we took legal action."

Out of the corner of her eye, she saw Jake stride through the front door. Spying her, he shot her a questioning look, which she did her best to ignore, but Sean caught their brief exchange before Jake disappeared into the kitchen.

"Friend of yours?"

"Sometimes," Maggie acknowledged before pivoting. "Do you think Vivian was in on the swindle?"

"I didn't, at first. She was mortified when I confronted her. And I was inclined to be sympathetic, considering her background. Chef was intolerable on his best days, but I don't think any of us expected him to be a crook."

"Having had my own legal run-ins with him, I'd have to say describing him as a crook is generous."

"You're probably right. He had the nerve to counter-sue."

"You're kidding?" Maggie gasped, shaking her head in disbelief. "He sure kept his attorney busy."

"That was when I decided to pay him a visit here in Duxbridge and lost my cool."

"What happened?" Maggie asked, knowing the answer but waiting to see how candid he was willing to be.

"It was a short but heated meeting. I almost pushed him into a swimming pool." He shook his head at his impulsiveness. "Not one of my finer moments. I guess I'm lucky I have a rock-solid alibi, or I would be at the top of the police suspect list. There were more than a few witnesses to our disagreement." He glanced in the direction of the kitchen.

Julie made a stop at the table to top off their coffee. Maggie smiled at her to allay her subtle look of concern. She didn't appear to be reassured.

"How is everything?" she asked.

"It is amazing. Miss Kitty was correct when she said your breakfast was the best in town," Sean beamed at her.

"Thank you," she replied flatly. "Let me know if you need anything else." She moved onto another table, greeting an older couple warmly.

Sean leaned across the table and whispered to Maggie, "Did I say something wrong?"

Maggie laughed. "No," she whispered back. "She's just being overprotective." He looked relieved and nodded. "You were saying how you didn't murder Devon," Maggie quipped.

"Murder isn't exactly my style. Now, ruining him financially, that was something I could sign off on, and I suspect you might feel the same."

Maggie was warming up to him, despite her misgivings. "Oh, I would have been happy to make him pay my legal bills and go away."

"When I heard he was murdered and read that Vivian was his fiancée, it raised a bunch of red flags. In all my interactions with them, Devon never appeared at all committed to her. I attended the funeral with the intention of adding Vivian to the lawsuit if I felt she was a participant in Devon's shady dealings."

"What did you decide?"

"I'm still not sure. I'm skeptical Chef had the expertise to do it on his own. I'm treading lightly with Vivian, assuming she'll share more information with a friend than a combatant. Without a doubt, she is wrangling to benefit from his death financially."

"Well," Maggie confided, "I'm not sure there are many assets left. I think he was deeply in debt, and Devo's was in trouble financially."

Sean nodded. "That aligns with the information I've garnered. I'm not sure about the farm property. I have people checking on that."

"Do you think she's in the will?"

"Honestly, I don't know. I don't even know if he had a will. I haven't found a discreet way of bringing that up with her yet. But if Vivian is as cunning as I think she is, she's devised some way to acquire access to whatever assets he had remaining - or hidden."

"If they were engaged, maybe she's actually on the deed," Maggie speculated.

"I have serious doubts they were engaged. The Friedrickson family seemed more than a bit surprised by the idea he was contemplating marriage."

"Yeah, my sources doubted they were living together, much less engaged. Devon seemed more interested in sampling the menu."

"I'm going to keep in touch with Vivian and working my sources. See if I can determine her motives. And do my best to clear your name."

He was growing on Maggie. Seeing as how he wanted to help exonerate her, she decided to take a leap of faith. "My brother was removed from the case, but I'm still getting information. I'm doing my utmost to clear my name if only so my brother can go back to doing his job, which he loves. If I find out anything useful about Vivian, I'm willing to exchange information with you."

Sean looked genuinely pleased with her declaration. Maggie suspected he wasn't used to having to work so hard to persuade someone. He had a solid charm offensive game going.

"So the sleuthing gene runs in the family," Sean said, impressed.

"Can't let my little brother have all the fun."

"I'm going to stay in town for a while and continue to console our bride-to-be. See if I can get her to reveal anything about Devon's finances. See if I can figure out how much she knew about the shoddy NOLA deal. I'll keep you in the loop."

"I appreciate that," Maggie replied while she pushed her mostly uneaten plate away and placed her napkin next to it. "I have no idea how I would get close to her otherwise. She practically incinerated me with a look at the funeral. I'll continue to explore other avenues of information. Maybe between the two of us, we can decode her motives."

"Whatever you do, be careful," he said, concern in his voice, "because someone out there murdered Chef."

"You sound like my brother," she laughed. "It's not as if I'm running around town, tracking down suspects. I'm just asking a few questions."

Sean did not look convinced. "Still, I'd hate it if something happened to you," he said, pushing away from the table. "I should get back to the hotel. I have to rearrange a half dozen meetings if I'm staying in town. You know," he added as he stood, "I was surprised there weren't any places to stay in Duxbridge proper. I would think there would be a few B&Bs or quaint little inns."

"Funny you would say that. Jules and Miss Kitty are negotiating to create a Bed and Breakfast next door. All Miss Kitty's idea."

"That does not surprise me," he said with a chuckle.

Sean paid for their meal, and Maggie walked him to his car. They exchanged numbers, and he assured her he would be in touch. As he drove off, Maggie couldn't decide which was sexier, the man or the car.

She immediately returned to the café kitchen, knowing the gang would want a debriefing of her brunch. The trio was gathered around the prep table, waiting. Maggie smiled and walked outside to the picnic table, the three of them following her like ducklings.

"You best be spilling all the tea," Juliet demanded.

"Do you think it wise to be so familiar with a possible murder suspect?" Jake added, looking annoyed.

"I don't think he had anything to do with it," Maggie replied.

"Do you think you can trust him?" Bria asked.

"I'm not sure who to trust, but he had some interesting information," Maggie answered and then shared their conversation.

"I can't believe Vivian. Accusing you at every turn." Juliet was visibly angry. "Do you think she could be the one who killed Devon?"

"I don't know. But if she did, I think it's unlikely she could drag a two-hundred-pound man out to sea. She would have to have help. I know I would have."

"Sean looks like he could heft a body without much effort," Jake interjected.

"I'm sure he could. I'd be very disappointed if that were true."

"Me, too," Juliet agreed, and Bria nodded.

Jake made a derisive sound, stood, and explained he needed to pick up a special order before departing. Carl poked his head out the door, and Juliet went inside to help him with a mini-rush.

"Let's go over the plan for tomorrow one more time," Bria said after the screen door banged shut.

Back at the gatehouse, Maggie did her laundry in her Aunt's basement, but her thoughts remained fixed on Devon. She was missing something, and it gnawed at her.

After finishing the laundry chores, she put together a bowl of fresh lettuce, radishes and chives from her garden for her Aunt. She took them over to the house and promised they would have a proper Sunday dinner next week, including Mike and any of the cousins who might be around. She tried to remain optimistic that by then, life would be back to normal, and she would not have to dodge a bunch of inconvenient questions.

She returned to her kitchen and found nothing to inspire her for dinner. She cursed Devon for impeding her creativity with his untimely death, then quickly chastised herself for her flippancy. The man was dead, after all. A rap on the door interrupted her self-recriminations.

SEVENTEEN

When she opened the door, Jake was standing there, holding a large bag of takeout from China Sails that smelled divine.

"I was unaware you moonlighted as a delivery driver for the Chow family."

"Don't laugh. I adore Helena, and if she needed me, I'd be the best delivery driver they'd ever had," he laughed as he moved past her to the kitchen. "If it's not obvious, I've brought dinner. I hope you haven't eaten yet."

"I haven't even begun to think of cooking anything. Being a murder suspect is really interfering with my job," she lamented. "That smells heavenly."

Maggie realized she was hungry. She had barely touched her meal with Sean Park Lee, too interested in the conversation to pay attention to her berries and crème fraiche tucked into a lighter than air Belgian waffle. And that had been hours ago. Jake began to take containers from the bag, and Maggie grabbed plates and chopsticks.

"I'm starved."

"Great. I grabbed a variety of entrees, so there should be something here you like. And egg rolls, lots of egg rolls."

They filled their plates and ate in silence. Maggie felt that Jake had something on his mind, and she gave him space to decide if he wanted to broach it.

"Look, I don't want to overstep..." Jake began, breaking the silence.

"I've been dragging you all over looking for a murderer. I don't think there is any overstepping at this point," Maggie reassured him.

"I don't trust that Lee guy. I genuinely don't. I'm afraid he has ulterior motives and the way he assumed you'd be willing to sit for his inquisition."

"It wasn't an inquisition," Maggie protested. "He doesn't strike me as someone who hesitates. It makes sense that someone with his background who has become so successful would be direct. I'd think you would understand that. You headed out, far from home, to explore the world and then found a place you loved and set up shop, creating your own successful business."

"Well, I'm no multi-millionaire," Jake stammered, deflecting the praise.

"Not many are. It takes a certain personality to do what Sean Park Lee has done. And the willingness to work with some unsavory characters," Maggie explained from experience. "Real estate developers, hedge fund managers, trust funders…there are a lot of sociopaths hiding in those professions. Not that I think Sean Park Lee is any of those."

"Is that why you left the world of finance?"

"I left because my personal life was a disaster zone. But when I took a step back, I realized I didn't want to play in that world any longer."

Jake nodded. "So, after talking to this Lee guy, have you decided? Is Vivian your prime suspect?"

"She's something, that's for sure," Maggie replied. "But it's a big leap from gold digger to murder." Maggie paused, lost in thought. "Now that restaurant manager, he's interesting. He might have a strong motive, and he's missing. With vendors and staff unpaid, maybe he was embezzling, and Devon discovered it."

"How do you know he's missing?"

"After the staff told me he hadn't been seen since Devon was murdered, I went over to his condo, and no one was home. As far as I know, he hasn't returned to Devo's. It's suspicious."

"Well, I'm up for an adventure. If he's not at Devo's, it might be a great time to catch him at home."

Maggie eagerly agreed. She made a quick call to Devo's. It sounded quiet when the hostess answered. Maggie inquired about Ricky Daniels, and the terse response confirmed he was not on the premises. Jake and Maggie jumped in Jake's Jeep and drove to the condo complex.

Once they parked near Daniel's building, they slipped in as another couple exited. Upstairs they found his door open and a real estate agent walking a young couple through the now empty and clean apartment.

The agent greeted them amiably. "Are you here to look at the condo?" she asked.

"Oh, no, we are…friends of Ricky's. We were stopping by to surprise him," Maggie responded deftly. "We had no idea he had moved. Do you know where he is now? I'm afraid with his busy job, we haven't connected as often as we liked."

"He was always so busy at the restaurant we rarely had the chance to get together," Jake added to bolster the tale.

"He had a sudden job change that took him out of Duxbridge and moved quickly. Showings started this afternoon." The agent lowered her voice but ensured the young couple could still hear her. "It's a quick sale and an exceptional deal. I don't expect it will remain on the market long." She nodded knowingly at them, hoping to entice the young couple into a decision.

"Well, thank you so much. We won't take up any more of your time. We appreciate the information."

In the elevator, Maggie pulled out her phone and texted Mike that she needed to talk with him.

"I don't like to ask him many questions, in case I'm arrested. I don't want anyone to think he was helping me. But I need to know if he's aware of Daniel's status."

The elevator doors opened, and they walked back to the Jeep.

"You should probably keep your distance, too. Don't want them to think you're an accomplice to whatever misdeed they accuse me of, like murder."

"I'll take my chances," Jake said as he opened the door for her.

As Maggie settled in her seat, her phone buzzed. She pulled it out and read Mike's response. He explained he was too busy to talk just then, so Maggie invited him over for an after work beer. He said he would try, but he couldn't make any promises. He was buried, but he would check in later in the evening. Maggie texted him that there would be a plate of leftovers to take home and a cold beer waiting if he was able to get away.

Back at Maggie's house, she handed Jake a beer and began putting together a plate for Mike of the copious Chinese leftovers.

"I'm discouraged," Maggie told Jake. "If the police let Daniels leave town, then they either don't believe he's a suspect, or they've cleared him somehow. But without a crime scene, I don't see how anyone could be cleared."

"Hang in there. Something is bound to break soon. And the good news is, the police haven't questioned you, so despite what Vivian is telling everyone, there doesn't seem to be any rush to judgment by law enforcement."

Maggie nodded in agreement as she packed the remaining food for Jake and began cleaning the counters. Jake watched as she worked around the cramped quarters.

"Have you thought any more about moving?"

Maggie was startled. "You mean out of Duxbridge?" she responded, her head tilted slightly.

"Oh, no, I meant buying your own place."

"Looking for a new client?"

"Always. But I was thinking more about how you'd appreciate a spacious, well-equipped kitchen."

Maggie looked around. She enjoyed living steps away from her aunt, and the cozy cottage had been comforting when she had moved back to Duxbridge, but she had to admit that over the past few months, it had begun to feel cramped and confining.

"I suppose. But I wouldn't know how to begin, and I'm already behind on all my deadlines. Maybe once this mess is cleared up, I'll give that more thought." She looked around. "It would be nice, though, to spread out a bit."

Satisfied he had moved her thoughts away from murder, Jake recycled his beer bottle, gave Maggie a quick peck on the cheek, and said, "Then we'll revisit this topic soon. I may have some ideas." He grabbed the bag Maggie made for him, tipped an invisible cap, and before he ducked out the front door, turned and reminded her, "I'm available for any additional snooping." Then he left, closing the door behind him.

Maggie leaned her elbows on the counter, resting her chin in her hands, and stared at the front door, wondering what it all meant. Especially that quick kiss. She would be lying to herself if she didn't admit it gave her a little flutter.

Mike arrived quite late, looking weary.

"Do you need a beer?" Maggie offered.

"No, I'm working tonight. But the food looks amazing. Thanks for putting it together," he said as he picked up the containers. "I wish I could stay, but I need to get back out onto patrol. Everyone is working overtime with everything that's going on."

"Any updates on the investigation?"

"Nothing noteworthy. Unless someone confesses, I don't think there will be much headway until they find the crime scene."

"Were you aware that Ricky Daniels, the general manager at Devo's, left town? His condo is empty and up for sale."

"I hadn't heard. I'll ask around and see what his current status is. I'm sure Madigan is keeping tabs on him."

"Unless Vivian has him convinced I'm a cold-blooded killer."

"Maddie's a good guy and excellent at his job. He'll need more than the ravings of a distressed partner to believe you could do something so vile."

Maggie had her doubts, still stinging from Mike's banishment to traffic stops and nuisance calls. But she trusted her brother, so she acquiesced. "I'm sure you're right. I'm just tired of being the prime topic on the gossip circuit."

Mike wrapped his arms around her for a long, reassuring hug, then took his leftovers and went back to work. Maggie was left alone again to wonder about her life. Despite all the chaos around her, her thoughts drifted back to Jake's question about houses. Why hadn't she bought her own home?

She had the resources, but something stopped her from even beginning the process. She looked around her current residence. What had once felt like a cozy, classic Cape Cod, with paned windows and chair rails, now felt cramped and dark. She resolved to begin a serious search for a house to purchase once the Devon matter was unraveled.

Feeling hopeful, she readied herself for bed. Maybe she'd even get a cat, she thought before falling into a dreamless sleep.

As Monday dawned, Maggie was at her usual spot at the Duck, essentially to keep Jules from calling out the cavalry. She stayed long enough for a cup of coffee and a bagel. During a minor rush, she filled her travel mug and waved goodbye before Jules could interrogate her on her activities for the day. Maggie was sure Jules would disapprove of the plan she had devised in the shower.

She drove to the police station and traded her car for Mike's. They each had keys to the other's car and homes, along with their parents. Before she drove away, she texted him about the switch without disclosing why and was well on her way before her phone chimed with a reply.

Her plan for the day was to follow Vivian. She wasn't sure what she expected to accomplish, but she wanted to know more about the woman who was vexing her. She was curious to know where she lived when she wasn't camped out at Devon's and what her day looked like now that the funeral business was completed. She assumed her bright red car was not practical for such surveillance, hence the sibling switch. Mike's much more practical dark navy SUV would blend in with all the other dark-colored SUVs she saw everywhere.

She began her quest at Devon's, cruising past the estate just in time to see Vivian toss her purse into the sporty sky-blue convertible BMW in the driveway. Maggie assumed that it was another one of Devon's vehicles. Vivian pulled out onto the road, and Maggie followed her at a safe distance as she drove out of town to the interstate. Vivian took the second exit and turned into the parking lot of Sean Park Lee's hotel. Maggie camouflaged herself between two other dark-colored SUVs. She was close enough to hear Vivian on her phone as she sat in the car, angrily chastising the caller about work matters.

"Listen, I cannot book any new events right now. I can't believe people are even asking after what's happened. You and Jolene will have to handle this weekend's wedding." She opened the door and exited the car. "And don't screw it up. I have a reputation to maintain," Vivian snarled before disconnecting, shoving the phone in her bag, and slamming the door. She turned, and her entire demeanor changed. Maggie followed her gaze and saw Sean Park Lee striding across the lot from the hotel entrance.

Vivian smiled and walked toward him, her arms outstretched. She embraced him warmly, and he returned her hug. To Maggie, he didn't look at all suspicious of her. Instead, she thought he looked delighted to be meeting with her.

"Sean, darling, I'm so glad you wanted to meet for coffee this morning," Vivian practically cooed as she hooked her arm in his and walked with him to the coffee shop. "I'm so glad you decided to extend your stay."

He smiled down at her. "I'm happy to have more time to spend with you." He patted her arm and asked somberly, "Anything new on the investigation?"

She sighed heavily and stopped for a moment. "Nothing. I have serious doubts about the ability of the local police to handle a case of this…prominence."

"Well, don't despair. I had a meeting yesterday that you might find very interesting," he opened the door for her, and they slipped inside before Maggie could hear the remainder of his remarks.

Her heart sank, thinking she had been all wrong with her assessment of Sean Park Lee. She wanted to leave and forget she'd ever met him. She also wanted to go inside and confront the two of them, catch them plotting how they would frame her. Instead, she sat and waited while they met for about thirty minutes, giving Maggie sufficient time to imagine various scenarios with Sean Park Lee as the lead villain. By the time Vivian exited the coffee shop, Maggie was discouraged by the entire situation and questioned what she was doing, pretending to be some kind of investigator.

Yet, she followed Vivian out of the parking lot, hoping her next stop would be more revealing. It was not. She ended up back at Devon's house, working on squatter's rights, Maggie assumed.

She parked again on the narrow road next to the cranberry bog, hoping the low brush and modest rise would be enough to obscure the large profile of her brother's SUV. She rolled down the windows, turned off the vehicle, and reclined the seat just enough to wait comfortably. Forty-five minutes later, her butt was asleep, and her legs ached. She was not built for undercover surveillance. She decided to watch the house for a few more minutes and then call it a day and get some lunch.

Just as she was gearing up to leave, a dark Lexus turned into the driveway and parked under the portico. A man and a woman, clad in expensive suits, exited the car. The dark-haired man carried a briefcase and followed the woman as she stepped up to the door and rang the bell. Maggie assumed they were Boston lawyers. Whoever they were, they were not local.

She settled back in to see if anything of interest developed. After about twenty minutes, Maggie concluded they were in it for the long haul, probably conspiring how to defraud the Friedrickson estate. Since she was hungry and stiff, she decided to give up on the stakeout in favor of food. She could stop back later in the day to see if anyone else showed up.

After trading Mike's car for her own, she went to the Duck for a quick bite. She also needed to consult with

Jules about Sean Park Lee and get her opinion on his morning meeting. She wanted another perspective. Hopefully, one that would tell her she was overreacting.

When she arrived at the Duck, Bria was there picking up lunch for her office.

"Good timing. Do I have some news for you," Bria said when she saw Maggie walk through the door.

"I have news, too. But you first."

They walked behind the counter and into the kitchen, where Juliet was pulling rolls from the oven.

"Oh, hey, two of my favorite people." She set the rolls on the cooling rack. "Carl, your burgers are a hit today. I'll slice these up as soon as they are cool enough."

"Busy today," Maggie noted.

"Yes, all the families in for graduation descended on us before leaving town. It's been steady since breakfast."

"I'm just grabbing some lunch to go, and then I'll be out of your hair," Maggie told her.

"Bria, honey, it'll take me a few minutes to ready your lunch order."

"No worries, I have some good gossip to share with Maggie to keep me busy."

EIGHTEEN

"Well, don't keep me in suspense; I could use some good info after this morning."

"Oh, no, did something happen?" A worried Juliet asked as she ladled tomato bisque soup into two large mugs and added them to plates with sliced turkey club sandwiches. She handed them off to Amber.

"Nothing much, except I saw Sean Park Lee and Vivian Larkspur having breakfast together."

"How did you stumble upon that...wait, I don't want to know." Juliet raised her hand to stop Maggie from elaborating.

Maggie laughed. "What did you find out, Bria?"

"I talked to someone in Vivian's office, and they told me they do host parties on boats, but they either rent the boat or use the client's."

Maggie tried to hide her disappointment. After all that had transpired, she was rooting for Vivian to be a cold-blooded killer. However, without access to a boat, that was highly unlikely.

"I still have a list of her clients to work through, and I'll tackle those after work," Bria continued. Maggie didn't expect anyone to dish any dirt on Vivian's homicidal tendencies. References are usually highly vetted before a savvy business hands out their numbers. "Even better," Bria added, "I have a client who attended one of Vivian's soirees, and there was big drama involving Vivian and some other woman." Bria's eyes sparkled as she reveled in this news. "She couldn't give me all the deets because we were heading into a design meeting, but she said she couldn't wait to share the juicy gossip. I inferred from her glee that she is not a fan of Ms. Larkspur. We are going to grab a drink after work, and she's promised to spill the tea."

That bit of news lifted Maggie's spirits. At least the lying snake had some skeletons in her business closet.

"I'm eager to hear any revelations. She's a mystery, for sure. I'd love to know what's up with Devon's estate. She met with a couple of lawyerly-looking people this morning at his house." Juliet raised an eyebrow but said nothing. "That was after she and Sean had their coffee klatch."

"You realize you are following around a potential murderer? What if she realizes it and comes after you? Why didn't you at least call Jake to go with you if you were going to do something foolish?" Juliet asked, exasperated.

"Don't worry so much. I didn't drive my car, so there isn't much of a chance she recognized me. And I didn't want to bother Jake when he had so much work to do. At least he's productive, unlike me, since I haven't written a decent word since this mess began."

"I'm happy to tag along with you next time," Bria interjected. "I'm always up for a bit of an adventure."

Juliet slammed the serving spoon onto the butcher-block table. "Look what you're doing, getting Bria involved in this nonsense. You should both let the police do their job and stay out of it. We're talking murder here."

"Does that mean you don't want to go on the next mission?" Maggie teased. "You can bring the stakeout snacks. Come on, you know I wouldn't put Bria in danger. It's not like I'm kicking in doors and searching for a murder weapon. All I want is to know more about the woman who has made my life a living hell."

Juliet finished putting together Maggie's to-go bag and looked from her to Bria. Bria tilted her head and said, "I think I'm perfectly capable of taking care of myself."

Juliet relented. "Of course you are, honey. I think I'm still reeling from having someone we knew murdered." She handed Maggie the bag. "But it would give me great satisfaction if we were the ones to bring that evil witch down, so count me in for the next reconnaissance mission."

Maggie hugged her and Bria before taking her lunch bag and exiting through the kitchen door. She smiled, thinking about how conspicuous they would be as they piled into Mike's SUV and tried to stifle their laughter while munching on croissants and drinking lattes.

Instead of walking to the parking lot and driving home, Maggie detoured through the alley walkway and down the street to Miss Kitty's shop. The bell chimed, and Miss Kitty appeared from the back.

"Maggie! How good to see you. How are you doing today?"

"Better, Miss Kitty, better. I was hoping you had time to join me for lunch. I had Jules pack a couple of turkey clubs and two of her raspberry tarts."

Miss Kitty put up a vintage Out To Lunch sign on the door and turned the deadbolt. "That sounds lovely, dear," she replied and led Maggie to the back room.

Maggie unpacked the food and placed it on the table. Miss Kitty pulled two bottles of flavored seltzer out of the mint green 1950s refrigerator, handing one to Maggie before sitting down.

"The Duck was buzzing. Have you been busy with all the post-graduation crowds?"

Miss Kitty opened her takeout box and picked up half of her sandwich. "This looks delicious. So thoughtful of you to think of me. No, I haven't been terribly busy today. Most folks did their shopping over the weekend." She gazed at the triple-decker in front of her, studying it.

"I'm not at all disappointed for the quiet." She tackled the overstuffed club and nodded her approval.

Maggie opened her box, picked up her sandwich, and then put it back into the container. She opened the bottle and took a sip. She wasn't hungry. Food made her think of Sean Park Lee and Vivian's breakfast, and the thought of him conspiring with Vivian made her queasy.

"What's the matter, dear?" Miss Kitty asked, setting the club down, looking concerned.

"I saw Sean Park Lee having breakfast with that awful Vivian Larkspur this morning, and I feel as if I was absolutely taken in by him. What if he's working with her to frame me, Miss Kitty?"

"Oh, nonsense." Miss Kitty dismissed her concerns with a wave of her bottle of seltzer before taking a sip. "I'm an excellent judge of character, if I do say so myself, and that young man is no more involved in anything nefarious then…well, then you are. I'm sure there is a perfectly reasonable explanation, and you should ask him about it."

Maggie's eyes widened at the thought of brazenly questioning Sean Park Lee about his meeting with Vivian. A meeting she shouldn't even know took place.

"Of course," Miss Kitty added with a smile, "I could be blinded by his good looks and excellent taste in antiques."

"I'm hoping you're right and there's an innocent explanation. He did say he wanted to stick close to her until he could figure out her game, and he did contact me when he realized she was telling everyone I was the one who killed Devon."

"What? Why that scheming wench!" Miss Kitty slammed down her tonic bottle so hard it fizzed, and bubbles slipped out the top and down the sides. She grabbed a napkin and mopped up the errant liquid.

"It's okay, really," Maggie assured her. "I didn't do it, so there is no evidence that could incriminate me. Eventually, they'll find out who did this, and the idea I might have had anything to do with it will evaporate like so much morning mist."

"Well, I'll keep an ear out for any hot leads. You know this store is a hub for Duxbridge gossip. The town has eyes, and they aren't shy about sharing information."

They continued with their lunch, leaving behind the dark business of murder, and chatted amiably about the upcoming summer tourist season, the Roost remodel, and the prospects for the Red Sox this year. Once they finished, Maggie helped Miss Kitty clean up and thanked her for listening.

Back home, Maggie sat at her computer, attempting to focus on the menus. When that didn't work, she organized her recipe cards for the book and pulled out a few she decided she would work on once she could concentrate again. Once completed, she made a quick call to her attorney. She wanted to confirm that with Devon's demise, his lawsuit was no longer an issue. Her attorney assured her that she had filed a stay in the case and because it was on shaky legal ground, to begin with, she couldn't imagine a scenario where it would not be dismissed. She told Maggie to rest easy, the nightmare was over.

If only that were true, Maggie thought when she hung up. Before she had even put the phone down, it trilled, and she looked at the screen. Her parents. She had been dreading this and wondered how she would ease their concerns regarding her current situation. She could just ignore them, let it go to voice mail, and return the call when she had a plausible answer to any questions they might have. Instead, she pulled out her adulting diploma and slid the green button over.

"Hi!" she said, trying to sound like someone who did not have a care in the world.

"Maggie, darling," her mom's voice rang out clear.

"Hi, honey," her dad joined in, sounding a bit further away. Maggie imagined him standing behind her mom, his hands on her shoulders, lovingly pressing his cheek to her salt and pepper curls. "We are just checking in. Making sure everything is okay at the house. Mail getting picked up? Anything look urgent?"

Maggie felt a pang of guilt. She hadn't been over to her parents' house since the murder.

"Has the landscaper shown up? He needs to mow twice a month and keep the weeds under control. It doesn't take long for them to take over the yard. His number is on the refrigerator."

Maggie reassured her dad she would check up on the landscaper. Since she had known him since high school and saw him at the Duck at least a couple of times a week, she would have no trouble contacting him. She was also sure he was taking excellent care of the yard while her parents traveled.

Her parents regaled her with tales from their most recent stopovers, and after about twenty minutes, when they had yet to bring up Devon or express concerns about her being a possible murderer, she breathed a sigh of relief. It appeared that Aunt Carol had not called them and ratted her out. She owed her big time for that. She was surprised they knew nothing about the murder but suspected they were staying unplugged while on their first big retirement excursion. After assuring her dad again that she would follow up with the landscaper and declarations of love all around, they said goodbye.

Once she disconnected, Maggie hopped in the car and hightailed it over to her parents to collect a week's worth of mail. She pulled into the driveway and strode down to the street to remove the mail from the box. Rifling through it as she walked to the porch, it appeared to be mostly junk mail. She pulled the house key from her pocket and let herself into the entryway.

She tossed the envelopes into a large wicker basket on the antique Queen Anne hallway console. She made a quick walk-through of the house to ensure that nothing was leaking or smoking and then walked around the yard, noting how well-manicured it was and that nothing was leaking outside, either. That's when she noticed the dark sedan parked across the street. The hair on the back of her neck tingled. Even though she could not see past the tinted windows, she felt someone watching the house…or her. She walked to the front of the house and down the stone walkway to the sidewalk to catch a glimpse of the license plate. When she reached the sidewalk, it sped off too fast for her to get a plate number.

Unnerved, Maggie called Mike. When his voicemail picked up, she disconnected and sent a text describing what had happened. She suggested an extra patrol in the neighborhood might be warranted and asked him to call her when he had a moment.

After double-checking all the window and door locks, she slid back into her car and noted the time. She made an impulsive decision to drive to Devo's and get takeout for dinner. She wanted to see how they were all holding up and also ask a few more questions. Maggie assumed Jo would be interested to know what happened to Daniels and that she shouldn't expect his sudden return.

As she drove out of town, she kept a lookout for the dark sedan. While she worried it was someone surveilling her parents' vacant home, she couldn't dismiss the idea that it might be someone watching her. She could only hope it wasn't the police.

As she pulled into the Devo's parking lot, she saw her two favorite employees, Pacey and Celia, standing outside by the delivery door. She waved to them as she exited her Fiat.

"Hi," she said with a smile. They did not smile back. "I thought I'd get some takeout ."

"Don't bother," Celia said gloomily as she took a drag off her cigarette.

Maggie gave them a quizzical look.

"We're almost out of food," Pacey explained. "Daniels and Chef were the only ones with signature power on checks, and all the vendors are COD now. We can't buy supplies or food."

"Luckily, the last payroll went through. Thank God for small favors," Celia said.

"Jo decided we should open for one last night, serve until everything was gone, and split the cash," Pacey added.

"Then we'll lock the doors and walk away." Celia dropped her cigarette and stubbed it out with more effort than required. "Good riddance."

"Do you know where you'll go? Do you have any positions lined up?"

"Huh! Maybe if we want to drive for hours each day. Most of us have long-term leases, so we either find something close, break our leases, or have a hell of a commute." Celia said fatalistically.

"Oh, I'm so sorry to hear that. I'll let you know if I hear of anything, I promise," Maggie said with genuine sympathy. She decided now was not the time to prod them for additional information regarding Devon. They exchanged numbers, and Maggie returned to her car. On the way home, she picked up a pizza from Tony's.

She popped the pizza box into her oven and turned it to warm, then grabbed a colander and went to her garden to harvest snow peas, radishes and lettuce for a salad. She texted Mike that she would have leftovers for him again if he wanted to stop by on his way home. He must have been besieged with calls because he had not yet replied to her message regarding the dark sedan.

After she ate a slice of pizza and a big bowl of salad, she packed up the leftovers for Mike before going out to water the garden. Deep in thought, she sprayed the hose absently over the rows of vegetables. She worried about Jo, Celia and Pacey. They deserved better than to be left high and dry by Devon's poor business skills. She decided she would let Aunt Carol know about their plight. With her contacts, Maggie was sure she would be happy to help.

She turned off the hose, wiped the dirt from her hands, and looked to the big house to see if Carol Ann's car was there. The sky glowed with the setting sun, creating an intense glare. Maggie held up her hand to shade her eyes and couldn't believe what she saw.

NINETEEN

Maggie was startled to see a dark sedan driving slowly down the street. Her heart pounded as she tried to tamp down the sudden alarm. If it was the same vehicle, then they were not targeting her parents' empty house. Her first fear was the police were watching her and her second was Devon's murderer was stalking her. Both thoughts were equally disturbing.

She was walking back to the gatehouse to call Mike when Carol Ann arrived. Maggie strode down the path to the house to greet her. She decided she was being irrational about the sedan but was still comforted that her aunt was home.

"Bridie's knitting group was canceled tonight," Carol Ann explained as she locked her car.

"Is everything all right?"

"Yes, but one of her ewes went into labor, and she wanted to be there for the delivery," Carol Ann replied and then hugged her niece. "How has your day been?"

"Same old, same old," she lied. Carol Ann gave her a look that meant she knew Maggie was lying, but she didn't push it. "I talked with mom and dad today. They're having a grand time."

"That's good. I haven't had a chance to speak with them this week. It's been hectic, what with summer tourist preparations and all," Carol Ann said with a wink. "We should try to find time for a family dinner next weekend. What do you think?"

"I think that would be great," Maggie agreed. "By then, I should have new recipes, and I could use guinea pigs."

Maggie didn't mention the sedan to her aunt before going back to finish up in the garden. She was feeling foolish for her reaction, and by the time she had rolled the hose and put away her weeding tools, she had talked herself out of any concern. Back in her kitchen, she decided against calling Mike again. He hadn't returned her earlier message, and he hadn't come by for pizza, so he must be inundated at work. She didn't want to add to his burden.

It was a small town. She probably saw the same people and cars several times a day and never gave it a thought. Just because she didn't recognize this car, it did not mean some crazed murderer was stalking her. One of her neighbors probably bought a new car.

However, she knew better than to ignore her intuition. Still, she pushed aside the thoughts of undercover cops and killers following her and focused on her plan for the next day.

She couldn't follow both Sean Park Lee and Vivian, so she decided to follow Vivian. She had to go to her office at some point, Maggie reasoned. And if she did go, and it looked like an ordinary day at the office, then Maggie would check if Sean wanted to have lunch with her. See if he vibed as a liar and a murderer. She would have to stick to her morning routine at the Duck, or else Jules would worry and send Jake after her again.

Not that his presence would be unwelcome, She enjoyed his company. He was smart, funny, and easy on the eyes, and he wasn't opposed to a bit of adventure. With thoughts of Jake to distract her, she drifted off to a peaceful night of sleep.

Maggie arrived at the Duck Tuesday morning just as Juliet flipped on the dining area lights. Wonderful aromas of pastries and breads baking filled the café. She grabbed a cup of coffee, followed Juliet into the kitchen, and sat at the prep table to watch her begin prepping the daily special, Washday Beans and Rice.

"You look like you slept well last night," Juliet remarked as she expertly made short work of dicing an onion and tossing the pieces into a large skillet.

"Finally," Maggie replied as she snatched a chunk of carrot from the cutting board. "I love your beans and rice." She saw the lights go on next door at the Roost, and thoughts of Jake rushed back. "How is the remodel coming along?" Maggie sipped her coffee casually. Juliet was not fooled.

"It's progressing. Jake is doing a great job." Juliet used a metal scraper to scoop up diced carrots and celery and add them to the pan with the translucent onions. She stirred them briefly with a large wooden spatula. "You should ask him to have lunch with you. I'm sure he'd welcome the break. Then you can fill him in on whatever ill-advised plans you have today."

Maggie smiled. She should know better than to try to slip something past her friend. "I promise I'm not going to do anything risky. But I was thinking of asking Sean Park Lee to join me for lunch, so your plans at matchmaking will have to be postponed until another day."

"He's not a bad choice," Juliet teased as she added large pieces of Andouille sausage to the skillet. "I mean, as long as he's not a murderer," she added with a grin.

"That's what I'm hoping to determine." Maggie replied and then added, "If he's a murderer, not if he's dating material." She grabbed a plate and helped herself to a bagel and cream cheese. She spread cheese over half. "Jules, are you okay with Bria's involvement? I didn't mean to cause problems when I dragged her into this." She bit into the bagel and observed Jules carefully, looking for any sign she had crossed a boundary unintentionally.

"She's making a few phone calls, having coffee with a client, and she's happier than I've ever seen her, so I'm fine with it." Juliet held up the large chef's knife she was using to cut up more sausage and pointed it at Maggie. "But that's as far as it can go. I don't want her going all Velma and Daphne, exploring places she shouldn't be, or following suspected killers. Got it?"

"Got it," Maggie took another bite of bagel and sipped her coffee, happy her friend wasn't cross with her and pledged to keep it that way.

By the time Carl arrived, Maggie had briefed Jules on the latest on Devo's and the staff there. Juliet vowed to pass along any job opportunities.

"Devo's closing will make quite a few vendors angry if they get stiffed. I'll have to give Bridie a call and make sure she knows what's going on in case de Luna's has any open invoices with Devon."

"You know," Maggie mused, "if Devon was into a vendor for a large sum, that could be motive for a crime of passion. Especially if they realized that he put all that money into his home reno while letting his restaurant bills languish."

"Don't tell me you think Bridie or Johnny offed Devon, do you?" Juliet was aghast.

"No," Maggie laughed. "I was thinking more like one of his wine vendors or those specialty meats he had on the menu. Those weren't local and definitely pricey."

"Killing wouldn't get them their money," Juliet countered.

"It might have been a moment of anger. Devon had that effect on people."

"Yes, he did," Juliet agreed.

"Although, if he carried a celebrity chef insurance policy, that could be used to pay off all the restaurant debts. That could be a solid motive."

"Is there such a thing?"

"Good morning, ladies," Jake sang out in his New Zealand lilt as he came through the kitchen door. "Staying out of trouble?" He didn't wait for an answer as he passed through the swinging doors to fill his travel mug.

"With high profile chef branded restaurants," Maggie explained, "investors require it because their assets would be lost if something happened to their celebrity chef. Devon's partners could have made him purchase it before they would fund his establishments. Depending on the policy, and if Devon didn't let it lapse after selling the other properties, it could be worth several million. If he had one, I bet Sean Park Lee would know its status. He seems the type who would be on top of something like that."

"That's probably why Devon cheating him on the buyout irked him," Jake chimed in as he came back into the kitchen. "Point of pride." He grabbed a plate and a bagel and sat next to Maggie.

"Definitely," Juliet agreed. "Do you want me to toast that for you?" Jake shook his head and borrowed Maggie's knife to slice the bagel in half.

"No thanks. I need to get moving." He snagged some of Maggie's cream cheese, spread it over the bagel halves, and sandwiched them together. Maggie found herself enjoying the casual familiarity. "My client is expecting to see some significant progress today."

"She's a real taskmaster, that's for sure," Juliet laughed.

"How are things going next door?" Maggie asked, savoring his proximity.

"Demo is done, and the hard work begins. What kind of trouble are you planning today?" he asked before taking a bite of his bagel.

"I have no idea what you mean," she replied and sipped her coffee, trying her best to look innocent and not burst into laughter.

He grabbed his plate and his mug and stood up. "I want an update on our investigation later today." He walked to the door as Maggie got up and stacked her dishes by the sink.

"I should get going, as well. I'm not in the mood to write today."

Jake held the door open and waited for her. She gave Jules a quick hug, and reassured her she would play it safe. Jake pushed open the screen, and they walked outside together, where the sun was peeking over the horizon, casting pink and orange streaks across the morning sky.

"So, in addition to avoiding your day job, what are you planning today?" Jake prodded.

"I'm going to check in on Vivian's movements, and if that is futile, which I'm sure it will be, I'm going to see if I can persuade Sean Park Lee to have lunch with me. I have some questions for him."

"I doubt it will take much persuasion," Jake noted. "Let me know if you need backup." He raised his coffee mug in salute and left.

Maggie returned home and looked up the location of Vivian's home and office. She was surprised to see that they were at the same address. She wasn't expecting a premiere event planning business to be operated out of Vivian's home. Although Maggie surmised it could be possible, there was a converted gatehouse on that property. They were not uncommon in Duxbridge. Maggie scribbled down the address in the event Vivian wasn't at Devon's.

Her first stop was her parents' house, so she could borrow their car, again to be less conspicuous as she followed Vivian. She made the quick drive out to

Devon's estate. Vivian was opening the door to a well-dressed man carrying a clipboard. Maggie recognized him immediately. Jim Morrow, owner of Morrow Realty. Maggie could see the roof of his emerald green Escalade peeking over the hedge, which obscured the "SOLDSMOBILE: See Today, Sold To-Morrow!" emblazoned on the side. He was wasting no time, Maggie thought. And neither was Vivian.

She settled into her parents' well-appointed car, enjoying the comfortable leather seats and ample leg room - definitely a step up from her sporty yet small Fiat. A variety of people came and went over the two hours that Maggie watched the house, but Vivian stayed put. By noon, Maggie gave up and returned her parents' car.

On the way back to town, she called Sean to see if he would like to join her for lunch. He agreed readily, and Maggie suggested they meet at the Stonebridge in Onset. She extolled its great views, excellent fried clams, and most importantly, privacy from prying Duxbridge eyes.

An hour later, he pulled out a chair for Maggie at a table with a view. The restaurant's large front windows framed the bay and the marina, where boats rocked on gentle waves of blue-green. The sunlight sparkled off the water as people spread blankets and towels and stretched out on the sandy beaches. Cape Cod cottages dotted the inlet in muted grays and vibrant whites with brilliant red roofs, not a pastel in sight.

Maggie picked up her menu and decided on their signature Thanksgiving sandwich: turkey, stuffing, and whole cranberry sauce on a grilled, fresh-baked roll, served with a side of dipping gravy. Sean chose shrimp and scallops on flatbread, garnished with mozzarella and spinach. He decided to start the meal with a stuffed quahog. Maggie passed on an appetizer but asked for iced tea with lemon. Sean ordered a glass of Sauvignon

Blanc. After the server took their menus, Maggie sat back with her tea and looked out at the peaceful bay.

Sean broke the silence. "This is a beautiful view, Maggie."

"And the food is excellent," she added. "I'm glad you had time for lunch."

"I'm assuming it was more than a friendly invitation."

"I admit to ulterior motives. I had additional questions about Devon and Vivian, and I thought you might have information or know someone who would be able to answer them."

The server set a plate of stuffed quahog in front of Sean.

"Thank you," he said as the server added his glass of wine. "This looks amazing," he said to Maggie after the server left. "Would you like a bite?" He pushed the plate toward her. She couldn't resist and dipped her fork into the steaming stuffing of quahog, sausage and bread crumbs. Sean slid the plate back and did the same. "Oh, this is delicious."

"It is," Maggie agreed. "I might have to see if I can recreate it." She sighed. "After I meet my deadline for this cookbook. I have enough recipes to write. I don't need to go looking for more."

"Work not going well?"

"It's difficult to concentrate. What with all the accusations of murder and all," she replied sarcastically.

"Tell me what I can do to help, besides trying to redirect Vivian's odious behavior. To no avail, I'm afraid."

"You've talked to her?" Maggie asked innocently.

"I had a quick and discouraging breakfast with her yesterday. I'm afraid my trust in her on business matters was misplaced."

The server brought their entrees and, after asking if they needed anything else, left them to their meal.

"Do you mean she was working with Devon to swindle his investors?"

"It looks that way. I was hoping it wasn't true," Sean said, shaking his head. "And nothing I said would dissuade her from her single-minded focus on you. I'm sorry. Even when I told her about the update I had from the investigator I hired after Devon counter-sued. He informed me that he witnessed a heated exchange between Devon and his general manager the Sunday before he was murdered."

"With Ricky Daniels? You're kidding. Did you know he left town?" Sean shook his head. "Have you informed the police? That information could help."

"I told him to give the Duxbridge police all the information he had collected on Chef. I'm hoping there is something in there that can help vindicate you. At least point them in a different direction."

Flustered by his attempts to intervene in her troubles, Maggie needed a moment to regroup. She picked up her knife and cut each half of her sandwich in half again. It was enormous, and she had visions of making a fool of herself as it spilled out all over her. Better to take precautions. "Vivian is an enigma, isn't she? I sure would like to know how I got on her radar in the first place," Maggie said as she picked up a sandwich section.

"Me, too. I suspect Devon had his share of detractors to choose from, with more motive than you, especially with the suspicious activities of the GM. It seems reckless to target the sister of a well-respected police officer." He bit into his flatbread and nodded his approval. "I'm curious about many things in regard to Vivian, but I don't think she'll be forthcoming with any real answers. Although, I'm going to keep prodding her."

"Don't give away the game, but I am interested to know anything you find out." Maggie took another bite of her sandwich before broaching another topic with

Sean. "Do you know if Devon held a death and disability policy to cover his business?"

"I know the partners required it on the properties in which they had a stake, to cover our investment if something happened to him. However, I'm not sure if he continued the coverage. It would have covered all of his properties in the event of his death or disability. It was a hefty sum."

"With his current financial difficulties, I'm betting he didn't, but if he did, who receives the funds?"

"They are generally distributed to the business to pay off debts and pay restaurant expenses until the business can be sold or shut down," Sean replied. "There wouldn't be a single beneficiary on that type of coverage, if you were looking for a motive."

"I'd be happy to point at any other suspects besides me, but honestly, I am more worried about the staff at Devo's. An insurance payout could help them. They didn't deserve this, and the closing will upend their lives if they can't find local work. Relocating will be a financial burden for most of them."

"You are a good person," Sean observed. "I wonder if Vivian will stick around or move her business back to New York or maybe to Boston?" He looked out across the water. "She has some good contacts here with the Hyannis and Vineyard summer season. I'm fairly certain that one of the events I attended last summer was at the yacht club across the water there." He pointed

"Really?" Maggie pulled out her phone and did a quick search. Bingo.

TWENTY

Maggie turned her phone around so that Sean could see it. "Was it the Point Onset Yacht Club? It's a small, exclusive marina that's been around about a hundred years."

"That sounds right. That was the last event I attended that Vivian hosted. She wanted me to meet another potential investment. But before the week was out, Devon's deception came to light, and I put some distance between myself and Vivian while the legal wrangling continued."

"Do you know if she rented the yacht? Or was it the client's?"

"It was definitely the client's yacht. It was something of an amalgamation of a housewarming and summer kickoff event. They had just completed the redesign, and they were enjoying showing the work to guests. And Vivian was very proud of the entire event, as she should've been because it was quite the affair."

He sounded wistful, and Maggie could see he took his friendships seriously. It didn't take a psychic to understand his disappointment in her betrayal. Maggie decided to take the bull by the horns. "Who do you think murdered Devon?"

"I honestly don't know. I mean, there are a few people I could imagine were angry with him, but it's always the question, angry enough to kill? I don't think it was premeditated. The way the body ended up on the beach, it was someone who didn't have a good plan."

"Or didn't understand tides."

"It's one of the reasons I don't think it was Vivian…or you. I mean, dumping a body into the ocean, that couldn't be easy."

"Well, the police think I had an accomplice."

Sean put down his fork. "They think you and your boyfriend plotted a murder and disposed of a body because Devon filed suit against you? Wouldn't that be a bit drastic?"

"Well, I did leave him an angry voice message once," Maggie replied sarcastically.

"The number of angry messages I left him could fill a detective's notebook."

"I'm sure we aren't the only ones," Maggie said with a laugh and then sobered. "Speculation is, my brother helped me. Which is why I need to put an end to this before it damages his career."

"Well, that makes even less sense. I mean, I could see you defending yourself if he was threatening you and he accidentally fell overboard. But you don't strike me as a stone-cold killer." He sipped his wine. "Vivian has proved herself to be someone who doesn't care who she destroys on the way up the ladder. But murder? I guess what I'm saying is, I don't know who killed Devon because I don't know anyone murderous."

"This is one messed up situation, isn't it?"

"It sure is. How about we talk of more pleasant things? Tell me about your latest cookbook and why you don't have your own cooking show." Sean took a bite of his shrimp flatbread and had to catch a bit of sauce as it threatened to land on his shirt. He smiled at her and shook his head at his gracelessness. She smiled back with empathy. Once he had regained control of his lunch, he added, "And I want to hear more about the staff at Devo's."

They spent the remainder of their lunch chatting amiably about Maggie's cookbooks, Devo's staff, and the remodel at the Roost, while avoiding any additional mention of Devon or Vivian. Sean shared with Maggie that he was on the lookout for new projects, something different from his usual real estate and business investments. He wanted something that felt more substantial, something creative. Maggie understood this desire. Working in finance was exhilarating and stressful, but at the end of the day, she wasn't sure what she had accomplished. Creating a delicious menu was so much more satisfying.

When the check arrived, Sean nabbed it and pulled out his wallet.

"Sean, I invited you to lunch. I should be paying."

"Nonsense," he replied, pulling a credit card from his wallet. "You introduced me to a pleasant new restaurant with an excellent view," he glanced up at her before placing the card in the sleeve along with the bill. "And I couldn't have asked for better food and conversation. Paying is the least I can do." He handed the folder back to the server. "I might let you pay next time," he said with a wink. Maggie blushed despite herself.

Once they had said their goodbyes and Sean drove off, Maggie sat in her car and stared out toward the water. A moment later, she was driving, not home, but to the other side of the bay. She knew it was absurd, but she wanted to check out the yacht club.

She drove over the stone bridge that crossed the inlet, past the summer rentals, turned right at the hundred-year-old stone church, and into an upscale neighborhood of larger homes with well-groomed landscapes. Streets were marked private and led directly to the inlet. The public road came to an end, and her choices were to turn right and continue down the private road that led to the exclusive yacht club or left and follow another public road back to Onset.

She turned right and proceeded to the water, where the yacht club sat at the edge of the small marina, dotted with large, luxury crafts. Everything was quiet, with little activity on the docks or at the clubhouse. She wasn't surprised, as it was early in the week. After the holiday weekend, it would be bustling with activity every day and continue through the summer months.

A quick internet search told her that the clubhouse was available for non-member event rentals. If anyone questioned her presence, that would be her cover story. She would explain she was surveying the location for a party.

She parked her car in a Clubhouse Visitor Only spot, exited, and walked up to the clubhouse door, only to see the Closed sign. Turning back, she followed the boardwalk to the docks. The lattice-covered entry stood between her and the private dock. She took a deep breath and put on her NYC financial whiz-kid attitude, threw her shoulders back, and turned the knob on the door, fully expecting it to be locked. Instead, it turned smoothly, and to her surprise, she gained easy access to the long, expansive dock, where boats of all sizes were moored.

"Well, so much for security," she said under her breath. Her brother would tell her that security measures are only as good as the people who remember to engage them.

She strolled the dock, not sure what she expected to find. The club was small, only about seventy-five slips, with two-thirds occupied. She wandered to the end, wondering about Vivian and her relationship with Devon. Any ideas she had of Vivian's participation in Devon's death were quickly evaporating. Her only access to a boat appeared to be business related. And piloting a yacht took some serious skill. She couldn't just borrow one on a whim, take it out to sea and roll a body overboard.

As Maggie turned around to make the journey back to the parking lot, she couldn't believe how callous she had become in the last week, disappointed that someone hadn't committed a murder. She attributed it to stress and weariness. With a sigh, she slid into her car, and drove out of the parking lot.

Despite a delicious lunch with good company, her mood darkened with the incoming spring storm as she drove home. Instead of turning toward her street, she changed her route for the Duck. She parked and looked at the threatening sky. She made a dash, not for the café, but for the Roost, just as the heavens opened up, making it inside before the deluge.

The Roost was abuzz with activity. The ceiling had been replaced, and the crew was busy putting up tin ceiling tiles over the drywall. Maggie was looking up and admiring the classic pattern when a familiar voice said, "beautiful, aren't they?" startling her.

"They are acoustic tin tiles," Jake continued with pride. "Real tin, as you can imagine, would make for an uncomfortable event experience. These are a bit more expensive, but Jules wisely understood the value."

"Well, they are gorgeous and fitting with the space."

"This entire venue will be a smart blend of traditional New England and modern aesthetic. Jules has a good eye."

"I'm sure Bria had a bit of input," Maggie laughed, knowing Jules trusted Bria's excellent taste.

"How was your lunch?"

Maggie looked around at all the workers. Jake jerked his head toward the stairs, and Maggie followed him as he walked to the small vestibule and held the door open for her. She stepped into the lobby and ascended the stairs with Jake close behind.

The upstairs was transformed. It had been stripped down to the studs and was now a wide-open expanse.

"Wow!" was all Maggie could manage.

"Miss Kitty has an agenda," Jake said with a laugh. "She is not one to wait."

"I'll say. I'd love to see the plans."

"I'll show them to you, but tell me about your lunch first."

"Not too much to tell. Vivian betrayed Sean's trust, but he can't see her murdering Devon and throwing him off a boat. And I have to say, I'm in agreement with him. We have no evidence she had access to any watercraft. I was at the yacht club near the restaurant -"

"You were what?" Jake frowned at her.

"I popped over after lunch," Maggie continued, ignoring the unspoken rebuke. "Sean said he had attended a yacht party Vivian's company hosted there, and I was just…curious."

Jake raised an eyebrow but remained silent.

"Anyway, even if she had access to a client's boat…all those yachts would take a master pilot."

"Maybe she had an accomplice, like Daniels, who lit out of town pretty quick. Or a friend with a small power boat."

"I suppose. Bria is doing research on her business. Maybe something will turn up. If the police would just find the damn crime scene, I could let this whole mess go and get back to writing."

"Any word from Mike?"

"Radio silence. Which is worrisome."

"Well, maybe I can distract you."

Maggie gave him a startled look and tried not to blush at her own thoughts.

Jake, ever the gentleman, pretended not to notice. "Let me pick you up after work. I'll take you on an adventure and then buy you dinner."

"How could I refuse such an intriguing offer," she replied before slipping through the door, walking downstairs, and dashing outside to the front door of the Duck. Despite the heavy downpour, her step was lighter with thoughts of Jake and his surprise. "Afternoon," she called out as she entered the café. It was nearly empty. Tina was busy refilling containers, and the bakery case was bare.

"Hi, Maggie! Hope you aren't hungry, we had a late rush, and they about cleaned us out."

"Just came by to see Jules. It's good to see you back. How was graduation?"

"Surreal. Can't believe it's over, and college starts in a couple of months." She put the stopper into the duck saltshaker she had been filling. "Have you heard from Mike? I texted him yesterday and haven't heard back."

Maggie shook her head. "They must be knee-deep in summer tasks and this murder case. He'll surface eventually," she reassured her, though she was not as confident as she pretended. "Jules in the back?"

"Yes, she and Bria are going over plans for the Roost."

"Oh, good, Bria's here," Maggie said, quickening her step and pushing through the kitchen door.

"Maggie! How was lunch with that hottie, Sean Park Lee?" Juliet cut right to the chase.

Maggie laughed. "It was fun, but I didn't learn anything new, except maybe that Vivian and Devon's betrayal cut him deeply."

"Speaking of betrayal," Bria chimed in. "I spoke with my client. She had some juicy insights."

"Front is all prepped for tomorrow," Tina said as she came through the swinging door. "Oh, we talking about that witch, Vivian?" Jules and Maggie exchanged looks. Corrupting the youth of Duxbridge seemed bad. Juliet was about to warn Bria when Tina, seeing their expressions, interjected. "Hey, remember I'm the one who found the body. I'm well-versed in the aspects of this case."

Maggie shrugged, and Bria continued. "At an event this winter, Vivian became physically violent when one of the guests turned out to be someone Devon was rumored to be dating. Recently, from the description of the argument that ensued. He may have even bought her an expensive Valentine's gift, according to the shrieks from Vivian."

"Oh, boy. I wonder if they were supposedly engaged when he was stepping out," Maggie mused.

"That did not appear to come up, and from what my client said, the woman Vivian was attacking didn't even know why she was so angry. It ended when Vivian picked up a tray of stuffed mushrooms and threw them at the poor guest. Staff members pulled her away and into the kitchen. No one saw her again that night."

"Wow, that couldn't have been good for business," Juliet said.

"Oh, it wasn't. According to my client, other guests began sharing stories of her volatility. I guess she has a reputation of being very…passionate."

"I'm telling you, everything about that woman is suspicious," Tina said, shaking her head. "I mean, blaming Maggie and now camped out at the murdered guy's house."

"How do you know-"

"Cop's daughter. I have sources," she laughed.

"Rumor has it she followed Devon to Duxbridge," Bria said in a conspiratorial whisper. "And despite some high-profile events, her business has been floundering here."

"I wonder if she'll stay now that Devon is dead?" Juliet mused.

"I wonder if the police are as well versed on Vivian's history as Bria here is," Maggie said.

The front bell jangled.

"I'll take care of it," Tina said and crossed the kitchen to the swinging doors just as Mike strode through. "Mike! Your ears must be burning. We were just talking about you."

"You look like hell," Maggie said with concern.

"It's been a grind, that's for sure. Wolinski is out on maternity leave, and the preparations for the summer influx have us all on overtime."

Juliet handed him a full coffee mug and a bag with sliced turkey on a baguette and some pastries. "I set aside your favorites in case you stopped by today."

"Thanks, Jules. Between you and Maggie, I will never starve. I've got to get back at it." He looked over at Maggie. "Walk me to my car, sis?"

Maggie followed him out to the street. The rain had subsided, and the skies were clearing, but there was a damp chill in the air. Maggie shivered as she stood next to his patrol car. "Are you getting any rest at all?"

"Getting home to shower and sleep a few hours each day, but that's about it. It should ease up next week. We'll have summer prep completed." He opened the passenger door and placed the mug and bag on the seat. "Look, I'm sorry I haven't been able to do any investigation. I swear the chief is keeping me busy, so I can't interfere. You're behaving, aren't you?"

"I have kept my inquiries to a few questions and a bit of useless surveillance. I've curbed my inner Nancy Drew and Trixie Belden, I swear."

"Give me your word you'll stay out of this. It is serious business."

Maggie avoided the plea. "Is there any progress at all? I mean, that would absolve me."

Mike shook his head. "Without a crime scene, the investigation is stymied. Whenever I encounter Madigan, he is more taciturn than the previous time, and he's snapping at everyone. My well-honed detective skills tell me things are not going well."

Maggie gave him a quick hug, and he was on his way. She hurried to her car and drove home to get ready for whatever surprise Jake had for her.

By the time Jake texted he was on his way, Maggie had changed into blue checked pedal pushers and a sleeveless white crop top. She topped it with a navy linen blazer, slipped on a pair of white sneakers, and waited. Five minutes later, Jake was in her driveway.

Maggie pulled the door closed and jogged over to the Jeep. Jake hopped out and opened the passenger door. "Ready for a little adventure?"

TWENTY-ONE

Maggie slid into her seat and adjusted her seatbelt. Jake jumped in and put the Jeep in gear.

"So, where are we off to this fine evening?"

"You are going to have to wait and see," Jake replied, turning to look at her before returning his focus to the road as he pulled out of the driveway. "That is part of the adventure."

"Uh-huh."

"You're not having second thoughts, are you?"

"No, not at all," Maggie laughed. "I'm just hoping I wore the appropriate footwear. If you're dragging me on some remote turkey hunt, I'm underdressed."

"Your shoes are cute, and I promise not to get them scuffed," Jake said as he dropped the sun visor. Maggie did the same as the early evening sun peaked beneath the trees lining the road.

Turning right onto Courtland, Jake drove slowly down the street, past a few houses, and then pulled into the driveway on the right side of a charming two-story duplex. It looked to be about at least one hundred years old and in excellent condition. The two sides shared a large covered porch. Each side banked by two-story bay windows.

"Are we visiting someone?" Maggie asked as Jake turned off the Jeep.

"Nope, it's empty."

Maggie unbuckled, unsure of what to expect as she exited. Jake took her hand, led her up the stairs to the porch and over to the duplex on the right. He pulled a key from his pocket and opened the door.

A musty smell greeted them that spoke of age and secured windows. To Maggie, it told the tale of history and lives well lived. Jake led Maggie into a large entryway, stairs leading to the second floor on the left, living and dining rooms to the right. The entry boasted a large brick fireplace with a built-in mirror above it, easily as old as the home. The rooms all had impossibly high ceilings, giving an expansive feel to the spaces.

Ancient roller shades, yellowed and cracked with age, covered the windows. Jake stepped through the arched threshold and into the spacious living room. He walked over to the bay windows and retracted all three shades, letting in the light, filtered through substantial elm trees.

Maggie followed him and marveled at the original wood floors and decorative trim. The paint was peeling in a few places, but she noticed as she walked that nary a board creaked beneath her.

"This place is beautiful," Maggie said in hushed tones, awed by the beauty before her.

"Wait until you see the kitchen." She followed him into the dining room, where he again opened all the shades. It was smaller, but it had a beautiful built-in china hutch, and outside, large lilac bushes shielded it from the neighbors. "The kitchen has a covered porch that opens to the backyard," Jake said as he stepped into a kitchen that looked as if it was last remodeled in the fifties.

"Wow, I'm not sure when I last saw Formica trimmed with aluminum outside of a diner," Maggie said with a laugh. The light was magnificent, even at the late hour, with ample windows. She could see a lot of potential here. "Okay, I give up. Is this your next restoration?"

"It could be," Jake grinned mischievously. "I know a secret about this place."

"Well, don't keep me in suspense."

"This entire house is going up for sale soon. Salvadore Vercellio owned it, he and his family lived in it, and then he rented it out after the kids all grew up and scattered. He and his wife lived in Florida near their oldest. She died several years back, and he passed a few months ago. His children are looking to sell it now."

"Wow, this could be quite the investment property."

"Uh-huh. Or a very nice home."

"Wait, you're not thinking I should buy it? I'm sure I could never afford this and the rehab that would go with it." Maggie felt the regret, even as she understood the impossibility of ownership.

"I had a different idea," Jake began. "And before you say no, give it some serious thought." Maggie was intrigued, so she remained quiet and waited for him to finish. "I was thinking we could buy this together, complete the remodel on both sides and live in the duplexes. Even with the renovations, it would be comparable to rent in the area." Jake took a breath and stole a glance at her before continuing. "I've checked it out. The bones are good, and the electrical and heating systems have all been upgraded in the last few years. The biggest cost would be giving you your stellar kitchen." Excited, he slapped his hand against the plaster. "And this isn't a load-bearing wall, so we could take it out and make the dining and kitchen one large area," he added to tempt her.

Maggie took a deep breath, walked around the dated kitchen, and continued to the front of the house. Jake followed and paused when Maggie stopped to look up the stairs.

"Don't you think I should see the upstairs before I make any kind of decision?" She laughed as she sprinted to the second floor.

After they had examined the bedrooms and popped into the mirror image space next door, they sat on the stoop to discuss logistics.

"Are you interested?" Jake asked.

"I think I am," Maggie replied, looking back at the house. "I really am."

"I'll put together numbers on everything. My real estate agent friend can put together comps, and if it all looks reasonable, we can put in an offer. If we do it all before they have to go to the trouble of listing it and readying it for viewings, we might get ourselves a deal," he finished hopefully.

Maggie sighed. It was a lot of ifs, and she didn't want to get her hopes up, but she was warming to the idea of her own home, and this place could be stunning. She didn't mind the hard work to bring it to life, that made it all the more appealing. She imagined the potential of a spacious, beautiful kitchen filled with light.

"Where would you like to get dinner?" Jake interrupted her reverie.

"I'll let you choose, but I would like to make a stop before we eat," Maggie said cryptically

"More sleuthing? We may need to acquire a Great Dane if this keeps up," Jake said with a wink. "Where to, Daphne?"

"I think I'm more of a Velma. I want to drive past Vivian's office. Turns out it's at her house." Maggie gave him the scrap of paper on which she had written down the address. It was across town, not far from Maggie's parents' house.

"Are we looking for anything in particular?"

"I'm just curious. Everything about her move to Duxbridge and her business feels out of character for someone who had created a successful following in New York."

"You moved here, despite a successful career in New York," Jake countered.

"True, but mine was more out of necessity and reinvention. Vivian appears to have maintained her business model but with new clientele. It had to be like starting over. And being this far south of Boston, it doesn't make sense."

"Well, she seems to have a good summer season with the Cape and Islands."

"True. And I suppose if she downsized her staff when she moved, it could be enough to sustain her until she built up a reputation in Boston. Still, it feels off," Maggie concluded.

"Maybe it's as simple as love," Jake countered.

"Jake Taylor, you're a romantic."

"Don't let that get around," he laughed.

"If it was love, it doesn't appear it worked out well for her."

"Devon's infidelity makes for a good motive."

"So does fraud and money troubles," Maggie said. "But infidelity and betrayal, that's classic for a crime of passion. I would think it was her, except I can't get past the logistics. How would a hundred-and-twenty-pound woman get a two-hundred-pound man into the ocean?" Jake slowed and pulled to the curb. "Everything is just speculation until the police find where the murder happened." Maggie peered out the window and pointed, "It's over there, the small saltbox. The one with no lights on," Jake turned off his headlights and crept down the street until they were across from the cottage.

The houses in this area were on acre lots. Vivian's detached garage was down a short gravel driveway, offset from the house, which was further back on the property. For such elaborate events, the garage was rather mundane. A small placard proclaimed: Elegant Events By V in a delicate script, tacked next to the Dutch door, framed on both sides by six-paned double-hung windows. The oversized garage door had been converted to a wall of windows, which looked like they might still roll up. Light spilled onto the ground from a window at the back of the garage.

Maggie opened Jake's glove box and pulled out his binoculars.

"Do you see something?" he asked.

"I think there is someone in the office." Maggie peered through the binoculars, adjusting the focus until she had a clear view of Vivian, on the phone, pacing. When she started to shout into the phone, Maggie strained to hear what had her so upset. Frustrated that she could only catch a word or two, she quietly slipped out of the Jeep. She could feel Jake's reproach as she crept over to the enormous lilac bush at the corner of the driveway and the garage. Vivian's voice rang out clearly from the open window at this distance.

"Listen, he owed me a lot of money. And that stunt he pulled in New Orleans almost ruined me. I didn't work this hard to regain my reputation to have him f -" Maggie squelched a squeak when Jake placed his hand on her shoulder to let her know he was behind her. He stepped in close to listen with her. "...I moved my entire life here for that fraud, and I'm not leaving that house until I get what I deserve. You're my attorney," Vivian snarled into her phone. "I'm paying you good money to take care of this. You do whatever it takes to get me his estate." She finished the call with an expletive and then began slamming things around the office. She appeared to be looking for something. Jake tapped Maggie's shoulder and led her back to the Jeep.

As they crossed the street, car tires squealed as a large SUV turned onto the road and sped past them. Jake pulled Maggie into his chest and out of the way. He cursed under his breath as the vehicle came uncomfortably close. Once the road was clear, he opened the door for her before climbing in himself. Maggie looked at the office, checking if Vivian had spotted them.

They decide on fish and chips at the Cabin for dinner. When their drinks arrived, Maggie took a long sip of her beer to calm her jangled nerves.

"Do you still think she couldn't do the deed?" Jake asked, carefully framing the topic, in case they were overheard.

"She sure seems volatile enough," Maggie conceded. "But we are back to the same problem. How did she do it?" She took another sip of her beer as the server placed salads in front of them. She realized she was famished and dug in. "I am curious what exactly her attorney could do about her predicament. If there's no will and they weren't married, no judge is going to award her his estate." Maggie took a bite of her spinach salad before continuing. "I believe the only way she could lay claim to the house is if she can provide documentation she invested in it with a promise of repayment. But even then, she'd probably have to get in line with all his other creditors."

"Would that include the restaurant's debts?" Jake asked.

Maggie thought for a moment. "It's not my area of financial expertise, but I think it would depend on how the business was set up. Even then, some vendors require a personal guarantee, especially in an enterprise as volatile as a restaurant." Maggie took a bite of salad and nodded her approval before continuing. "I think she's screwed if she was looking for a financial payout, which would make her an unlikely suspect. She had nothing to gain and an awful lot to lose."

"Unless it wasn't premeditated," Jake speculated.

"And Bria confirmed she does have a quick temper," Maggie agreed.

Their entrée arrived, and they put aside talk of murder and enjoyed their meal.

"How are you feeling about the house?" Jake asked as they relaxed with coffee after dinner.

"I like the idea. I like the house. I'm not exactly good with a hammer and saw," Maggie admitted.

"I can teach you the basics, and there are many other things to handle: bookkeeping, managing material orders, hauling scrap, painting, staining. All things I'm sure you could easily handle. It needs some updating, but it has a solid structure."

"Honestly, I'm trying to talk myself out of jumping impulsively into this because I'm excited about the entire prospect." It wasn't just the house that excited Maggie and gave her serious pause. "And I think I will be mightily disappointed if it doesn't work out." Jake grinned at her. She tilted her head slightly and asked, "What?"

"That's *sweet as*. I was afraid you'd think I was a *muppet*. It'll be hard *yakka*, but worth it. It will all work out, and you'll be much happier in a house."

"You just want me next door, so you'll have free meals," she said with a grin.

"Not gonna lie, that'll be choice."

Once Jake dropped her back home, Maggie found herself thinking more about Jake's proposal and the house than suspected killers. She smiled as she pulled out one of her ubiquitous notepads to begin a pro and con list. Jake was right, this was a good distraction, and she was grateful for the reprieve. She scanned the property details on the real estate website, finding it still listed as not for sale. She breathed a sigh of relief. As Jake had pointed out, getting in before it was listed would be an advantage.

Maggie was deep into financial calculations when there was a knock on her door. Startled, her mind went to dark places of search warrants and handcuffs before realizing it was Mike.

"Hey, sis, sorry it's so late. I should have texted," Mike said when she opened the door.

"No worries," she replied.

"That's not what your face says."

"I was deep in thought, and you startled me, that's all," Maggie lied.

"Uh-huh."

"I'm sorry, I'm low on leftovers. I haven't done much cooking. This entire matter has made me completely lose focus on my job. Can I get you something to drink? I can scrounge up some coffee cake, and I have half a turkey sandwich from Stonebridge."

"I'm good. I grabbed dinner earlier. I wanted to stop by and see how you were doing and ask about the car you saw at mom and dad's."

Maggie had almost forgotten the suspicious vehicle, and now that she had to relay the information to Mike, it felt silly. She was on tenterhooks and convinced she was overreacting as a result.

"Oh, it's nothing, honestly. I thought there was a fishy dark sedan parked across from the house. They drove off when I went outside. I'm hypersensitive right now. I'm sorry if I worried you."

"I trust your instincts. If it didn't feel right, I'm inclined to believe you. Keep an eye out and let me know if you see it again."

Maggie nodded. "I will. Any updates?" she asked hopefully.

TWENTY-TWO

"Madigan is getting pressure from the mayor to either name a suspect or bring in the State Patrol."

"It's only been a week. The mayor has been watching too many crime shows," Maggie scoffed. She wondered if the mayor knew his Chief of Staff's niece was at the top of that suspect list.

"It's a small town. I think everyone believes it should be easy to narrow down a suspect," Mike explained.

"Great. And everyone has chosen me. Did it occur to any of them that it might be someone from out of town? From what I'm learning, Devon was not short on people he antagonized," Maggie argued, even though she knew Mike was aware of all of it. Her frustration was palpable.

"That's because of that damn Vivian. Every chance she gets, she points the finger at you."

"Isn't the significant other always the more likely suspect?"

"Yes, but Vivian doesn't own a boat," Mike said flatly.

"Well, neither do I!" Maggie slammed her hand on the counter.

"I'm worried she's going to ratchet up the heat by accusing you of having an affair with Devon."

"Yuck," Maggie said, and they both laughed. The absurdity of that idea instantly eased Maggie's tension.

"They are searching all the marinas in the area for the crime scene. Without it, there are a lot of possible suspects but not enough evidence to arrest anyone. The search is taking up a lot of patrol officers."

"Which is why you're running flat out, taking up all the slack."

"And also why I can't find time to do any digging on my own, but I will, I promise, as soon as things ease up. The temporary summer officers arrive at the end of the week. That will give me some relief," Mike said as he stood up and wrapped his arms around Maggie. "Hang in there, just a bit longer. The cavalry is on the way."

Maggie knew one thing for certain as she closed the door, turned the deadbolt, and watched Mike back out of the drive. She wasn't going to wait for the damn cavalry.

Wednesday morning dawned cold and foggy, with the threat of rain. Spring in New England, Maggie thought as she fought the urge to pull the covers back over her head and avoid the day. Once she dragged herself into the shower, she had decided today would be the day she would find where Devon had been murdered. She had no clue how, but if optimism and pluck were valid investigative tools, she had those in spades.

The Duck was already open and humming with customers when Maggie finally arrived, giving Jules a quick wave and making a beeline to the coffee. After pouring a mug, she turned to survey the early morning patrons and was surprised to see Sean holding the door open for Gwen Fellowes and Georgia Robinson as they exited with coffees and a large box of baked goods. He gave her a wave, and she lifted her mug and smiled at him. He came to the counter.

"Good morning. Nice to see you. Want to join me for breakfast?"

"I'm good with coffee right now, but I'd be happy to join you," Maggie replied and followed him to an empty table by the front window. Maggie looked out on the damp street, feeling less gloomy now that Sean was in the picture. He pulled out her chair, and Maggie sat down. He sat across from her and followed her gaze.

"I prefer a hot summer day," Sean mused. "But rainy days have their perks." Tina came up, and Sean ordered an omelet. Maggie indicated she was good with coffee for now. "Do you come here often?" he asked and then laughed, realizing how that sounded. "Sorry, didn't mean to make that sound like some cheesy pickup line."

Maggie laughed with him. "I find I'm most productive in the morning and usually arrive before Jules opens the doors. I enjoy the quiet before the rush, listening to the kitchen sounds while I write." She looked around at the quickly filling dining room. "This morning, I got a late start, but it looks like half the town decided to make the Duck their first stop on this dreary day."

"So you write your cookbooks here?"

"I start them here, then I go home and test the recipes. Depending on my mood and Juliet's schedule, sometimes I film my videos here. Otherwise, I film them in my tiny kitchen." Maggie couldn't help but think of the possibilities of a new kitchen, an idea that hadn't even crossed her mind twenty-four hours ago.

"It sounds like you have a thriving enterprise."

"I do okay. I'm very lucky. One of my old clients is an agent and took me on when I put my first cookbook together. He's been invaluable in setting my course."

"That's excellent," he paused as Tina set a mug on the table. "I was hoping to talk with you while I was still in town. I have a business proposition."

"Oh?" This took Maggie by surprise.

"I'm looking into buying Devo's, either from the estate or from a bankruptcy sale. I was hoping you would think about partnering with me. Becoming the new head chef there."

Maggie was stunned into a moment of silence. Never would she have thought Sean would be proposing something like that. "No," she said, shaking her head. "No, no, no. It's not that I am not flattered at the offer, but I'm no chef. The best I can do is cook for my family. I wouldn't have any idea how to serve a crowd. And doing what Jules does completely stresses me out. But I am excited that you're considering investing in Devo's."

"I understand. The restaurant business isn't for everyone."

"Definitely not me, that's for sure. I like my quiet mornings writing and having my evenings free," she laughed. "I'm surprised you'd consider another restaurant after New Orleans," she added thoughtfully.

"I find the idea of succeeding where Devon was failing oddly satisfying. Besides, I have taken a liking to Duxbridge, and as you pointed out, there is an excellent staff that needs employment."

"You know, if you're looking to invest in Duxbridge, Jules is working on a brilliant expansion." Maggie proceeded to give him the details on the Roost and The Nest.

"She is ambitious and quite the businesswoman," Sean said with admiration.

"She is, and if you were looking to invest in a sure thing, anything she's involved in would be it."

"I'll talk to her. She is an excellent chef," he said as he forked up a bite of his omelet. "But, and don't say no right away, I am still interested in working with you to build your brand. Promise me you'll think about it."

"I will. I'm intrigued by the possibilities." Maggie looked down at her empty cup. "Right now, I need a refill, and I should get back to work, or I won't have a brand." She stood up and pushed in her chair. "Enjoy your breakfast. We'll talk soon."

Maggie filled her mug and slipped into the kitchen to share her conversation with Jules.

"Hey there," Juliet greeted her. "You and Sean appeared to be having an interesting conversation. Did you solve Devon's murder?"

"I wish," Maggie sighed. "No, we were talking business. He wanted me to become the new chef if he acquires Devo's."

"What?!"

"Don't worry. I told him I was neither capable nor interested in running a restaurant." She sipped her coffee. "But I did tell him about someone very good at both cooking and business who might be interested in a partnership."

"You didn't?!"

"I most certainly did. Imagine the things you could do with an influx of cash and Sean's business skills. Jake could use only the finest materials for the project."

"Well, I'm flattered, but I'm probably small fish compared to his other investments," Juliet said. "Oh, and speaking of Jake, I'm concerned. He hasn't stopped by yet. I can hear them working next door. I'm worried he hasn't grabbed his coffee and pastry because something is going wrong over there."

"I'm sure everything is fine."

"I'd take these over myself," Juliet indicated the travel mug and white pastry bag, "but this rush needs my attention." She gave Maggie a plaintive look.

Maggie laughed. "Okay, little Miss matchmaker, I'll take it over. But just so you know, I see right through your intentions." Juliet smiled and handed Maggie the delivery. "Meanwhile, don't let Sean leave without at least talking with him about your ventures."

Maggie exited through the kitchen door and was pleased to see the back door to the Roost open. That meant Jake's crew was making progress, as the door had previously been hidden behind drywall. Maggie peeked in, ensuring it was safe to enter, and was surprised to see the biggest German Shepherd she had ever seen following Jake around the room.

She caught Jake's attention and raised the mug and bag to entice him. He and his companion made their way to her, dodging pallets of flooring and buckets of paint.

"Who's your friend?" Maggie asked as she handed him his delivery.

"This is Anahera. It's Maori for angel."

"Well, hello, girl," Maggie greeted her as she enthusiastically scratched the pup's ears. "Where did she come from?"

"Someone dumped her near my foreman Sabo's house. He lives outside of town, off Wood Street. Dog just showed up. No chip, no tags, no response from lost and found ads placed in the Gazette, no one looking for her at the Humane Society. He even put up a poster of her at Fellowes."

"Oh, my gosh, poor baby, who would do that to you?" Maggie said as Anahera leaned into her, looking for more scratches.

"He didn't have room for her – he has a house full of critters and kids – and he was asking around to see if anyone could take her. I took one look at her, and it was love at first sight." Maggie looked at the two of them, standing together, and was sure the feeling was mutual. "We have a veterinarian appointment later today, and once she has a clean bill of health, I'll introduce her to my landlady. Fingers-crossed." Maggie had no doubts that Jake and Anahera would charm her.

She was almost afraid to ask her next question, but she had to know. "Any word on the house?"

Jake grinned, obviously pleased she was excited about the idea. "My agent friend is reaching out to the family today. He has a good feeling about it. I'll let you know as soon as I know."

"I guess I better put 'find a mortgage broker' on my list today," Maggie replied, feeling a flutter of excitement. "Are you okay with using someone I know? We'll need to do the financing together."

"What? Trust a big city financial wizard? That's crazy talk," he said with a laugh.

"I should let you get back to work," Maggie said.

"What's on your crime-solving menu today?"

"Honestly, I'm not sure. But I'm tired of all of this, and I'm determined to find a way, once and for all, to put an end to speculation of my involvement," Maggie explained. "And, one way or another today, I'm either going to implicate or eliminate Vivian in Devon's murder." Maggie wasn't sure how yet, but she was resolved.

"That sounds ominous," Jake said with concern. "Promise me, you'll bring me along on any excursions."

"Don't you have a lot of work to do here?" Maggie felt guilty about distracting him when she knew how much Jules needed the Roost completed so she could begin booking events by late summer.

"I think you can imagine that Jules would prefer I keep an eye on her friend before I keep a schedule here. Besides, Sabo is excellent, and I trust him to supervise in my absence. He's actually so good I'm thinking of expanding, taking on more than one project at a time."

Maggie assured him she would keep him in the loop as she left him and sweet Anahera to return to the Duck. The kitchen was empty, so Maggie stepped out front. The café was abuzz with chatter and visible excitement. Juliet rushed over to her, grabbed her elbow, and led her back to the kitchen.

"What's going on?" Maggie asked, concerned, suddenly imagining a warrant had gone out for her arrest.

"There's a rumor going around that Ricky Daniels has been arrested."

"The former GM at Devo's? Are you sure?"

"I don't know. Have you heard from Mike?"

Maggie grabbed her bag off the coat hook by the back door. She dug out her phone. It was devoid of any texts or missed calls. "Not a word," she said as her fingers flew over the keys, texting Mike. She asked him if there was any truth to the rumors. She sat down at the big prep table and waited for a reply.

"This would be great news if it were true," Juliet said as she placed a fried egg sandwich in front of Maggie.

"Oh, my favorite, what a treat!" Maggie exclaimed, realizing she was famished. "What's the occasion?" she asked before biting into the toasted, bacon-layered goodness.

"A well-deserved reward for convincing Sean Park Lee to look at investing in the Duck, the Roost, and the Nest," Juliet replied excitedly. "We had a good chat before he left. As long as he's not a murderer, this could be good."

"Oh, that's great. He'd be smart to invest in you." Maggie's phone buzzed. She put down her sandwich and checked her message. It was Mike.

Are you at the Duck?

Maggie replied in the affirmative.

I'll be right there.

A few minutes later, Mike came in through the back door, arriving just as Maggie finished the last bite of crust. Juliet and Tina immediately joined them at the prep table.

"Well?" Tina asked impatiently.

"It's true. Daniels has been arrested." Mike began.

"Do they think he's the murderer?" Juliet interrupted.

"Right now, it's on suspicion of financial crimes. Now that the restaurant is closed, seems Joanne Sanchez, the sous chef, decided to use her downtime to go through the books. She had a cousin, who is an accountant, help her. They managed to find the bank passwords and get into the account to see recent transactions. It was all very suspicious, so they contacted Madigan, and sure enough, it looks like Daniels was embezzling." Juliet handed Mike a mug of coffee. "Thanks. The big red flag…the morning Devon died…Daniels withdrew over fifty grand."

"Oh, my," Maggie exclaimed.

Mike nodded. "He claims it was back pay."

"He must be the murderer," Tina said adamantly.

"Again, no crime scene. And the rest, well, he did have signature powers on the bank account, so without Devon to say it wasn't back pay, it may be difficult to prosecute. It does appear he created a fake vendor account and paid that account while others went unpaid. If Devon discovered that, it would be a motive for murder and at least enough to focus the investigation on Daniels."

"Murdering Devon would solve a lot of his problems," Maggie speculated.

"I'm assuming that's what Madigan is thinking. Now it's just a matter of finding evidence to back up that suspicion. It'll be a slog, but it gives them a solid place to begin looking." Mike snagged a croissant from a baking tray. "Best part, though? You are no longer a person of interest, sis."

"Hallelujah!" Juliet said as she clapped her hands together. "It was pure insanity to think Maggie was involved."

Unexpected tears came to Maggie's eyes. She had underestimated the stress of the entire ordeal. Now that it was over, a boulder had been lifted from her chest.

"I've got to get back out onto patrol. I'll stop by tonight," Mike said as he kissed the top of Maggie's head.

Relieved to have her life back, Maggie bid goodbye to Juliet and Tina and decided to go on a shopping spree.

Her first stop would be Miss Kitty's to share the good news.

Although she had no doubts, Miss Kitty was already privy to the latest developments.

TWENTY-THREE

The bell at the antique shop chimed as Maggie entered.

"Darling!" Miss Kitty called out when she saw her. She weaved her way through the many antiques to embrace Maggie. "Such fabulous news!" Maggie returned the hug and wondered how many stares they were eliciting until she realized the store was uncharacteristically vacant. "Come, sit down and tell me everything you know."

"Where is everyone?" Maggie asked. "It's awfully quiet."

"Once the news broke, everyone scattered to their favorite gossip locale. Fellowes and the Duck." Miss Kitty directed Maggie to a pair of wingback chairs.

"I'm grateful the chatter is no longer about me."

"I'm sure they will prattle about how you were unjustly suspected and turn their attention to what is going on with you and the handsome Kiwi."

Maggie laughed. "If that's your subtle way of asking, Miss Kitty, there is nothing going on. Oh! Except we are looking at a property together! A cool duplex to renovate." The sale had completely slipped her mind, pushed aside by sheer relief.

"What? The Vecellio place?" Of course, Miss Kitty would know which duplex, Maggie laughed to herself. "That's a lovely idea, you and Jake revitalizing it. Let me guess, it was all Jake's idea? I'm ashamed I didn't think of it!"

"You don't think I'm crazy, going into this deal with someone I hardly know?"

"Oh, honey, Jake has been smitten with you the moment he first laid eyes on you. I'm surprised it took him this long to make a move," she said with a twinkle in her eyes. "I think any project that young man is involved with will be successful, and you'll have a beautiful home when it's completed."

"I have to tell you, I'm more excited than I expected at the idea of renovating the place and having a home of my own. Well, after a few hundred mortgage payments."

"I'm very impressed with Jake's work at the B&B. His workmanship is impeccable, and he does not believe in shortcuts."

"Sean Park Lee may be investing in the Duck and its many expansions," Maggie confided.

"That would be a windfall. He could help us make the Nest a destination. I have many ideas, and working with Sean would not be a hardship. Not. At. All." Miss Kitty winked at her, and Maggie smiled back. "How smart of that young woman at Devo's to figure out the embezzlement scheme. She might be a great addition to the Roost and Nest operation."

"I don't know, as a sous chef, she may want to advance in the kitchen. But it wouldn't hurt to ask her. I hate thinking of the staff left high and dry there because of all of this."

"Do you know, did he have life insurance or a contingency plan for the restaurant if something happened to him?"

"Sean said that at one time, Devon carried insurance to protect his investors. He doesn't know if he let it lapse or not. If it was still active, it could be used to pay off all the vendors, and I think the staff could make the case for a severance package."

"That might make a compelling motive for that Daniels fellow, too. Embezzle, get caught, kill and then embezzle the insurance payout."

"I agree. And he'd be the one to know if there was a policy. I do wonder, though, if he was expecting an insurance payout, what compelled him to leave town so quickly."

"Fear, darling, fear. It's one thing to think murder is the answer. It's quite another to live with those consequences. Just ask Edgar Allan Poe."

The bell over the store's door rang brightly, and two customers gave Miss Kitty a quick wave before wandering the aisles.

"Duty calls," Miss Kitty said, standing. Maggie stood as well and gave her a quick hug before making her way home.

Standing in her compact kitchen, Maggie felt better than she had in days. Excited by the idea of a kitchen of her own design, she contacted a mortgage broker friend. She explained the circumstances and asked him to send her a list of what she needed to do to get the ball rolling. Her friend expressed concern about partnering with someone she didn't know well. Maggie was unfazed, explaining that he came with excellent references, and besides, she reminded him she would get to see Jake's credit report. "And isn't that the most important item in any business dealings?"

Once she concluded that task, she dove headlong into two new recipes, Sweet and Sour Meatballs, and Sautéed Mushroom Salad. As she was pulling the meatballs from the grill, Mike drove into the drive. Maggie waved for him to follow her into the house.

"Good timing," she said when he walked into the living room. "Give me five minutes, and you can test this new recipe." She slit two hoagie rolls down the middle to butterfly them before buttering them and placing them under the broiler. Mike grabbed iced tea from the refrigerator, poured two glasses, and set them on the table. Once the rolls were toasted, Maggie added the meatballs and a serving of the salad to each plate. It wasn't until she set his plate in front of him that she noticed the solemn expression on her brother's face. "What's wrong?" she asked, immediately concerned about their parents and the myriad of other family members.

Mike took a sip of tea before breaking the bad news. "Daniels has a rock-solid alibi."

"What?!" Maggie almost dropped her plate. She pulled out her chair and sat down hard.

"He was in New York, shadowing the current general manager at his new restaurant job. He was there until well after closing time, around three a.m. There is no way he could have murdered Devon or even helped someone dispose of him."

Maggie was crushed. "Damn, I didn't even have a full day of relief before becoming a suspect again."

"The good news, if there is any from this, is that it clarifies that there are a substantial number of people out there with strong motives."

"But none that the grieving fiancée is accusing daily," Maggie sighed. "How are your meatballs?" She had completely lost her appetite. Her one bite tasted like cardboard.

"They are excellent. I might add a side of the sweet and sour sauce," he replied. "And the mushroom salad is great with them." The review heartened Maggie. She wrapped her hoagie in waxed paper and put it in the refrigerator for later. "Sis, don't worry. Madigan is going to get to the bottom of all of this. He's a good detective, and I have serious doubts he's relying on Vivian's accusations alone in his investigation."

"And yet, here you sit, sidelined, and the entire town is awash in suspicions about me. I just need this to go away." She slammed a glass container onto the table and began scooping the mushroom salad into it. "I need them to find that crime scene."

After Mike left, Maggie decided it was time to implement her original idea. She needed to either discredit Vivian, or find the crime scene, or if things would finally break her way, both. And she required Sean's help to do it. She picked up her phone, paused a moment while she rehearsed in her head what she wanted to say, and then tapped the icon next to his name.

Sean was eager to help, and they decided to meet at Miss Kitty's shop. They would have privacy there. Maggie was still paranoid that someone was watching her, and no one would think anything of her going to Miss Kitty's, even if Sean showed up at the same time.

When she arrived at the antique store, there was only one customer. Maggie didn't recognize her and assumed she was from one of the nearby towns. Maggie caught Miss Kitty's eye and then walked to the back of the store. Miss Kitty followed, and she quickly filled her in on her plan to have a discreet conversation with Sean. She didn't elaborate on the reason why, and Miss Kitty did not ask.

"Help yourself to something to drink. I'll send Sean back when he shows up," Miss Kitty said before returning to her customer.

Maggie grabbed a bottle of water from the refrigerator and waited nervously for Sean. She jumped each time she heard the bell chime. Finally, he appeared in the doorway. Maggie gave him a friendly wave.

"Hi, thanks for meeting me here," Maggie said before opening the refrigerator door. "Do you want something to drink?"

Sean shook his head. "I was happy to do it. I'm as anxious as you to get to the bottom of this. What can I do to help?" he asked, getting right to the heart of the matter.

Maggie looked out the door to make sure no customers were within listening distance and then closed it gently. She gestured to the small table, and they both sat. She took a sip of water, gathering her thoughts. She knew she needed answers before she involved him.

"I need to know something. Did you have anything to do with Devon's murder? Did you help Vivian or anyone else?" She tried not to shake as she waited for his answer.

"No, I didn't," Sean said without hesitation. "And I know why you need to ask me that," he reassured her. "Now tell me how I can help."

Maggie carefully laid out her idea. The police needed a crime scene, and once they had that, she would be in the clear. Her idea was to either reveal Vivian's involvement or clear her by feeding her information. If she was involved and took the bait, Maggie would discreetly follow her and then alert Mike. If she did nothing, then Maggie could focus elsewhere. However, she wasn't sure who had as much to gain from Devon's death as Vivian seemed to, by her own admission.

"What's the bait?"

"We are going to convince her that the police were able to use Devon's waterproof smartwatch to track his movements, and they tracked him back to the marina. Where he was at the night of his death, and they are working on obtaining a warrant to start looking at the various craft docked there to look for any evidence of blood or broken glass. No matter how clean a suspect thinks they've left a scene, there's always some minute spatter or fragment they've overlooked."

"You're hoping she was involved, and she'll lead us to the marina," Sean said.

"If you are convincing enough, if she was involved, I think she will. If only to make sure there's no incriminating evidence left behind. If she does nothing, then I believe we can eliminate her as being involved and just chalk up her behavior to a grieving lover lashing out inappropriately."

"That's gracious of you, considering how she's behaved."

"I'm having difficulty believing she's a murderer. Maybe I'm naïve. I've seen enough true crime shows to believe scorned lovers are capable of heinous acts, but I can't get past the physical aspects of the crime. Devon was stabbed and most likely delivered a fatal blow with a glass bottle, then dumped out in the bay. It screams crime of passion. But I've put myself in the scenario a dozen times, and I can't work out how I would have done it," Maggie paused, worried about how that might sound. "I mean, without help of some kind. And besides," she quickly added, "I don't know how to drive a boat."

"Vivian does," Sean said solemnly. "She definitely knows how to operate a small boat. We used to go out on Lake Michigan in school, and she'd take her turn at the helm."

"Hmmm, well then, fingers-crossed, she leads us to the crime scene. After that, I'm happy to let the police figure out the rest."

With Sean eager to help, they concocted the story he would tell Vivian. Having overheard a conversation at the Duck, he decided to share it with Vivian to "help ease her stress and reassure her" that the police were about to break the case. He would frame all the information as "good news." Explaining that the police were confident that with a crime scene, they would soon have the killer in custody.

"I'll call her later from my hotel. I'll ask to meet her, and I'll let you know when and where."

"I hope this works," Maggie said after they finished their preparations.

"Me, too." Sean agreed.

Once Sean was on his way, Miss Kitty joined Maggie in the back room.

"You and Sean get everything worked out?"

"We did. And hopefully," Maggie added as she tossed the bottle into the recycling, "I can end this nightmare. I'll fill you in on the details when I know something concrete. Thanks for letting us use your shop for clandestine matters."

"Anytime," she said with a sly smile.

Maggie left and went directly to the Duck. She was sure Juliet had heard the news by now and would want to talk to her. Juliet was in the kitchen doing prep work for the following day. The dining area was gleaming, and the staff had left, so even though Maggie would have loved a strong cup of coffee, there was none to be had.

"Oh, honey," Juliet said when she saw her.

"You've heard." It wasn't a question.

"It went through the café like wildfire," Juliet said. "Are you okay? Stupid question. Of course, you're not okay. Damn Vivian and her evil accusations."

"It was not the news I wanted to hear," Maggie agreed. "But I'm not going to sit around and wait any longer."

"Oh, no, Maggie, what are you planning?" Juliet asked, her concern palpable.

"Nothing dangerous, honest," Maggie reassured her. "Sean and I have a plan that, hopefully, will challenge Vivian's credibility, rendering her accusations moot."

"You're working with Sean Park Lee?" Juliet aggressively kneaded an innocent mound of dough. "Are you sure that's a good idea?"

"He's kept it friendly with Vivian, despite his suspicions surrounding her business dealings. So he's the logical choice."

"And you trust him?"

"My instincts say to be cautious, but yes, I trust him," Maggie said. "Besides, Miss Kitty thinks the world of him, and you know how she is."

Juliet nodded. Everyone knew Miss Kitty had impeccable instincts when it came to people.

"What about Jake?"

"What about him?"

Juliet raised an eyebrow in disapproval. "How do you think he will feel about you working with Sean?"

"Sean and I are enticing Vivian to reveal her real motives, not running off to Atlantic City for a hot weekend."

"Uh-huh."

"All right, I'll fill him in on the details," Maggie acquiesced. She snitched a raspberry from the batch Juliet was using to garnish a tray of lemon tarts. "It's not like we're dating, you know. I mean, if Sean wanted to take off for a hot Atlantic City weekend, I'm available."

"Marjorie Katherine Stellino, are you going to stand there and tell me you aren't interested in Jake Taylor?"

Maggie hesitated. She enjoyed his company, had a lot of fun with him, but she had to wonder if they had anything in common besides a desire to solve the mystery of a dead celebrity chef. She supposed she should figure that out before diving headlong into business with him.

It could get awkward quickly if there were unwanted feelings on either side. Maggie filched another raspberry before answering. "I do like him, Jules. I'm just not sure we are compatible. I mean, my last relationship was with a driven financial shark. What if a sweet, kind and completely laid back, extremely handsome contractor and I have nothing in common?"

"Well, if you're too dense to realize he's the best thing to happen to you in ages...I'm not sure how I can help you with that. But you better figure it out before you sign onto a mortgage and remodel with him. It might be all business for you, but I can assure you, it's not for him. Anyone with two eyes can see how he feels about you."

The back door swung open, and both women fell silent.

"*Kia ora*," Jake said as the screen slammed behind him. "Oh, hi Maggie, I heard you were cleared of murder today."

Maggie sighed. "Unfortunately, my reprieve was short-lived. The prime suspect has a rock-solid alibi."

"I am so sorry. What can I do?"

"Do you have a minute to talk?"

TWENTY-FOUR

Juliet put the finished tarts into the walk-in cooler, giving Maggie a stern look as she walked across the kitchen.

"I am so very sorry. I can't imagine what a roller coaster you've been on today," Jake told her. "I need to have Jules sign off on something, and then I'm all yours." Juliet returned and wiped down the prep table. "Jules, if you have a moment, I have a change I want to run by you real quick."

The three of them walked over to the Roost, and Jake held the newly installed 9-lite wood panel door open as they walked through. Maggie was amazed at the transformation. The ceiling was covered in the pressed tin tiles, and the walls were painted a creamy white.

"Oh, Jake, this looks lovely."

"Thank you. This is just the bones. Wait until we add the fancy trims and embellishments." He turned to Juliet. "Which is what I need you to see. I would like your opinion on a few cabinet selections. You don't have to choose today, but it would be good if we could narrow it down to a couple of styles."

Maggie's phone buzzed, so she stayed behind to check her messages. She hoped it was Sean giving her a time and place, but it was just Aunt Carol, worried about her and wanting an update. Maggie texted her to let her know she was fine and put her phone back into her bag.

"Maggie, help me out here," Juliet called. Maggie crossed the expanse to look at cabinet faces and pointed to the one she thought fit the space best, but her heart wasn't in it. All she wanted was for her phone to buzz and see a text from Sean letting her know the plan was a go.

Juliet narrowed her choices down to two and then left to finish the next day's prep.

"How are you doing, really?" Jake asked when they were alone.

"I'm okay," Maggie reassured him. "Mike insists it's all going to be fine, and I have no reason to doubt his assessment."

"And yet you look like you're wound so tight a loud noise would shoot you into the stratosphere."

"Ha, ha. Look, I need to tell you something," Maggie began, then her phone buzzed. "Excuse me, I have to check this." She pulled the phone from her bag and looked at her texts. It was Sean.

> Meeting with Vivian set.
> In an hour at Devon's
> house

"I have to go. But I want you to know that Sean and I have put a plan in place to get to the bottom of Vivian's involvement."

"What? Are you sure you can trust him?" Jake protested.

"I don't know, I think so. He's my in with Vivian, so I have to, at least for now."

"I don't want you going alone," the concern in Jake's voice was unmistakable. "I have to wait for a delivery. After that, I can go with you."

"I have to go now. Don't worry, I won't do anything stupid, and I'll call you as soon as I know something," Maggie assured him. Jake looked skeptical. "I promise." Maggie began to leave and then turned back to him. "Oh, I almost forgot. I contacted a mortgage broker I've known for years. He will send me a checklist of everything we'll need to gather to begin the process. I'll forward it to you." And before he could respond, she was out the door and hurried to her car.

She pulled out of the parking lot and sped over to her parents' house to trade vehicles again, to remain discreet. After that, she made a beeline for Devon's estate. She hit all the traffic lights right and managed to pull onto the road across from the house and park before Sean arrived. She hoped that the trees and bushes camouflaged her well enough. She was afraid Vivian was getting desperate, and Maggie suspected the car she had seen the past few days was, indeed, Vivian keeping tabs on her.

It didn't take much imagination to believe if Vivian became aware of Maggie's surveillance, she would try to convince Madigan that Maggie was stalking her to do her harm. All she needed was a visit from Duxbridge's finest to slap her with a restraining order. Or worse, claim her behavior was probable cause to issue a search warrant. Not that they would find anything, but she didn't have time to clean up the mess that would make.

Maggie had a horrifying thought. If they took her computer and tablet, they would see her search history, and that would not cast a kind light on her behavior. This entire ordeal had turned her into a super-stalker. She made a mental note to wipe her search history and back her recipes up to the cloud, just to be prudent.

She watched anxiously, wishing she had transferred the binoculars from her car to this one. Her wait was short as she saw Sean's red Mercedes speed past her hideaway and slow to turn into the drive. He parked under the porte-cochere, where he stayed in the vehicle. Maggie wondered if he had lost his nerve when her phone vibrated. She grabbed it out of her bag and answered.

"You ready for this?" Sean asked.

"Yes, are you?"

"More than ready to put an end to the mystery. I'm going to leave the line open. Mute yourself and listen in."

"Roger that," Maggie replied as she turned the call volume up and pressed the mute button. She listened to Vivian's friendly welcome and Sean's pleasantries. He didn't waste any time, sitting at the dining room table, declining her offer to join her for a drink before explaining the reason for his visit.

"I was at the Duck for lunch today and overheard an intriguing conversation. I thought you would be interested because it might mean your wait for the estate and insurance to be settled could be over."

There was a long pause, and Maggie was afraid the connection had been lost, but then Vivian spoke.

"Really? That would be great," Vivian said, though Maggie noted she didn't sound excited by the development. "What did you hear?"

"The table next to me was populated with uniformed officers who were very excited. One of them told the others they finally had a break in Devon's case. He explained that Devon's watch was not only waterproof but turned out it was a smartwatch, and after getting a warrant," Maggie smiled at Sean's thoroughness, "they were able to trace his movements the night he was murdered. They found the marina where they believed he was killed. The officer said the detective on the case was obtaining a warrant to search the boats docked there that night for any evidence. He was confident they would find something…small drops of blood, DNA left on a rope or broken pieces of glass from the murder weapon. They said once they located the crime scene, they were sure they would have a suspect in custody shortly." Maggie heard Vivian gasp, and her heart raced. "Oh, I'm sorry. Have I upset you with the details?" Sean sounded genuine in his concern. Maggie was impressed, if not a little troubled, by the ease with which he lied.

Oh, well, she thought, *I asked him to do this, and he rose to the occasion.*

"I'm just glad that this could soon be over and that horrible woman, Maggie Stellino, will be brought to justice," Vivian said with venom.

"I wanted to be the one to give you this good news. If the police find the crime scene, your situation should resolve rapidly. And you know you can contact me if you need anything going forward. I know some good real estate agents and a few high-powered attorneys who can handle any complications."

"Thank you, Sean. I appreciate that. If you don't mind, I should make some calls to share this information. I know a few people who would be…happy to hear the news."

"I understand. I can see myself out," he replied. Maggie heard a chair scrape and, a moment later, the brush of a heavy door across a tile floor. Then silence. She watched as the Mercedes pulled out of the drive and slowly made its way past the cranberry bog. She unmuted her phone.

"Are you there?" Maggie asked.

"Yes. Were you able to hear the conversation?" Sean asked

"I was. She seemed…surprised by the news."

"If you could have seen her face, she went sheet white when I told her about the marina. She obviously knows something."

"Agreed. I'm going to hang out and see if she does anything. She may not make a move until nightfall, which means I could have a bit of a wait."

"I want you to let me know if she leaves and let me know where you end up. I don't want you putting yourself in danger. I'm convinced after this conversation that she is involved somehow, and I don't want you finding yourself tangled up with her or a potentially dangerous partner."

"I'll be careful. And I'll let you know what happens," Maggie said without committing to divulging any location she might uncover. She was grateful for his efforts, but everyone was right that she didn't know much about him. He might want to find Vivian at a crime scene for his own purposes. "I'm going to call Mike now and catch him up on events," Maggie lied. She had no intention of calling Mike until she knew something for certain.

"Okay. Talk to you soon," Sean said before disconnecting.

Maggie settled in, expecting a tedious late afternoon of sitting and staring out the windshield. She was glad her parents' car was roomy and comfortable. She hoped her bladder would hold out and wished she'd thought to bring snacks. She hadn't eaten earlier with Mike, and now she was famished. *Oh, well,* she thought, *small price to pay to put an end to all of this.*

Despite her expectation, Maggie did not have to wait long. Vivian wasted no time, virtually flew out the door, hopped into the BMW, and sped out the driveway. Maggie followed at what she hoped was a safe distance. She couldn't risk losing Vivian as she careened recklessly down the narrow two-lane road, where a thick tree line obscured several dramatic curves.

Several turns later, Vivian reduced her speed as she reached the edge of Duxbridge proper. Maggie breathed a sigh of relief. A slower pace and heavier traffic meant she could keep a safer distance. Eventually, Vivian turned off Main, and Maggie knew where they were going.

"Damn," Maggie cursed under her breath. Vivian was driving to her office. She gripped the wheel until her knuckles turned white, slowing to a crawl to let Vivian turn and make her way down the street, keeping enough distance to remain undetected. Maggie's frustration mounted. She had set her hopes on this plan working, and now it looked like it was going to be a bust.

Once Maggie was sure Vivian had enough time to exit her car, she turned the corner. She parked the car three houses away from Vivian's and waited. The sun was getting low in the sky, and the glare threatened to obscure Maggie's view of Vivian's house until she repositioned the car, and the sun was hidden behind a tall maple. She settled in, expecting a long, unproductive evening.

She was wrong. Before she could even push back the driver's seat and stretch her legs, Vivian scurried out of her house carrying a five-gallon orange bucket. She tossed it onto the passenger seat as she got into the car and then turned around in the large parking area by her office. Gravel scattered in all directions as she picked up speed and fishtailed onto the street.

Maggie waited to start the car until Vivian turned right. She pressed down on the accelerator and sped to the corner, not wanting to miss her if she made another turn. Luckily, Maggie caught sight of her as she blew through a stop sign and proceeded right on Main Street, headed for the interstate. Vivian took the southbound onramp onto I-495. Maggie tamped down her excitement as the drive was taking them straight to Onset.

Fifteen minutes later, with Maggie carefully keeping several cars between them on the interstate, Vivian veered right onto Route 25. She drove toward Onset Boulevard, and Maggie could barely contain herself. She had no doubts Vivian was headed to one of the marinas in the area. Vivian turned onto Onset Boulevard, and once she crossed the long stone bridge into Onset Village, Maggie knew where they were going.

"Gotcha," Maggie said as she lifted her foot slightly off the accelerator, not allowing her excitement to translate to her speed. She watched Vivian turn right onto Independence Lane and then Hammond. Maggie decided to hang back until she was sure Vivian was in the marina, then she turned onto Hammond and drove until she had a clear view of the Point Onset Yacht Club. She watched Vivian park her car near the entry gate, grab the orange bucket, and disappear behind the fencing.

The parking lot was sparsely filled, and the club itself still looked closed. Maggie would have preferred more people milling around in case things went sideways. She could blend into a crowd. She needed a plan. If Vivian were going to a boat with the intent of destroying evidence, Maggie would have to find a way to stop her. There was no doubt in her mind that Vivian was involved in Devon's death, and Maggie knew that made her dangerous. She decided it was time for backup.

She picked up her phone and called Mike. She was betting his anger with her would be fleeting, and he would be as excited as she was that this could be it. The call went directly to voicemail. She disconnected and typed out a quick text.

> I'm at Point Onset YC.
> This is the crime scene.
> I'm sure of it. Call me
> ASAP

Maggie pulled latex gloves from her purse and stuffed them into the pocket of her jeans. She pushed her bag under her seat, took a deep breath, and put the car in drive. She proceeded at a crawl to the clubhouse, parking close to the building behind a large forsythia that gave her a bit of cover.

She exited her car and walked to the gated entry, keeping an eye out for Vivian as she did. The sun was low, and Maggie knew she would have to act fast to implement her plan. She intended to track Vivian and film whatever she was going to do, praying it would be enough to connect her to her crimes. With luck, Vivian would be too engrossed in her endeavors to notice Maggie's presence.

Before she was halfway across the parking lot, her phone buzzed. Expecting Mike, she answered quickly and said hello in hushed tones.

"Where are you?" Jake asked. It sounded like an air horn in contrast to the quiet lapping of waves against the dock and the occasional seagull.

"Hold on," Maggie whispered as she fumbled to turn the volume down on the call. "I'm at Point Onset Yacht Club, following Vivian."

"You're what?" Jake shouted.

"Shhhh, keep your voice down. Sound really carries out here. Listen, I can't explain, but I'm positive she's involved now, and I'm going to make sure she doesn't destroy any evidence. If you want to stay on the phone, that's great, but you must mute yourself. I'm going to film everything. It may be all the evidence we'll have if she decides to do something drastic, like torch a multi-million dollar yacht."

"You shouldn't be -"

"Don't make me end this call. I'm doing this, and it would be better if you were listening, but you have to mute yourself now."

"Jules, call Mike, you are not going to believe -" was all Maggie heard before the phone went silent. She looked at the screen to make sure they were still connected. She was relieved to see he was still there, listening.

Maggie pulled the gloves from her pocket and put them on before opening the door. She breathed a sigh of relief when the door was still unlocked. Turning on her camera, she scanned the dock looking for Vivian. She was afraid she'd have to inspect all the boats, but then she saw a blonde head bob quickly up a short gangplank to a very large yacht. It was Vivian, and she was carrying the orange bucket.

Maggie watched her climb aboard and then disappear.

TWENTY-FIVE

Maggie surveyed the situation. There was minimal cover along the dock leading to the slip. If she was careful, she could conceal herself intermittently with the pilings and then stay close to the larger boats making it difficult to see her as she approached Vivian's yacht. That still left a large expanse where she would be exposed.

Her other choice was to walk down the boardwalk like she belonged and hope Vivian was so preoccupied with destroying evidence she wouldn't notice.

"Jake," Maggie whispered. "Vivian is aboard the largest yacht at the marina. It's moored at the last slip." She hoped Jake could hear her.

"Maggie," Jake responded quietly, startling her. "Jules is calling Mike, and I'm driving to you right now. Wait if you can. Do not hang up this call," Jake pleaded before muting his phone again.

Maggie checked her phone to ensure it was recording and slowly made her way to the first piling. She waited a moment. When no one screamed obscenities at her, she stepped back into the open and quickly walked to the next piling. She tried to spot Vivian, but she was still hidden somewhere on the enormous craft. All Maggie could hope was that Vivian did not have a clear view from her position.

As Maggie closed in on the yacht, the sun sank deeper in the sky, creating intense sun glitter behind her. She held her breath and stepped onto the long, open distance leading to the gangplank, praying the sun glare was enough to obscure her movements. A motorboat raced into the inlet, and Maggie used the noise to cover her entry onto the yacht, still cringing at each creak and moan of the ramp as she boarded.

Once on board, she was overwhelmed by the size of the vessel. She had never been on a yacht, not even a small one, and this one looked immense. She began to have misgivings about her plan. She worried Vivian would dispose of any evidence before Maggie found her.

Stairs on both port and starboard led to upper and lower decks. She decided to stay on the covered lower deck, despite the upper one providing a better vantage point. She was concealed enough to take a moment to get her bearings and adjust her plan. There was a large seating area in front of her, opposite an enormous bar with two big-screen televisions. While she was deciding her next move, she heard a loud scraping sound, like something heavy being dragged across a deck. She held her breath and listened, hoping to hear it again, to be able to pinpoint the location. She was confident it was aft, but what deck?

Then she heard the clatter of metal hitting wood, and Maggie realized it was coming from below. She crept to the railing and peered over. There was Vivian, on the swim deck, tipping over a chaise, examining it closely before setting it upright and scanning it again. She must have descended the port side companionway after Maggie boarded. Otherwise, she certainly would have seen her.

Shaken by how close she had come to being discovered, Maggie had to steady herself as she filmed the activity below. The pool deck jutted out of a covered lounge area. The lounge was furnished with a teak table and four matching chairs. The chaises were also stored there, and Vivian dragged them out one by one, flipping each one over, frantically checking it before retrieving another.

From her position, Maggie could not see fully inside the lounge, so despite her better judgment, she inched over to the port stairs, carefully stepping down one step at a time until she had a better view. Vivian was still partially obscured by the stairwell, but Maggie did not dare get any closer. Vivian was now dragging the teak chairs out and repeated her examinations. After she had examined all four chairs, Maggie watched Vivian fall to her knees and peer closely at the deck, running her hands in a wide circle, looking for something. Maggie held her breath when Vivian stood and walked toward the stairs, but it was only to grab the orange bucket she had brought with her, along with a giant sponge.

Vivian walked over to the edge of the swim deck, and Maggie quickly crouched down to avoid detection. Vivian dropped the bucket over the edge, dipping it into the water to fill it. She carried it into the lounge, and water sloshed over the sides when she set it down. She dipped the sponge into it and began to wash an area of the deck, vigorously scrubbing like someone filled with rage or terror.

Maggie had a horrible thought. That could be the place where Devon took his last breath. And Vivian was washing away any evidence that remained. Maggie fought the urge to stop her. She knew that if there had been blood there, the chances Vivian could eradicate it all were slim. It was conceivable some would have seeped under the decking.

Vivian stood, picked up the bucket, and dumped the remaining water onto the deck before disappearing deep into the covered area. Maggie waited for her to reappear, but when she didn't, Maggie slowly continued down the stairs to the swim platform. From there, she could see the entire area. No Vivian, but cushions and ottomans were strewn everywhere. There was a door on the starboard side of the lounge, and it was ajar. Maggie cursed her curiosity and cautiously crossed to the door, stepping gingerly around the mess strewn on the floor.

She took a deep breath and looked through the opening. When she didn't see Vivian, she slipped through the door into a compact garage. That's when she saw Vivian examining the backseat of one of the two sizable, multi-person WaveRunners. Maggie ducked behind the dinghy positioned close to the door.

As Maggie continued to film, she was convinced Vivian was guilty and acted alone. Vivian probably killed Devon in a fit of rage and then drove the body out to sea on one of the two personal watercraft. She expected that Devon would drift out to sea and no one would ever suspect what happened on a yacht soon to be summering far from the mainland. The tide was her enemy on the first assumption, and Maggie's subterfuge thwarted the second.

Maggie had no idea how the pieces would all come together, but she was sure the police would have no problem untangling this because Vivian was neither clever nor careful. Deciding she had enough to help the authorities, she turned off the camera and saved the file to her cloud account. It was time to take herself out of harm's way. As she carefully retreated from the garage, the quiet was shattered.

"Maggie," Jake's whisper sounded like a bomb going off in the cavernous space, "We're here. We'll be right there."

Vivian whipped around and made a strangled sound. She blindly charged Maggie, and Maggie escaped to the pool deck. She slipped her phone into the front pocket of her jeans so she would have two hands free to fight off Vivian if needed. She looked around for something to use as a weapon, but other than furniture, the deck was clear.

"Get out of here," Vivian yelled as she charged around the cushions and overturned chairs strewn everywhere. Maggie did her best to keep furniture between Vivian and herself. Vivian picked up one of the teak chairs and raised it above her head. Rage made Vivian strong. Self-preservation made Maggie quick. She dashed to the stairs as Vivian launched the chair in her direction.

"Vivian, it's over," Maggie tried to reason with her as she scrambled up the stairs. Vivian pushed the chaises out of her way and continued to pursue Maggie. "The police are here. They know everything."

"You're lying! And if you disappear, they'll never know anything," Vivian screamed at her, her wet shoes causing her to slip just as she reached the stairs. Maggie used the opportunity to run the remaining steps, but just as she reached the top, Vivian, having regained her footing, clambered her way up the stairs and body-slammed Maggie into the deck. "He deserved it," Vivian said breathlessly, holding Maggie down by the shoulders. Maggie pushed back, but Vivian had her full weight and fury as leverage. The more she struggled, the stronger Vivian seemed to get.

Maggie wasn't sure what Vivian was capable of, but she knew help was on the way. Instead of fighting Vivian, Maggie decided to try a different tact. "Why did he deserve it, Vivian?" Maggie asked quietly, trying to disarm her with empathy. "What did he do?"

"What did he do?!" Vivian howled. "What did he do?! He stole my life! He ruined my reputation!" She let her iron grip loosen, and Maggie tried to free herself, but Vivian slammed her to the deck. "I brought him out here, made him a romantic dinner, and suggested we finally move in together, and do you know what he said?" She was kneeling on Maggie now, and Maggie was finding it difficult to breathe. "He said he had no intention of being with me. I was just a means to an end, a fun time. He told me we were good friends but nothing more! Nothing more? He was a lying, cheating bastard, so you know what I did? I stabbed him, and when he grabbed the knife away from me, I picked up the wine bottle and hit him! And then I hit him again and again!" Vivian was shrieking and sobbing.

She was distracted enough by the memory that Maggie took that instant to strike. She used all of her strength to roll Vivian off and scramble to her feet. She could see Mike, Jake and Juliet running down the dock, with Jake's dog Anahera in the lead. She started to shout for help when Vivian grabbed a heavy metal tray from the bar and slammed it into her back.

Maggie stumbled but did not lose her footing. She whirled around and deflected another blow with a raised arm. "Stop it, Vivian! Just stop it!" Maggie yelled and tried to grab the tray from her.

She could see the trio dash across the gangway, and before Vivian could react, Anahera tackled her to the ground and latched onto her arm with a ferocious growl. Jake grabbed her collar, praised her, and pulled her away so Mike could cuff Vivian before she put up a fight.

"Vivian Larkspur, you are under arrest for the murder of Devon Friedrickson."

It had been two days since Mike put an angry, spitting, and kicking Vivian into the back of a patrol car. Maggie, Mike, Juliet, Bria and Jake sat in the empty café after hours and relaxed with coffee and cookies. Anahera lay peacefully across Maggie's feet, snoozing. Everyone was still processing all that had happened and what they had learned about Devon's death.

The police techs had found traces of blood all over one of the WaveRunner seats and down into the storage compartment. Blood and glass were embedded in the decking, and Devon's fingerprints were all over the yacht. Confronted with that evidence, Maggie's video, and Jake and Mike hearing her admissions on the still connected phone call, Vivian confessed to everything.

According to her statement, the yacht owners were friends and clients. They had asked if she could help them out. They had to go out of town for a family emergency but had already scheduled a week of maintenance on their boat to prepare it for summer at the Vineyard. They wondered if one of her staff could stay on the craft while technicians came and went. Vivian was more than happy to handle the situation herself. A week on a luxury yacht sounded like a mini-vacation. On that fateful Monday, she invited Devon to the boat for a romantic evening of dinner, drinks and hot tubbing under the stars.

She admitted to killing him in a moment of rage and then rolled his body onto one of the WaveRunners, tethered off the pool deck, waiting for a pre-summer test run. She took him far out into Onset Bay and dumped him into the water. Then she went back and cleaned up the blood and glass.

Since no one, including her friends, knew she had been staying on the yacht, she hatched a plan to play the grieving fiancée. Still angry at Devon for damaging her reputation with Sean and Winthrop, she decided she would do everything she could to lay claim to his estate. She spent her days at his house, going through his accounts, looking for a will or insurance. Planting the idea that she had been living with him for a while, she hired lawyers to begin a claim on his estate.

When asked why she fixated on implicating Maggie, Vivian replied it was a way to manipulate the police and keep them on her side. She didn't care one way or another if they believed Maggie was involved as long as they didn't suspect her.

Mike said that along with murder charges, they would probably be able to get her on fraud, as well. She had unsuccessfully tried to access Devon's accounts but had managed to put the estate title in her company's name.

There was a rap on the café door. Maggie looked up to see Miss Kitty and Sean. Miss Kitty gave a little wave as Juliet walked over to let them in.

"How is everyone fairing today?" Miss Kitty asked.

"I think we are all still coming to terms with everything," Jake replied.

"I bet," Sean said. "I've known Vivian forever, and I'm still having difficulty believing all of this."

"Did that awful Madigan apologize to you, I hope," Miss Kitty said to Maggie while patting her arm.

"Ha!" Maggie responded. "You mean after he lectured me for putting myself in the middle of a police investigation and in harm's way?" She laughed. "He did tell me that I was never a serious suspect. He just needed to gain Vivian's trust. He was suspicious of her from the start, but, of course, they had to build a case. And while they did it, if letting her hurl accusations at me kept her distracted, he was fine with that." Maggie smiled at Sean. "They didn't have a trusted associate who could exploit her like I had."

Mike rolled his eyes. "I'm assuming, going forward, you'll leave the police work to me."

"Maybe," was all Maggie would promise.

"Sean has some news," Miss Kitty interjected.

Everyone looked at him expectantly. "Well, first of all, as you know, Jules, Miss Kitty and I have formed a partnership for the Roost and Nest. And since that means I will happily be spending more time in Duxbridge, I have begun the process of buying Devo's, and I'm going to open a new restaurant at the location. I'll keep any staff that wants to stay and start looking for a new chef." He looked over at Maggie. She smiled, shook her head, and waved him off.

"Nope," was all she said.

Maggie and Jake's phones buzzed. Maggie flipped hers over on the table, as Jake pulled his from his pocket.

"Choice!" Jake said as he pumped his fist in the air, smiling at Maggie.

"Oh, boy," she agreed, smiling back. "Our offer on the house has been accepted," she explained to the table.

"Let the adventures begin!" Jake added.

An hour later, Maggie, Jake and Anahera drove by the Courtland house. They parked in front and looked upon their new venture. Then Jake took Maggie back to the gatehouse.

"What a wild week," she said as she tossed her coat on the couch.

"I'll say. You must be knackered. I'm hoping you'll take a few days off and relax."

"I'd like to. I could definitely use a spa weekend, but there is so much to do, and I'm so far behind on the cookbook." She bent down and kissed Anahera on her snout. "I guess I need to include a dog biscuit recipe now, since you did save my life." Anahera wagged her tail enthusiastically. Maggie stood up. "I hope you're hungry because there are going to be a lot of recipes to test in the next few weeks."

"Always," Jake said. "I'll let you get to it." He kissed her on the cheek and walked to the front door, Anahera at his heels. He opened it and was about to leave but stopped and turned back to her. "What would you think if we went on a proper date?"

"I'd like that."

RECIPES

French Market Chicken:

- 1 cup rice
- 1 cup water
- 2 cups chicken broth
- 3 boneless chicken breasts, cut into large cubes
- ½ onion, chopped
- 2 stalks celery, chopped
- 8 oz diced carrots
- 1 green pepper, chopped
- 1 red pepper, chopped
- 8 oz jar sun dried tomatoes
- 1 tsp red pepper flakes
- ½ tsp crushed garlic
- Herbs de Provence to taste
- salt & pepper to taste

saucepan, skillet

In saucepan, add rice, water & 1 cup chicken broth. Bring to a boil, cover, reduce heat and let simmer 20 minutes until all liquid is absorbed.

Meanwhile, in skillet, heat oil, brown chicken & onion, add remaining chicken broth. Add celery, carrots, peppers, tomatoes, & spices and simmer until carrots are tender.

Add chicken mixture to cooked rice and let simmer 10 minutes.

Blueberry Coffee Cake:
- 2 cups flour
- 1/2 cup sugar
- 3 tsp baking powder
- 1 tsp salt
- 4 tbsp cultured buttermilk powder
- 1 egg, beaten
- 1 cup water
- 1 tsp vanilla
- ½ cup vegetable oil
- 8 oz frozen blueberries

Topping:

- ½ cup brown sugar
- ¼ cup butter, softened
- ½ cup flour

8x8 baking dish, greased, 2 bowls

In bowl, add flour, sugar, baking powder, salt, buttermilk and mix well.

Make a well in the center add egg, water & oil.

Stir quickly until all everything is mixed well, but don't over mix.

Fold in blueberries. Spread batter evenly in baking dish.

In bowl, mix topping ingredients until crumbly. Sprinkle evenly over the top of batter.

Bake at 400° for 25-30 minutes, until toothpick comes out clean

Butternut Squash Pasta:

- 1 large butternut squash
- 1 tbsp olive oil
- ¼ lb spicy Italian sausage
- ½ lean ground beef
- 2-14 oz can diced tomatoes
- 2 tsp basil, crushed
- 2 tsp oregano, crushed
- 2 tsp crushed garlic
- salt & pepper to taste
- 12 oz bowtie pasta

deep skillet, saucepan

Peel and cube butternut squash.

Heat olive oil in skillet and add squash.

Sauté about 10 minutes. Remove from skillet.

Add sausage & ground beef to skillet and brown.

Add squash, tomatoes & spices.

Let simmer on medium heat until squash is tender, about 20 minutes.

Meanwhile, prepare pasta according to package directions. Drain and toss with sauce mixture and serve.

Grilled Sweet & Sour Meatballs:

- 1 lb 80/20 ground beef (not lean)
- 1 egg
- 1 tsp crushed garlic
- 3 green onions, finely chopped
- ¼ cup sweet & sour sauce
- ½ tsp salt
- ¼ tsp pepper
- ½ tsp red pepper flakes

Bowl, 4 metal skewers

Combine all ingredients and form 12 balls.

Place 3 on each skewer and grill about 8 minutes until cooked through, turning frequently.

Serve on toasted rolls.

Washday Beans & Rice

- 1 cup rice
- 1 cup water
- 1 cup chicken broth
- 14oz can red kidney bean
- 4 links Italian or Andouille sausage (sweet or spicy) - slice each link into 4 pieces
- 1 tbsp olive oil
- 1 tsp to 1 tbsp Cajun Creole Seasoning (start with teaspoon and work your way up to taste)
- 4 green onions, chopped
- 2 celery stalks, chopped
- 1 large green pepper, chopped
- 1 large tomato diced (or 14 oz can)

2-quart saucepan and skillet

Combine rice with water & chicken broth in a saucepan, cover.

Bring to a boil, reduce to simmer, cook until all the liquid is absorbed (about 20 minutes).

Over medium-high, heat oil in skillet; add onions, celery, green pepper & sausage, cook until sausage is done in the center.

Add sausage, beans, seasoning and tomatoes together into the saucepan.

Keep the heat low and let cook 10 minutes to let flavors blend.

You can add shredded, cooked pork to the beans if desired.

Chocolate Chocolate Chip Cookies

- 1 cup + 2 tbsp butter
- 1 cup dark brown sugar
- 1/2 cup sugar
- 2 eggs
- 2 tsp vanilla
- dash of salt
- 1 tsp baking soda
- 2 cups flour
- 1/3 cup unsweetened cocoa
- 2 cups semi-sweet chocolate chips
- 1 cup nuts (walnuts, hazelnuts, almonds or peanuts), chopped

mixing bowl and cookie sheet

Preheat oven to 350 degrees (the lower temperature is because dark cookies can burn easily)

Cream together butter and sugars.

Add eggs and vanilla, mixing well.

Sift together salt, soda, flour and cocoa, then add to butter mixture, blending well.

Add nuts and chocolate chips.

Spoon onto cookie sheet and bake at 350 degrees for 10-12 minutes.

Cool on cooling rack.

ABOUT THE AUTHOR

Annie DeMoranville has lived all over, including Boston and Los Angeles. She now resides in the shadow of the Rocky Mountains with a menagerie of critters. She loves to travel with a goal to see the most beautiful beaches in the world. **Duxbridge Mysteries: Recipe for Murder** is her third book and the first in the **Duxbridge Mysteries** series.

Up next: The third book in the **TJ Wilde Trilogy. Full Sail.** And **Blackout,** the first book in the new **Jennifer McCaffrey Mysteries** series.

For more information on her upcoming novels, visit
www.AnnieDeMoranville.com

Connect with her:
Facebook/AnnieDeMoranville.com
@AnnDeMoranville on Twitter
#annieshortstories on Instagram

ACKNOWLEGMENTS

Special thank you to **Larissa G.** for being a terrific editor, and an amazing cover artist. Couldn't have done it without her.

Much thanks to **Lari M.** for always encouraging my progress, and demanding *MORE PAGES!* to read.

Thank you to my brother **Gary R** for working with me on the sailing lingo…and just for being my brother

And thanks to **Carol R.**, for heading out to take the photos we needed when travel was not possible

And **Eli G.** for taking a red pen to page to make it better

Coming Soon

FULL SAIL

The third book in the **TJ Wilde Trilogy**

For more **recipes and menus** go to:
www.AnnieDeMoranville.com/category/recipes/